BENEATH THE SHEETS

SHANDI BOYES

COPYRIGHT

ALSO BY SHANDI BOYES

Perception Series

Saving Noah (Noah & Emily)

Fighting Jacob (Jacob & Lola)

Taming Nick (Nick & Jenni)

Redeeming Slater (Slater and Kylie)

Saving Emily (Noah & Emily - Novella)

Wrapped Up with Rise Up (Perception Novella - should be read after
the Bound Series)

Enigma

Enigma (Isaac & Isabelle #1)

Unraveling an Enigma (Isaac & Isabelle #2)

Enigma The Mystery Unmasked (Isaac & Isabelle #3)

Enigma: The Final Chapter (Isaac & Isabelle #4)

Beneath The Secrets (Hugo & Ava #1)

Beneath The Sheets (Hugo & Ava #2)

Spy Thy Neighbor (Hunter & Paige)

The Opposite Effect (Brax & Clara)

I Married a Mob Boss (Rico & Blaire)

Second Shot (Hawke & Gemma)

The Way We Are (Ryan & Savannah #1)

The Way We Were (Ryan & Savannah #2)

Sugar and Spice (Cormack & Harlow)

Lady In Waiting (Regan & Alex #1)

Man in Queue (Regan & Alex #2)

Couple on Hold (Regan & Alex #3)

Enigma: The Wedding (Isaac and Isabelle)

Silent Vigilante (Brandon and Melody #1)

Hushed Guardian (Brandon & Melody #2)

Quiet Protector (Brandon & Melody #3)

Enigma: An Isaac Retelling

Twisted Lies (Jae & CJ)

Bound Series

Chains (Marcus & Cleo #1)

Links (Marcus & Cleo #2)

Bound (Marcus & Cleo #3)

Restrain (Marcus & Cleo #4)

The Misfits

Russian Mob Chronicles

Nikolai: A Mafia Prince Romance (Nikolai & Justine #1)

Nikolai: Taking Back What's Mine (Nikolai & Justine #2)

Nikolai: What's Left of Me (Nikolai & Justine #3)

Nikolai: Mine to Protect (Nikolai & Justine #4)

Asher: My Russian Revenge (Asher & Zariah)

<u>Nikolai: Through the Devil's Eyes</u>(Nikolai & Justine #5)

<u>Trey</u> (Trey & K)

<u>The Italian Cartel</u>

Dimitri

Roxanne

Reign

Mafia Ties (Novella)

Maddox

Demi

Rocco

Clover

Smith

<u>RomCom Standalones</u>

Just Playin' (Elvis & Willow)

<u>Ain't Happenin'</u> (Lorenzo & Skylar)

<u>The Drop Zone</u> (Colby & Jamie)

Very Unlikely (Brand New Couple)

<u>Short Stories - Newsletter Downloads</u>

Christmas Trio (Wesley, Andrew & Mallory -- short story)

Falling For A Stranger (Short Story)

<u>One Night Only Series</u>

Hotshot Boss

Hotshot Neighbor

<u>The Bobrov Bratva Series</u>

Wicked Intentions (Katie & Ghost)

Sinful Intentions (April 25)

Devious Intentions (June 13)

WANT TO STAY IN TOUCH?

Facebook: facebook.com/authorshandi

Instagram: instagram.com/authorshandi

Email: authorshandi@gmail.com

Reader's Group: bit.ly/ShandiBookBabes

Website: authorshandi.com

Newsletter: https://www.subscribepage.com/AuthorShandi

DEDICATION

My one and only.
I love you, Chris.

ONE
HUGO

Present Day

My hand trembles as I yank my cell phone out of my running shorts' pocket. My body is slicked with sweat, and my heart is pounding fitfully against my chest. There's only been one time in my life I haven't wanted to make a call. It was when I had to tell my best mate that my sister, his wife, had been critically injured in a tragic accident. If that wasn't bad enough, the same accident claimed the life of their unborn son.

My plan was to wait until Hawke's feet touched home soil before telling him about Jorgie's accident, but I didn't have the chance to wait that long. He knew something wasn't right the instant he heard me speak. I'll never forget the howl of a broken man that resonated down the line that day. It was a soul being shattered with no possibility of being repaired.

Against the doctor's advice, we kept Jorgie on life support for three days so Hawke could return from duty in Iraq and say his final goodbye to the love of his life in person. Jorgie was buried the day after his return with their son, Malcolm, cradled in her arms.

Part of me died the day my sister did. We were two peas in a pod, rebels cruising through life one adventure at a time. Her life was perfect. Until it was brutally ripped away.

Now, for the second time in my life, I have to tell a man the woman he loves is gone, snatched under my nose by men who wish her harm. Protecting Isabelle is my job, the most vital task of my employment contract, but even if it weren't, I'd still protect her.

Izzy has a lot of the same qualities as my sister Jorgie. She's the same age as Jorgie was when she passed away. They have matching dark hair and fair skin, but instead of Izzy having Jorgie's cornflower blue eyes, hers are a rich chocolate brown. But the biggest similarity is their personalities—little firecrackers who keep everyone on their toes. They ensure life never gets boring.

I wouldn't necessarily say my life has been dull over the past five years, but when Izzy crashed into Isaac's life, things certainly became more dynamic. Before she arrived in the picture, I'd spent the past five years as Manager of Operations in the background of Isaac's empire, hidden from prying eyes. I handled acquisitions and proposals presented to his company and assessed the capabilities of any nightclubs he considered purchasing.

Isaac knew the instant he met Izzy she was his game-changer, so he took measures to ensure she'd be protected. The very first task he undertook was altering my job description.

Most would see my transition from Manager of Operations to a Protective Detail as a downgrade. I don't. Knowing Isaac trusts me enough to take care of Izzy when he can't is more rewarding than any fancy job title could ever be. Not only do I get the opportunity to thank Isaac for saving my life, but I left the stuffiness of a boring nine-to-five office job that was becoming as tedious as folding my overflowing laundry basket every Sunday morning.

The only bad thing that came from Izzy's inclusion in Isaac's life is realizing what I sacrificed by not taking the time to consider the consequences of my actions. Instead of evaluating how greatly my life would change from the mammoth decision I made five years ago, I once again became a bull in a china shop, charging first and asking questions later.

I live with the repercussions of my decision every day but seeing the way Izzy looks at Isaac makes the demise of my life even more apparent, but I can't change the past. I can only shape the future. And right now, my focus needs to remain on Izzy.

The muscles in my thighs burn as I sprint down 42nd Street, chasing the white Range Rover with an unconscious Izzy splayed in the back seat. I tried to get her out. I smashed the back window of the Range Rover with my fists trying to save her, but I failed. *Again.*

My feet stomping on the sidewalk drown out the thumping of my heart as I dial a number I know by heart. Lifting the cell phone to my ear, I push it in close, making sure I can hear Isaac over the shrill of my pulse in my ears.

"Hugo," Isaac greets me.

His tone is stern, like always, but with a slight hint of playfulness. I knew he would have seen it this morning, the spark in Izzy's eyes that told him she was coming back to him. I've seen it emerging over the past few days. The way her ears pricked when my untraceable cell phone rang, her long stares into space that ended with her arms prickling, and the way she finally stood up to the two-faced bitch, Clara.

Izzy finally having the gall to go against Clara was all I needed to know she was ready to forgive and forget. To let love win. To stop fighting fate. Now, she may never get her opportunity.

"They have her. They've taken Izzy." My words are barely audible in my breathless state, but Isaac must hear them.

He inhales a sharp breath, no doubt his heart freezing in ice-cold fear. It's the same feeling I had when he told me I had to walk away from Ava nearly five years ago when we stood out in front of my sister's house.

"Walk away or risk her life. The choice is yours," he said that day.

To me, there was no choice. I would *always* protect Ava, so I walked away. Not just for a moment but for a lifetime.

Although Ava and I were only together for mere weeks, I gathered enough memories to last me a lifetime. I watched her sleep for hours, absorbing and categorizing every look that adorned her beautiful face. Every smile and frown were assessed in great detail. They're the memories that have kept me going for the past five years. Our time together was short, but I'm grateful I got to experience those moments with her. Not many people meet their soulmate. I did, and I'll be forever grateful for that. Memories can't compete with real-life moments, but when they're all you have, you take what you can get.

"Who has her?"

Isaac's low tone drags my thoughts back to the present. "I don't know. They pulled her into a white Range Rover at the bottom of St. Thomas Street." My words are as breathless as my lungs. "Fuck, boss, I'm sorry, I only left her for a minute."

With the remnants of a nightmare clinging to my skin, Izzy's assumption that I'm cowardly hiding from my family hit harder than normal. Although nightmares have become a rarity the past five years, as the anniversary of the incident in Afghanistan creeps closer, they've resurfaced stronger than ever, so instead of absorbing the sting of Izzy's words like a man, I stormed off in anger, too overwhelmed to continue our argument.

That was all it took for them to snatch her.

Mere fucking seconds.

My eyes lift to the Range Rover when it slams on its brakes and mounts the curb to avoid missing a blue sedan suddenly pulling out in front of it. I barge through the dense foot crowd that forever clogs the sidewalks of Ravenshoe, pushing past a throng of people unaware of the danger surrounding them. In any other town, chasing a car by foot would be a fruitless effort, but thankfully for me, Ravenshoe has as many traffic issues as New York City.

Isaac's breathless grunt sounds down the line, reminding me I have my cell phone pressed against my ear. "Where are you now?"

I cut across the T intersection of Tivot and Mark, my brisk pace slowing when a truck comes out of nowhere. It is charging straight for me. It slams on its brakes, infusing the air with burning rubber and smoke. The best parts of my life flash before my eyes as the grill of the truck inches toward me. Tires bounce across the asphalt and a horn honking shrieks through my ears. Time freezes, and everything goes deathly quiet.

When the truck narrowly misses hitting me, I release a ragged gasp then recommence my chase. I jump over the tray of the truck before increasing my speed. Motorists honk as I sprint by, and my lungs heave, incapable of securing a full breath, but adrenaline and determination keep me going.

"I'm tailing them on foot," I inform Isaac, my words winded.

My body is exhausted, screaming in pain, but I can't give up. I can't fail... *again*. The fear in Izzy's eyes when she thrashed against her attacker as he held a white cloth over her mouth will haunt my dreams.

Another item added to the already exhaustive list.

"They just pulled down Tivot," I advise when the Range Rover mounts the curb, barely missing a pedestrian waiting to cross.

The veins in my neck thrum when the passenger of the Range

Rover dangerously leans out of the window. He's a brute of a man, easily my height but a good twenty pounds heavier. A snake tattoo slithering up his right arm leads to a face only a mother could love. His mouth curves into an arrogant smirk at the same time he produces a black pistol.

While inhaling a sharp breath, I scope the area. "Fuck. Get down!" I scream at the mass gathering of people in the firing zone.

The gunman takes aim, not the slightest bit concerned for the safety of the bystanders enjoying their Sunday morning. I sprint to a middle-aged woman frozen in fear at the bus stop. A rustle of air escapes her lips when I push her out of the line of fire.

Burning lava scorches my veins as a jolt of pain shreds through my chest. I fly backward, hitting the concrete sidewalk with an almighty thump. I try to get up, to fight through the pain pinning me to the asphalt, but my body refuses to cooperate. My breathing slows to uneven gasps as a chill runs down my spine. The smell of copper mixed with sweat lingers in the air as my eyelids become heavy. A short time later, a shadow hovers over me, blackened by the bright sun. Its harmful rays bounce off the stranger's golden hair, haloing him like an angel fallen from heaven.

"My name is Brandon James. I'm an FBI Field Agent. My number is 443567. I need an ambulance sent to the corner of Tivot and Welsh."

"Blondie?" My words are garbled as the air from my lungs bubbles into my chest.

I cough, splattering my lips with blood. A string of incomprehensible words rumbles from my mouth when someone pushes down on the pain burning through my chest and shoulder. Hot, sticky blood puddles around me as my eyelids droop.

When the blackness overtakes me, my first thoughts go to her. *Ava.*

TWO

AVA

While washing my hands in the sink, I catch my reflection in the vanity mirror. I grimace. Thanks to getting caught in an afternoon shower, my hair is a frizzy mess. The mascara I coated my lashes with this morning is gone, and my eyes are plagued with dark bags that haven't budged an inch in nearly five years. *I'm wretched.*

After fluffing out my wild, messy hair, I grab my powder compact out of my purse and set to work on concealing years of restless sleep.

"I guess that will have to do," I mumble while staring at a slightly improved Ava reflecting back at me.

Once I've applied a dab of lip gloss and spray of perfume, I rush out of my office's cramped bathroom then scurry down the hall.

"I know, I know," I apologize when I catch Belinda's, my dear friend and office receptionist, pursed lips.

While assisting me into a wool-lined trench coat, she cautions, "You know what he's like, Ava." She wraps a cashmere scarf around my neck as I slide my shaking hand into black leather gloves. "Being late is a way of saying you believe your time is more valuable than the time—"

"Of the person waiting for you," I interrupt, quoting the saying I've heard *many* times the past four years.

Belinda smiles while handing me a cashmere beanie.

"But isn't it better to be late than arrive ugly?" I quip, my tone as unconvincing as the concern hampering my vocal cords.

Her dainty chuckle warms my heart.

"Please come with me," I beg, my words barely a whimper.

As she pouts, the twinkle in her green eyes dampens. "I would if I could." She squeezes my arm before guiding me to the exit. "Be careful. The grounds are slippery."

I press a kiss on her cheek. "I will."

After giving her a tight squeeze, I slip through the door of the reception area. Bitterly cold winds pelt through me when I scuttle across the concrete sidewalk. The chill of winter has arrived early.

As I pace through a gathering of people eager to start their weekend, a buzz of excitement dashes through me. I've always loved the anticipation of waking up on a Friday morning and knowing I only need to make it through another eight hours before having two days of freedom to do whatever my heart desires. Slow, lazy weekends doing as much or as little as I please are some of my greatest joys.

When my cell phone buzzes in my clutch purse, I increase my already brisk pace. I don't need to look at the screen to know who's calling. My five-minute tardiness is all that's required to identify my caller.

"I'm so sorry, my last patient's crown took longer than expected," I say after squashing my cell phone to my ear. "I'm arriving now."

I hurry through the security turnstiles of the Belvedere Hotel, smiling a greeting to the elderly doorman welcoming me into the affluent foyer with a dip of his hat.

"We're in the west wing," my caller replies, his tone clipped.

My heart rate kicks up a gear when he abruptly disconnects the call, not allowing me the chance to reply. Generally, his mood can be quite curt, but his agitation at my tardiness would have increased his annoyance.

After removing my coat, scarf, and gloves, I hand them to the grinning coat clerk before gathering up my ticket and dashing for the west wing. My almost jog wanes to a brisk walk when the flash of a breaking news banner catches my eye. I halve my lengthy strides before redirecting my steps to the color television sitting on the counter of the Belvedere Hotel's reception desk.

Col Petretti, notorious businessman and suspected mob boss, has been killed in an FBI targeted sting, I read off the screen.

As my eyes skim the flickering screen, absorbing the snippets of information displayed, my throat tightens. A female reporter is standing at the front of an old manufacturing warehouse. It is similar to the textile mill in Graham, North Carolina. Flashing red and white lights bounce off the reporter's rich auburn hair as she hustles her competitors also vying for a prime position.

My pupils widen when a picture of Col Petretti pops up on the screen. Even though I'm looking at him through a monitor, his evil eyes still make my skin crawl.

I've never forgotten the devastation that bombarded me the night I first laid my eyes on him...

When I'm grabbed at the side and dragged deeper into the corridor, my heart leaps out of my chest. "You need to come with me," announces a raspy voice I don't immediately recognize.

My panic somewhat recedes when my head cranks to the side, and I'm met with the worldly eyes of Patty. He holds me close to his side, bombarding me with his feverish body heat. As he guides me down the corridor, his eyes drift around our location similar to the way Hugo's did at the club months earlier.

Without speaking a peep, he directs me to an apartment at the end of the hall. After ushering me inside, he secures a massive number of deadlocks into place on the thick wooden door. The queasiness hampering my stomach earlier returns full pelt when he spins around to face me. His pupils are wide, and his face is gaunt.

"What's going on, Patty?" I query, my voice trembling.

He props a steel baseball bat against the entryway table then steps closer to me. After seizing the crook of my elbow, he steers me into his kitchen, which is an exact replica of mine. He pulls out a wooden stool from underneath the counter then gestures for me to sit. I shake my head, too shaken to sit still.

Grunting off my dismissal, he moves through the kitchen, gathering sandwich supplies like I'm an invited guest for dinner, not ushered here against my will.

"Patty—"

Any further words preparing to leave my mouth are hindered in my throat from the wry glare he directs at me. My heart thrashes against my ribs when I spot the calamity in his usually gentle eyes. Upon noticing my frightened expression, his expression softens before he once again gestures for me to sit.

Not trusting my shaking legs to keep me upright, I plop onto the barstool and swivel to face him. With a kind smile, he places a loaf of crusted bread onto the countertop before he runs his hand along the edge of his jaw.

He looks uneased. I learn why when he asks, "The man who followed you to Hugo's floor. Do you know who he is?" His voice is stern, but the concern in his eyes is my greatest worry.

I shake my head. "I've never seen him before."

"His name is Col Petretti," Patty advises, his tone deep and raspy.

My lips purse, certain I've heard his name before, but before I can work out where, Patty adds, "He's a monster, Ava, a man who will decimate an entire family without a second thought."

My pupils enlarge as dread grips my heart.

"A brutal, heartless man who destroys everything in his wake, not stopping for anyone or anything."

"H-Hugo," I stammer out through the tears clogging my words. "He was at Hugo's apartment."

Patty steps closer to me, his face as hard as stone. "It is too late for Hugo. He made his bed, and now he must sleep in it."

I shake my head so fiercely salty blobs fling off my cheeks. After slipping off the barstool, I rush to the door, my frantic steps only impeded by the fear wreaking havoc on my body. I can barely breathe through my panic, but nothing can stop me. I need to get to Hugo to protect him from the real-life monster who has escaped his nightmares.

Before I reach the door, Patty beats me to it. He squashes his back to the thick wooden material before bouncing his remorseful eyes between mine. "It is too late for Hugo, Ava. If he isn't already dead, he soon will be."

*My eyes burn, unable to accommodate the moisture flooding them. I claw at my neck, struggling to contain the emotions crip-*pling me. This can't be happening. Surely. I'm only just getting a grasp on my loss. I can't go through that again so soon. It will destroy me.

Like he can hear my silent thoughts, Patty says, "He's gone, Ava. He can't come back from this."

Despair crashes into me when I see the candor in his eyes. His honesty is brutal to hear, but it's a frankness I appreciate when I recall what occurred earlier today.

"That's why he said goodbye." I hiccup through a stream of

tears, incapable of catching a full breath. "He knew he was never coming back. H-He knew he was leaving forever."

Patty's glossed eyes stare into mine for several painfully long seconds before he nods. When the fear paralyzing me becomes too much for me to accept, Patty catches me before he cradles me close to his chest. As he runs his hand down my sweat-drenched hair, he whispers soothing words while also encouraging me to breathe through the tears flooding my face...

"Ava!" shouts a voice across the room, breaking me from my memories.

I drag my hand under my eyes, removing any evidence of my tears before spinning toward the voice. My attempt to make myself presentable is fruitless when *his* narrowed eyes zoom in on my glistening cheeks. "She doesn't need to sign in. She's with me," he informs the receptionist standing behind me.

I smile warily at the stuffily dressed lady, grateful she didn't refute his inaccurate statement. As I quickly span the distance between us before she can announce the cause of my distraction, my high-altitude stilettos click against the marble floor. When his eyes slit while drinking in my Misha Collection Leyana dress, I run my hands down the knee-length skirt, smoothing out the invisible creases he *believes* are in my dress.

"Out of all the days to be late, Ava, you choose today," he grumbles before he adjusts the neckline of my dress.

"I'm sorry," I mumble, my words as weak as my reply.

After scrubbing his hand under my eyes to remove the mascara my tears smeared, he clutches my hand so roughly, a squeak of pain pops from my lips before he races us into an opulent ballroom. Once we're surrounded by elegantly dressed men and women, his stiffened posture softens, and the mask he regularly wears in public slips into place.

Over the next twenty minutes, I play the role of devoted

spouse to a T. I smile at important dignitaries, ignoring their depraved assessments of my body, and praise the pompous-looking ladies in their hideous ball gowns.

By the time we make it into the middle of the elegant room, my cheeks are burning nearly as much as my hip from his firm clutch on my body. "I said to smile at the important men, not gift them an open invitation to your bedroom," he snarls, his tone low enough so only I hear him.

"Believe me, no man in this room is getting an invitation to my bedroom tonight," I gabble under my breath before snagging a wine glass off the silver tray of a waiter ambling by.

"Sorry, what did you say?" From his tone alone, I know he heard me, but thankfully, the clinking of a wine glass interrupts our showdown.

After strengthening his clutch on my body, he glides his gaze to Mr. Gardner standing behind a podium in the middle of the ballroom. Mr. Gardner, both work associate and boss, looks dashing in a dark blue tailored suit and polished dress shoes. The vibrancy of his red tie matches the hue Mrs. Gardner's cheeks get when he shares the story of how they met and married the day they attended a dental conference in Las Vegas twenty-five years ago today.

My heart warms from the love projecting out of Mr. Gardner as he speaks about his fondness for his beloved wife. His eyes have the same gleam Hawke's always got when in Jorgie's presence, the same gleam Hugo's eyes had when he woke me every morning before Jorgie's death. The sentimental tears Mr. Gardner's speech elicits is the perfect concealment for the heartbreak I still feel for losing Hugo and Jorgie.

I force a smile onto my face when the clinking of wine glasses jingles through my ears at the end of Mr. Gardner's speech. The color in Mrs. Gardner's cheeks amplifies as she prepares to comply with her wedding anniversary guests' request. A giggle bubbles up my chest when wolf whistles bellow across the room as Mr. Gardner seals his lips over Mrs. Gardner's. Even though they're in their late-fifties and have been married for thirty-five years, their love for each other is still in that giddy newlywed phase.

The cheers only simmer when a deep voice at my side requests quiet. My heart hammers my ribs when the procession of elegantly dressed party attendees swivel to face me, then I can barely secure a full breath when my date releases his death clutch on my hip to kneel in front of me.

I shoot my eyes around the room crammed with our work associates and important dignitaries when his hand delves into the breast pocket of his midnight black suit. When he produces a black velvet ring box from his pocket, my eyes rocket back to his. The mad pulse raging through my body clusters in my ears when he cranks open the box to display the princess cut diamond engagement ring nestled inside.

"Marvin, what are you doing?" My voice is low to ensure the people surrounding us don't hear the fear in it.

Marvin's eyes snap up from the ring box to me. "Ava, will you do me the honor of becoming my wife?" His voice is as uneasy as the expression on his face. He doesn't want this any more than me.

As Mrs. Gardner's hand shoots up to muffle her excited squeal, I swallow, relieving the dryness impinging my throat. The room goes deadly quiet when I'm unable to comprehend what is happening, let alone articulate a response.

The longer I stay quiet, the more Marvin glares at me, wordlessly reprimanding me for the delay. He will never forgive me if I don't accept his proposal, so with tears pooling in my eyes, I hesitantly nod.

Marvin mouths, *"Finally,"* while pulling the diamond ring from its box. The shake of my hand trembles my arm when he slips the engagement ring onto my ring finger. When he stands from his kneeled position and wraps his arms around my shoulders, the sternness in his eyes eases.

The crowd erupts when he seals his lips over mine. The saltiness of the blobs streaming down my face mixes with the whiskey lacing his tongue when he slips it inside my mouth, sealing our engagement with what should be an emotionally-packed kiss.

THREE
HUGO

My back arches off the mattress as a tormented scream rips from my throat. I thrash against the sheets wrapped around my withering body, fighting to loosen their deathly tight grip. When another painful howl rumbles through my lips, my eyes snap open. As I rein in the panic scorching my veins, I drift them around the unfamiliar darkness swamping me. My body is covered in a thick layer of sweat, and my heart pounds fitfully as the dark shadows of a nightmare cling to my body.

With the mellow-toned walls and stark white sheets confusing me, it takes several long moments to gather my senses. For the past nearly five years, I've become accustomed to waking up in the bedroom of my apartment, not a hospital room.

Five hours on an operating table, four pints of blood, and more stitches than I can count were the aftermath of once again failing to consider the consequences, but thankfully, this time, my failure didn't have the same repercussions as my last debauched decision.

The relief I felt when I awoke to the remorse-filled eyes of Izzy staring down at me hit like a ton of bricks. I should have known

Isaac would have stopped at nothing to ensure she was safe. His protectiveness of Izzy is more vital to him than his next breath.

Ignoring my shoulder screaming in pain, I scoot across the hospital bed, desperately needing a shower to chase away the nightmare still clinging to my sweat-slicked skin. The ache hampering my shoulder turns lethal when I raise my arm to clasp the silver lift dangling over my bed.

I need the pain, though. It's a somber reminder of what happens when I don't take the time to evaluate my decisions before making them. My lack of judgment yesterday could have ended a lot worse than it did, adding another item to the exhaustive list of mistakes I've made in my lifetime.

Gritting my teeth, I hoist myself into an upright position. Dizziness clusters in my head, amplifying the swirls of my stomach when I throw my legs off the bed and balance on a pair of wobbly knees.

My shaky steps to the attached bathroom are hindered by the heart rate monitor strapped to my chest. After leaning on the wheeled side table to steady my sways, I use my free hand to rip off the heart monitor and defibrillation pads from my chest.

As soon as the first pad is removed, an alarm sounds from the monitor, shrilling in my ears. My fingers frantically punch at the buttons on the unit, trying to shut up its irritating shrieks. The shake impeding my legs switches to my hands when a flood of memories pelt into me at once.

You don't realize the significance of a ripple in a pulse line until you see one vanish before your eyes. When my anger gets the better of me, I rip the cords off my chest then stalk into the bathroom, dragging the IV stand with me. The pain shredding through my body is nothing compared to the ache crippling my heart.

I step into the tiled hob of the shower, not bothering to remove my hospital gown. After cranking the water on full pelt, I stand under the spray. The frigid water sends a jolt through my body, restarting my frozen heart. I lean my good arm on the sparkling marbled wall before using my spare hand to rip off my gown, then I step deeper into the spray. The chilly water blasting the back of my neck both relieves my overheated skin and chases away the remnants of my nightmare.

The subzero temps have only just cooled my feverish skin when the bathroom door swings open, and Raquel zips into the room. "What are you doing out of bed?" she reprimands me, her high-pitched squeal bouncing off the tiled walls and jingling into my ears.

Raquel is the nurse Isaac hired to look after me during my recovery. When Izzy spotted her sauntering into the room yesterday afternoon, her eyes popped as her elbow landed in Isaac's ribs. She reacted the exact way any woman would when a girl with cock-twitching good looks like Raquel enters a room.

Raquel is the exact vision every man conjures up when the term 'naughty nurse' is mentioned. She has straight blonde hair, defined eyes, and curvy lips that accentuate her beautiful face.

Although Izzy is fooled by Isaac's reasoning for hiring Raquel, I'm not. Isaac knows me well enough to know even though Raquel is gorgeous and has a body that would make most men fall to their knees, I'm not interested in purchasing what she's selling.

I'll never openly admit it, but I have a *slight* fascination for a certain skin tone. It isn't an absolute necessity when seeking a bed companion. I'm like every guy out there, but instead of my favorable characteristics being determined by their hair or eye coloring, my interests lie in the smooth richness of their beautiful skin.

Don't construe my admission the wrong way. Although my preferences lean toward tanned skin, it isn't the only feature required to gain my attention. Raquel is a prime example of that. Just watching her nibble on the end of her pen last night sent a mass injection of blood to the lower region of my body, and her complexion is as white as a hospital sheet. I don't mean slightly pale. She doesn't have a hint of a tan, whiter-than-Casper-the-Ghost white, but Raquel's pasty skin has nothing to do with why I'm not lining up to purchase the sweetness she's offering.

Raquel was hired as my nurse, but I've known her for nearly two years. I class her as a friend. Only once in my life have I crossed the fine line that separates friends from bed companions. I didn't just cross the line with Ava, I smudged it out with my foot on the way over, permanently erasing it from our lives.

Just like Ava is the only girl I've ever lusted over, asked out, and fallen in love with, she will remain the only girl I'll ever jump the friendship line for.

"You were told to buzz me if you needed anything," Raquel scolds, rushing toward me without the slightest concern for my nakedness.

She curls her arms around my waist before guiding me to a shower chair at the side of the stark white vanity.

"I was shot in the shoulder, not in my legs. I'm perfectly capable of walking," I remind her.

She snarls before pushing me into the chair, surprising me with her strength. She's too tiny to have so much gusto. Her eyes continue reprimanding me as she heads to my suitcase on a luggage table in the washroom so she can dig through the clothes laundered and packed by Catherine, Isaac's housekeeper. Suddenly, she stops rummaging through my belongings, cranks her neck, then looks at me, blinking and confused. "They didn't pack you any briefs," she murmurs, her nose screwing up.

I lick my dry lips, concealing the grin attempting to spread across my face. "I don't wear briefs." The scrunching of Raquel's nose amplifies. "Boxers, butt huggers, nut huts, Calvin Kleins, whatever you want to call them, I don't wear them."

Raquel's brow cocks. "You go commando with *that?*" she queries while gesturing her head to my crotch.

I don't have a chance in hell of stopping the shit-eating grin stretching across my face. I'm a guy. You *never* turn down a compliment to your manhood, deplorable mood or not.

A ragged gasp expels Raquel's lips when I nod. After returning her bulging eyes back to my suitcase, she yanks out a pair of cotton blue-striped pajama pants, straightens her spine, then saunters my way. "These will ensure there are no zipper incidents," she chides in a witty tone.

I gulp.

Upon noticing my panicked expression, a broad grin etches on Raquel's face. "Can you manage? Or do you need me to *shower* and *dress* you?" she quips while holding out the trousers.

I roll my eyes before snatching the pants out of her hands. "I've got this."

When I stand, my abrupt movements send a rush of dizziness to my head. I sway like a leaf in the hot summer breeze. Raquel grabs the tops of my arms, steadying my uncontrollable sways. Through gritted teeth, I use her and the IV stand as a brace so I can slip my legs into my pants and yank them up to my waist. I grumble about how pathetic I am since I can't even dress myself the whole time.

I got shot in the chest, for fuck's sake, not my legs.

"You had a class four hemorrhage, Hugo. That's well over four pints of blood lost. Your muscles not only need time to recoup from that, but you also chased a car for nearly five miles." Raquel's tone is sincere yet stern. "Even marathon runners need help getting dressed after that effort."

Once she secures my pants in place with drawstrings, she guides me back to my bed. Any agitation about my inability to care for myself dampens when I notice the strain hampering her face.

The heavy crease in the middle of her eyes and the way her lips are pursed, reminds me so much of a face Ava pulled years ago.

The groove crinkling Raquel's usually smooth forehead disappears when I flop onto the hospital bed. "There you go," she says while hauling my legs, which seem the weight of concrete, onto the bed.

"What happened to my belongings?" I try to keep my tone neutral, but my attempts are borderline.

Raquel's brows scrunch as her eyes shoot around the room. "Your clothing was given to a local detective, but your wallet should be here somewhere."

The heaviness weighing down my chest lightens at her admission. I have a very important item in my wallet I'd hate to lose.

Suddenly, Raquel's face lights up. "The triage nurse said she locked it in your drawer." I release the breath I'm holding when her hand plunges into the top drawer, and she produces my black leather wallet. "There you go."

She hands it to me before she returns to the bathroom. Once she slips out of my view, I crack open the wallet, inwardly sighing when a faded and cracked polaroid photo confronts me. I close my wallet and place it on the side table.

I don't need to see the photo to know what it looks like. I've studied it many times the past eleven years, so I recall it in photographic detail. It's a picture my mom snapped of Jorgie, Ava, and me on our last family vacation at Lake George before Ava and Jorgie left for college. In the photo, Ava is wearing a teeny yellow bikini under a hideous Rochdale Village T-shirt she stole from my suitcase, and her knock-your-socks-off smile is plastered on her face.

Her smile is the reason I carry the picture with me everywhere I go. That was the first time in the eight years I'd known Ava that I had seen her smile like that. If it wasn't rewarding enough being in the presence of such a beautiful smile, it was even more special because it was directed at me.

I'd spent most of the summer vacation hanging around Michael Scoller. Michael was a local boy who lived by the lake with his parents. He was four years older than Ava and Jorgie, but that didn't stop them slack-jawing in his presence. Jorgie nick-named him Junior because she swore he was an exact replica of Freddie Prince, Jr. from Jorgie's favorite movie at the time, *I Know What You Did Last Summer.*

Much to Jorgie's dismay, Michael only had eyes for Ava.

Unable to dampen the inane jealously that forever swamped me when men paid attention to Ava, I spent the month of my summer vacation acting as if I was Michael's new best friend.

Putting it bluntly, it was a fucking hard month.

Being slapped with a cold fish would have been more enter-taining than hanging out with Michael, but I did it. I gritted my teeth and spent the entire month talking about how dragonflies mate and the difference between the Harry Potter books and their motion pictures. It nearly killed me, but I would have done anything to stop him from getting close to Ava, and my dedication paid off the final night at the cabin.

Every year, a bunch of local teens and a handful of college visi-tors held a final hoorah to summer down by the water's edge. It was generally held in a tiny pocket away from the prying eyes of the parents of the underage teens. After *pretending* to celebrate a little harder than I actually did, Ava aided me in returning to the cabin.

While cackling like the teenage boy I was over the excited gleam in her eyes when we made it up two flights of stairs without incident, I stumbled on my monstrous feet right outside my bedroom door. In slow motion, I tumbled to the floor. Since Ava had her arms curled around my waist, she came crashing down with me.

I was frantic, certain I'd crushed her to death. After rolling off her, I raked my eyes over her face and every inch of her body. She remained silent, staring up at me wide-eyed and slack-jawed. When she spotted my mortified expression, she laughed hysterically. Not the dainty, girly laugh I was used to hearing, instead, it was a belly-crunching, full-hearted chuckle.

Like every time I heard her laugh, any hang-up I had about her being my little sister's best friend unraveled. Before I could blurt out that I'd been crushing on her for years, Ava leaped forward and planted her lips on mine.

Fuck, she tasted good.

The perfect combination of sweetness with the sourness of the watermelon punch she'd been drinking.

Unlike our first kiss, I let Ava control the pace of our exchange. That kiss was just like Ava—sweet and tender. We sat on the floor kissing for hours as if we'd never get the opportunity to do it again.

We didn't.

Only a few short weeks later, Ava walked out of my life with a stream of tears flooding her cheeks and a one-way ticket to San Diego.

That was by far one of the hardest days of my life.

My attention reverts to the present when my hospital door unexpectedly swings open. I inhale a quick, sharp breath when my eyes roam over the man filling the doorway. Even though nearly five years have passed since I last saw him, time has been kind to him. He's barely aged a day.

"Anyone would swear you just saw a ghost," Rhys mutters, pacing further into my hospital room. "I can understand your surprise. The only difference is, I have seen a ghost. A man who vanished without a trace five years ago. Missing, presumed dead." While walking to the end of my bed, he roams his vibrant hazel eyes over my body. "Imagine the shock of arriving in surgery to discover the patient you're there to save is already dead. Has been for years." A smirk curls on his lips. "Well, dead on paper anyway."

"You're the surgeon who saved my life?" My voice comes out heavily drawled as fragments of my past now crash into my present.

Although the full extent of my injuries hasn't been shared with Izzy, the bullet that entered my chest and exited through my left shoulder blade not only nicked my left lung on the way past, but it also rocketed through a vital artery. From what Dr. Jae has informed me, it was the combination of the medical treatment received at the scene and the hands of a gifted surgeon that saved my life. I remember the events leading up to being shot, but everything after being knocked onto my ass is a complete blur.

Rhys nods. "I did everything in my power to save you... just like I did for Jorgie and her baby."

His words slam into me harder than his back hit the wall during our last exchange. When he told me he'd done everything in his power to save Jorgie and her baby, but he had exhausted all avenues and had to let her go, I lost all rational thought.

Even though Jorgie's death was over five years ago, I'm still grieving.

The smirk on Rhys' face fades as his eyes bounce between mine. "You have the same look on your face Ava did when she collected your death certificate two years ago."

My heart freezes at the mention of Ava's name, but fortunately, my outward appearance doesn't give any indication to the treason of my heart. I'm also flabbergasted by Rhys' admission. Normally, when a person disappears, they have to be missing for seven years before declared dead in absentia of a body. I've only been missing for five years, so why did Ava collect my death certificate?

My head shifts to the side when Raquel enters the room. "Next time you decide on a three a.m. shower, can you at least—" Her words stop when she detects an additional presence in the room. A grin stretches across her face when her eyes lift from my drenched hospital gown to Rhys. Although Rhys is discreet, I don't miss his eyes running over Raquel's body.

"Hi, Dr. Tagget," Raquel greets, her tone higher than normal.

Rhys dips his chin in greeting before drifting his eyes back to me. "My employment contract stipulates that utmost diligence is to be given to any patients I serve in this hospital, giving me a clear conscience to pretend I've never seen you."

Raquel's brows scrunch as her eyes bounce between Rhys and me. The tension in the air is so thick, it's palpable. After dipping his chin in farewell to Raquel, Rhys spins on his heels and ambles to the door. Just before he exits, he cranks his head back to look at me. "My conscience is clear, Hugo. Is yours?"

Not giving me the chance to reply, he walks out of the door and closes it behind him.

FOUR
AVA

"Thank you," I say through gritted teeth before sliding into the back seat of an Uber.

The coolness of the leather as I slide across the bench seat does nothing to simmer the fiery rage burning out of control inside of me. While keeping my gaze planted on the dense flow of traffic, I attempt to latch my seat belt. A silent squeal bubbles in my chest when my rough yanks on the seat belt latch causes the safety mechanism to lock in place. I can't move it an inch from my shoulder. When Marvin leans over my shoulder, I stiffen as he gently pulls on the seat belt strap, then clicks it into place.

"Thank you," I say again with less sneer in my tone this time.

"157 McAllister Street," Marvin instructs the Uber driver like he's his personal chauffeur. His flat tone doesn't have a chance in hell of hiding his anger.

The driver nods before seeking an opening in the thick flow of traffic. We've only merged mere inches from the curb when I lose the ability to rein in the annoyance scorching my veins with feverish heat. "Why did you do that, Marvin?" I shift my eyes from the back passenger window of the SUV to him. "You bombarded me in there, leaving me with no other option than to say yes."

I thought having my impurity announced to a room of spectators would remain my number one most embarrassing moment, but Marvin's proposal is cutting it a close second. Not only was the room full of Marvin's family and friends, but it was also packed with people who could aid or destroy any dental career of their choice. Mr. and Mrs. Gardner alone are allies I can't risk as I continue to strive for a prominent place in the notable dental conglomerate of Rochdale.

My nails dig into my palms as I fight to bottle up my anger, needing to store it for a more appropriate time. "*We're* not ready for that." I keep my voice low, ensuring the driver isn't subjected to the awkwardness of our argument. "*I'm* not ready for that."

The last part of my sentence comes out with a quiver when Marvin swings his furious gaze to me. "It's been five goddamn years, Ava!" he roars as the veins in his neck bulge.

Four years, nine months, and three days, I gabble internally to myself.

"For fuck's sake, how much more time do you need?" He yanks on the bowtie around his neck, unknotting it until it dangles around his heaving shoulders. "He's *never* coming back. He left you high and dry. Or did you forget that? He's fucking *dead* yet you still can't let him go."

My heart painfully squeezes, but I'm not surprised by Marvin's outburst. He uses the same cruel words during every argument we have, not the slightest bit concerned about how they affect me. When my tearful eyes stray to the rearview mirror, my breath catches in my throat. The driver's dark eyes are staring straight at me. His gaze is full of worry but with a touch of empathy.

I return his compassionate watch as Marvin continues to

unleash a torrent of vicious words. "Without me, you would have ended up homeless, without a career, without a fucking thing. I fed you, clothed you, have taken care of you for years, but all you care about is a guy who left you. He *left* you, Ava."

His words are like a knife being stabbed into my chest but, unfortunately, everything he's saying is true.

Hugo did leave me.

He chose to go.

Marvin didn't.

After exhaling a deep breath to clear my body of nerves, I tilt my torso to face Marvin. "I know that, Marvin, and I appreciate everything you've done for me, what you still do for me," I say anything to lessen the tirade that always erupts when he drinks or when Hugo's name is mentioned. "I'm thankful for everything you've done, but you know as well as I do, marriage isn't the solution for us. Neither of us is ready for that. I'm not ready, and neither are you."

He stares at me, his chest rising and falling with every breath he takes. His gaze is vehement, and it has my pulse quickening. Not in a good way. It feels like hours pass, but it is mere seconds before he braces his hands on his knees then snaps his eyes back to the heavy flow of traffic, ending our discussion.

"Thank you." I hand the driver a bunch of crinkled notes from my purse. "Keep the change."

His pupils enlarge when he notices the generosity of my tip. A bonus is the least I can do for exposing him to the daily drama of my life.

After sliding out of the SUV, I walk up to my front door that's been left open, exposing my home to the chilly midnight temperatures. When I enter the foyer, I close the door and kick off my shoes. I hang my coat on the coat rack next to Marvin's then step further inside, seeking his retreating frame.

I discover his dark shadow standing in the middle of my compact kitchen. He's clasping a glass of hard liquor. Liquor is Marvin's go-to fix for any dilemma. Mine is a long, hot shower.

Deciding I don't have enough strength for another argument, I leave Marvin to wallow in solitude and head to the main bathroom. Hopefully, a good scalding of hot water will wash away some of the negativity choking my usually carefree attitude.

Upon entering my moderate-size bathroom, I remove my dress and place it in a dry-cleaning bag draped over the bathroom door. Once I've slipped into a satin knee-length kimono, I head for the vanity, deciding to make quick work of the heavy makeup suffocating my pores before having a shower.

As I run a cotton cloth drenched in makeup remover on the dark shadow on my eyelids, I roam my eyes over the new ringlets sprouting through my hair. Since I had my hair chemically straightened over five years ago, my curls are returning stronger than ever. In the past six months, I've made three separate appointments to have my unruly locks straightened again, but every time without fail, I neglect to attend my appointment.

Although it was well over ten years ago, the memories of Hugo twirling my hair around his finger as we watched reruns of *Friends* were in the forefront of my mind every time I was working up the courage to walk into my local hair salon. It might have been the smallest memory, but it still has the greatest impact on my suffering heart.

My reminiscing is interrupted when Marvin staggers into the bathroom. Whiskey and cheap cologne infiltrate my senses when he props his hip onto the vanity counter. "I'm going to head to my place."

"It's past midnight, Marvin—"

"I know," he interrupts, his tone surly. "But I have some paperwork I need to take care of."

I shift on my feet to face him. "It can't wait until morning?"

"No." His reply is swift, short, and demoralizing.

With his eyes locked on the vanity, he presses a kiss to my temple. When he pulls away, his eyes drift down to the engagement ring shimmering in the bathroom light. I'll give credit where credit is due. The ring is beautiful, a princess cut three-carat diamond of the highest quality, but just from looking at it, I know Marvin didn't choose it. He barely has time to look me in the eyes, let alone pick out my engagement ring.

Marvin lifts his bloodshot eyes to mine. "There could be far worse options for you than marrying me. You're lucky I came into your life when I did. You should remember that."

With that, he pivots on his heels and ambles out of the room.

I wait until my front door slams shut before I call him every curse name under the sun. I don't hold back. Words I swore I'd never speak come out of my mouth in a tirade a sailor on shore leave would be proud of. My rant is highly inappropriate but one hundred percent accurate. Every curse word I've heard in my life could describe Marvin in some form. *Asshole. Two-faced bastard. Motherfucker.* Those are a small handful of the words spilling from my mouth right now. And they're the tame ones.

After a long, boiling shower, annoyance is still firmly clutching my neck, asphyxiating me. I throw the frilly decorative pillows off my bed like they're missiles before diving under the thick down quilt. Even surrounded by softness greater than a cloud, the tension tightly coiling my muscles makes me restless.

I stare at the bedside table on my left, willing it to answer my silent questions as to whether it can calm the storm raging inside me.

There's only one way I can relieve this type of tension, and an item in the drawer is the perfect solution.

I scoot across the bed and fling open the cherry oak drawer. My heart rate quickens when I delve my hand inside to hunt through the drawer full to the brim with odd knick-knacks and ornaments. My breath hitches when my fingertips brush a smooth, cool surface. I grasp the item tightly in my hand, knowing it's what I'm seeking without needing to see it.

As my eyes dart around my room, I yank my hand out of the drawer like I've been scorched by an ignited flame. Once I'm sure the coast is clear, I slowly pry the shiny glass instrument away from my heaving chest.

As I twist the lid on the bottle, I snap my eyes shut, then urge my tears to stay at bay. Hot, salty blobs roll down my cheeks when the invigorating smell of Woods of Windsor aftershave fills the air. Even though it doesn't have the scent of his skin mixed with it, it is an energizing smell that sends a flurry of emotions coursing through my mind.

After placing the smallest dab of the aftershave Hugo left sitting on my bathroom sink nearly five years ago onto my pillow, I put the bottle back into the drawer then snuggle into the pillow.

No matter how hard I try, no matter how many days, months, or years pass, I can't forget.

My heart will never forget him.

When my eyelids become as heavy as my heart, my mind drifts.

My very first thoughts go to him.

Hugo.

FIVE

HUGO

"Hugo!" Izzy squeals at the top of her lungs when I wrap my good arm around her waist and hoist her off the floor.

I've just arrived at the annual Christmas Eve party billionaire Cormack McGregor holds every year. Cormack is one of Isaac's oldest and dearest friends. Even though he's filthy rich, he's one of the most stellar guys I've ever met. Just like Isaac, his heart is bigger than his bank account.

Although Cormack's party isn't as extravagant as his other functions I've attended over the past five years, it is my favorite. The atmosphere is relaxed, the focus more on guests having a good time than attempting to drain their pockets for the various charities Cormack and Isaac chair.

When I place Izzy back onto her feet, she spins around to face me. Her jaw is hanging low, and her eyes are open wide. After running her eyes over my face, she drops them to my body. She's done the same thing every day for the past week. No matter how many times I assure her my injuries resulted from due diligence, she still harbors guilt about what happened.

"Is the sling a necessity? Or are you trying to get sympathy points from the ladies?" she quips, her tone playful as she peers at the sling holding my injured shoulder in place.

I throw my head back and laugh. "A bit of column A, a bit of column B," I retort, loving that the guilt plaguing her eyes the past week is diminishing with time.

After drifting my gaze from Izzy's glistening chocolate eyes to Harlow, Izzy's best friend, I ask, "Are you going to share one of those?" I nudge my head to the bottle of tequila she's clasping. "Since I'm officially not on duty and can't get fired by Izzy misbehaving, I may as well have a little bit of fun."

My deep chuckle booms around the room when Izzy sticks out her tongue. If I squint, I could pretend she's Jorgie.

Harlow waggles her brows before pouring four shots of tequila into gold-flecked shot glasses. After handing me a shot glass, she playfully winks. "Bottoms up."

Just as the scent of tequila hits my senses, the shot glass is snatched from my hand. "Or not." Regan downs my nip of tequila.

I balk, surprised when she doesn't grab a wedge of lime from the round bar table after she swallows the nip of tequila in one quick gulp.

"Come on, Regan, one shot won't kill me."

Regan is Raquel's older sister. If that doesn't already make her a ball crusher, she's also Isaac's friend and lawyer.

Regan quirks her lips. "No, but Raquel might if she finds out you were drinking alcohol after taking pain medication."

I scoff. "If she stopped ramming them down my throat, I wouldn't have to worry."

Regan smiles a bright grin. As much as she would deny it, she loves that Raquel is following in her footsteps. Raquel's hard ass, take-shit-from-no-one stance has been wearing my patience thin the past week, but in all honesty, even with her busting my chops at every opportunity, I can admit, she's good at her job.

Without her pushing me, I'd most likely still be laid up in a hospital bed, stewing over my confrontation with Rhys.

Only now, years after the incident, do I realize I was in the wrong regarding the way I reacted when Rhys informed me Jorgie wasn't going to pull through her injuries. In my defense, part of me died the day Jorgie did. And no matter how hard I fight to piece back the shattered pieces of my heart, it never happens.

It will never happen.

My eyes float up from the floor when Isaac asks, "How did you get out of Raquel's clutches for the night?"

"I didn't," I grumble, my mood balancing dangerously between somber and playful. "She sent her evil twin in her place."

It swings to playful when Regan throws her clutch into my chest, winding me from the power of her hit. I chuckle while ribbing her with my elbow. Although Regan acts like she hates me, the tears that frequented her eyes every time she visited me in the hospital tells me she likes me a little more than she's letting on. But just like Raquel, as much as taming the beast raging inside Regan would be a compelling feat, she's too much of a friend for me to tread over that line.

I cringe when a high-pitched voice shrieks through my ears. "Holy crap! What is that?"

My eyes shoot to Cormack's little sister, Cate. Her bugging eyes are planted on a glistening of color sparkling on Izzy's hand.

Izzy's teeth munch on her bottom lip as she confesses, "We're engaged."

I can't hold back the grin that morphs onto my face. Although Izzy and Isaac have only been together a few short months, time is no barrier when you find your other half. It shouldn't matter if it is a week or a year, if they're who your heart desires, that's all that matters.

Oh god, would you listen to me?

Maybe I did get shot in the cock instead of my shoulder.

My brows furrow from the stern glare Isaac directs at me when I issue my congratulations to Izzy with a friendly hug. He knows me. I'd never cut another man's turf.

After shrugging off Isaac's newly acquired second green head, I slip away from the group and head for the bar. I lift my chin in greeting to the bartender preparing a spritzer for a slightly over-weight lady wearing a dress five sizes too big for her luscious body.

"Can I grab a beer?" I request after plonking on the barstool.

The bartender places a coaster in front of me before setting an open bottle of beer on top.

"Where have I seen you?" I ask while raising the beer to my parched mouth.

He seems familiar, but his name has been misplaced, which is unusual for me. I have a stellar knack for matching names with faces.

"Dante," he introduces himself. After wiping his condensa-tion-covered hand down a white tea towel hanging off his waist, he offers it in greeting.

I accept his hand. "Hugo."

He tries to mask his surprise, but I didn't miss his quick gasp that relays he knows who I am. Not the Hugo Jones everyone in Ravenshoe knows but the real Hugo who vanished from Rochdale nearly five years ago.

The pulse thrumming in Dante's neck increases when I squeeze his hand with more force than I was originally instilling. He tries to pry his hand out of my grasp, but his small frame is no match for a man of my size.

"Please don't break my hand. I'm starting my internship to be a surgeon next month," he begs, his eyes pleading.

"How do you know me?" My tone is low as anger envelops me. I've reached my quota of run-ins with people from my past. First, I had to deal with Col Petretti sniffing around Ravenshoe, then Rhys, now Dante.

"My brother," he stammers as the bones in his hand creak from my brutal pressure. "My brother is Rhys."

My eyes dance over his face—same mocha skin coloring, hazel eyes, and prominent nose. I don't know how I missed it. He's the spitting image of his older brother.

The strain hampering Dante's face relaxes when I free his hand from my grip. He shoots it across the counter, ensuring it isn't within my reach. When I swig on my beer, he eyeballs my every move.

I shift my eyes around the room to ensure no one witnessed my small confrontation with Dante. Isaac is talking to Clara at my left, and Izzy is strolling toward the makeshift dance floor with Cormack's younger brother, Colby, closely in pursuit.

Once I'm happy no one is watching, I shift my eyes back to Dante. "Why are you in Ravenshoe?"

"Rhys is my guardian," he mutters. "Until I finish my studies, I go where he goes."

My brows stitch together in shock. "What happened to your parents?" Mr. and Mrs. Tagget have been members of the Rochdale community as long as my parents. Mrs. Tagget was my fifth-grade teacher, and Mr. Tagget was the local obstetrician.

The devastation of his loss still weighs heavily in his readable eyes when he informs me, "They were killed in a traffic accident nearly five years ago."

"I'm sorry for your loss." Although my eyes issue my sympathies for the loss of his parents, they also deliver my repentance for my earlier overreaction.

Dante nods, accepting my apology before moving down the bar to serve another patron.

My attention lapses from perusing the dance floor when a flurry of red catches my eyes. "Hi," Peta breathes out heavily, slipping into the space beside me.

"Hey." I swig on my beer to conceal my assessment of her face and body.

Peta is Cormack's secretary and the *second* sexiest woman alive. She has flawless, rich, tan skin, unique light brownish-yellowish eyes, and a face hand-carved by sculptors. She's no doubt gorgeous, and even better than that, she's not a friend of mine.

"Did you want to dance?"

My lips purse, shocked by her request. Although we've openly flirted the past year, it's gone no further than a few corny one-liners. That may have more to do with the fact I refuse to ask anyone out. Not to a date, to the movies, or even to dance. I have never asked out anyone before Ava, and I will never ask anyone out after her.

When Peta runs a shaky finger over the curve of her top lip, I realize I failed to answer her question. "Sure, I'd love to dance," I say with a grin.

I guzzle down the last of my beer before guiding her to the dance floor by placing my hand on the small of her back. My eyes scan the area as we approach, ensuring it is clear of any encumbrances. Screening the premises is as natural as breathing to me. It is a habit that was engrained in me years ago, way before Ava and I reunited. Although I'd always done it, it became more important after Ava was nearly attacked in a dance club right under my nose.

Some may see my constant surveillance as an annoying practice. To me, it isn't. Keeping an eye out for safety means I won't get blinded by other people's bad habits.

After nearly an hour of dancing, my dress shirt is limp, weighed down by a mountain-load of sweat, my throat is parched, and my shoulder is wailing in pain, though I'd never admit the latter to Raquel. I lean into Peta's side, ensuring she can hear me over the loud rumble of music booming out the speakers. "I'm going to grab a quick drink," I shout in her ear. "Did you want anything?"

She spins on her heels, revealing inches of skin on her luxurious thigh when the split in her dress gapes open. Spotting her mouth-watering legs has me reconsidering what hankering to tackle first. My thirst or another irrepressible hunger only a woman can quench.

"A bottle of water?" Peta's unease makes her request come out as more of a question than a demand. "Then maybe we can get out of here?" she adds, her voice trembling.

As I peer into her famished eyes, my head slants to the side. The unsure grin curling her lips morphs into a full smile when I nod. Winking at the excitement crossing her face, I pivot on my heels and make my way to the bar. Dante's throat works hard to swallow when he notices my approach. If I weren't thinking with my lower head, I'd properly apologize for my earlier overreaction, but since I very much am, that apology will have to wait.

After gathering my beer and a glass of iced water, I amble back to the dance floor. My steps are fast, eager to wash off the funk I've been sporting the past week. My brisk strides falter when a deep voice says, "If I squint, I can see the similarities."

I crank my neck faster than a rocket launching into space.

Rhys is standing behind a round bar table. Unlike last week, he's forgone his surgical scrubs and stethoscope, choosing the classier look of a sleek black suit with a pale green dress shirt.

With the air saturated with mugginess from a large gathering of people in a small space, he's removed his suit jacket and rolled up his shirt sleeves, exposing his vast collection of tattoos. Just like my arms, every inch of skin on Rhys' forearms is covered in artwork.

Just seeing him floods my head with memories I try to keep buried.

Imagine what it would be like if I ever saw her again?

After lifting my chin in greeting, I continue with my initial objective.

"Poor girl. Does she know you're looking at her as a doppelgänger?"

I grit my teeth but continue walking, ignoring Rhys' taunt. I'm not the same man I was five years ago. I've learned to hide my spikes well.

"She may look like Ava, but you sure as hell know even someone as beautiful as her can't compete with a woman of Ava's qualities. No one can compete with Ava's sweetness."

I freeze halfway between the bar and the dance floor. I suck in quick, rapid-fire breaths to calm the anger bubbling in my veins, but no matter what I do, no matter how much I try to suffocate the jealousy building like an out-of-control wildfire, I can't squash it.

I've never been able to rein in my anger when it comes to Ava.

Before contemplating what I'm doing, I spin on my heels and charge for Rhys. He doesn't balk. He doesn't even blink when he notices me storming his way. He stands his ground like a man who is on a mission to unravel me one thread at a time.

"Even after all this time, she's still under your skin." His eyes bounce between mine. "She's right where you left her, Hugo. If you want her that much, why don't you go get her?"

"I left for a reason." My angry snarl booms over the blaring music.

"Yeah, and that reason is now dead."

I balk and take a step backward.

"Come on, Hugo. Give me some credit. I'm a lot smarter than I look." He takes a step closer to me, bringing us chest to chest. "The man who was charged with running down Jorgie goes missing the exact day the victim's brother falls off the face of the earth, never to be seen again."

In the corner of my eye, I catch Hunter watching the exchange between Rhys and me. He scrubs a hand over his scruffy beard, signaling he's positioned to step in at any time. I shake my head, advising him that I've got this.

Although Hunter moves deeper into the crowd, I can feel his eyes on me when I say, "Get your facts straight before you go running your mouth. We're not in Rochdale."

Rhys smirks, not the faintest bit intimidated by my threatening tone. "Col Petretti wanted your blood. When he couldn't get it, he went after the next closest thing."

"That is why I left!" I snap out, incapable of inhibiting my anger for a second longer. "That's why I stayed away. To protect my family!" *To protect Ava.*

Rhys's strong stance weakens. "I understand that, but you can't use that excuse anymore. Col Petretti is dead. I saw his body myself. So, if you want to keep hiding, pretending you're dead too, you'll need to find another excuse because your last one expired."

My nostrils flare as my lungs fight hard to cool my overheated body. Even though everything Rhys is saying is true, it doesn't stop the anger pumping my veins with ferocious heat.

Rhys rolls down his shirt sleeves then puts on his jacket. Once his coat is buttoned, he locks his eyes with mine. "It took courage to walk away like you did. To sacrifice everything to keep your family safe. To keep Ava safe, but a man who can admit he made a mistake would be even more courageous than that."

With a flash of an uneasy smirk, he exits Destiny Records' head office without a backward glance.

By the time Peta finds me standing where Rhys left me, her glass of water is sitting at room temperature, and my mood is woeful. Her unique light brown eyes dance between mine as she says, "I'll catch you at the next function?"

I nod, press a kiss on her cheek then make my way to my car. Everything Rhys said plays on repeat for the drive to my apartment building, but it isn't as simple as he's making it out to be. Just because Col is dead doesn't mean I can waltz back into my old life like nothing happened.

I'm also dead.

The Hugo Marshall who was born in Rochdale is dead. I can't come back from that. And even if I wanted to pretend those facts don't matter, there'd be no possibility a woman like Ava would still be single and waiting for my return. *Would there?*

Hawke's head lifts from his laptop when he hears me entering the front door of my apartment. Although Isaac offered him his own apartment, he was happy to camp in the spare bedroom of my place while I was recovering at Regan's.

When I rip the stupid shoulder brace off my body and dump it into the bin in the kitchen, he watches me cautiously but remains quiet. I grab a cold beer out of the refrigerator then crack it open on the marble countertop before his curiosity gets the better of him. "Good night?"

I grunt before flopping onto the white leather sofa in the sunken living room. After snagging a few extra beers, Hawke joins me. If I ignore the cracks in my heart, I could pretend we're sitting back in his den, laughing and drinking beers like we did every Sunday afternoon when he wasn't deployed.

As the hours tick by, the beers sloshing in my belly lessen the anger coursing through my veins.

"Come back with me," I blurt out, my mouth choosing to speak before my brain can object. "Come back with me to Rochdale."

Hawke stiffens but remains as quiet as a church mouse.

"I can't," he eventually replies while staring at a speckle of dust. "I can't go back there without her."

"Do you think she'd want this, Hawke? Do you think Jorgie would want us to live like this? If you can even call it living. You're fucking miserable." My volume rises as a surge of emotions pummel me. "Jorgie would be rolling in her grave—"

Before any more of my drunken tirade can escape my lips, Hawke drags me off the sofa and pins me to the wall of my living room by my throat. The veins in his neck bulge when he tightens his grip, and his nostrils flare as his broken, desolate eyes burn into mine.

"She's never coming back, Hawke," I sputter, my words cracking.

He yanks me forward before slamming me back with force. My body doesn't register the pain of my head slamming into the hard wall. It's too focused on the hurt projecting out of Hawke's lifeless eyes to register anything. I don't even put up a fight because I know he needs this even more than I do.

My watering eyes drift between his. "She's gone, Hawke."

"You don't think I know that!" he roars, the veins in his neck bulging. "I wake up every fucking day praying it was a nightmare, that Jorgie and Malcolm are still here, but it *never* happens. I *never* wake up! So you don't need to tell me she's gone. I'm stuck in this fucking recurring nightmare. I live it every fucking day, so I know she is gone!"

His jaw quivers as wetness floods his eyes. As he struggles through the same emotions that cripple me every time I think about the loss of Jorgie and my nephew... *and Ava,* his chest heaves up and down before he eventually loosens his grip on my neck.

"But you don't have to live in this nightmare if you don't want to. Ava can pull you out of it." He flicks his eyes between mine. "But only you can choose if you want her to save you." My feet return to the floor when he takes a giant step back. "I'd give anything for another day with Jorgie, to have her in my arms, to hold my son, but I don't have that opportunity." He waits a beat to settle the emotions in his voice before saying, "But you do, Hugo."

After picking up the reclining chair he knocked over as if it is weightless, he staggers out of the room, his steps as heavy as the weight on my chest.

SIX

HUGO

My hand darts down to the window crank of my car—*Jorgie's baby*. As I shift my eyes between the road and the window mechanism, I wind the window up, lessening the blast of cold air blowing in from outside.

It's colder here than I remember.

The crisp wind, chilled with sleet, has the tip of my nose turning a shade of red.

I didn't even pack a jacket.

Every mile I travel quickens my heart rate. Even though it's been years since I've been here, I know the way. It's engrained in me. I took the same route I used when I left—all back roads hidden from prying eyes. The candy apple coloring of my car is now murky brown, thanks to the dust flying off the roads I've driven on.

The tremble pounding my heart extends to my hands when the 'Welcome to Rochdale' sign peers over the horizon. I've been driving for hours, nearly nine straight. I only pulled over for gas before I continued on my mission. I couldn't give my brain the chance to formulate an objection to the rushed decision I made while licking my wounds from my tussle with Hawke.

Upon noticing the gauge is once again sitting close to empty, I pull into a gas station on the outskirts of the main town district. The quietness that surrounds me when I switch off the ignition and curl out of the driver's seat is disturbing. When there's too much silence, my mind tends to wander.

When I duck back into the cab to grab my wallet, I snatch a baseball cap and pull it down low over my head. While filling up the gas tank, I drink in my surroundings. Five years have passed, but it looks like nothing has changed. The graffiti on the brick wall attached to St. Mary's Church is still there, only faded and accentuated with new tags. The sign dangling out front of Gus's Grease Box is still rusted and askew, and the inquisitive gawks are still present.

Nothing's changed.

I place the gas nozzle back into the pump then enter the service station, eager to pay for my gas and continue with my trip. It's late, and I'm beyond tired.

My heart rate kicks up when the automatic glass doors swing open, and many pairs of eyes turn to me. I lower my shirt sleeves, concealing my tattoos that normally conjure nosey gazers, then make my way to the attendant. Several pairs of eyes track me as I walk across the tiled space. Even with a cap hanging low on my face and my appearance altered with age, I know their curious stares aren't associated with a stranger arriving in the middle of the night.

They come from recognition.

I was born and raised in Rochdale, the beloved quarterback of the high school football team that was crowned State Champions two years in a row under my leadership, and even if they're too young to remember my glory days or too old to care, my family are well-known members of the community.

I'm also the spitting image of my father. My eyes, my nose, hell, my entire face is an exact replica of his.

"Pump four."

I toss three rolled-up twenties onto the counter before spinning on my heels.

I always pay with cash. No cards mean no chance of being tracked.

My brisk strides slow when the cashier shouts, "You forgot your change."

After raising my arm in the air, I reply, "Keep it."

I stop frozen in my tracks when the cashier replies, "I can't do that, Hugo. It's against the rules."

The automatic doors open and close, unsure if I'm coming or going.

They aren't the only ones confused.

After exhaling a big breath, I spin on my heels. The walk back to the counter is painstakingly long, but when I reach it, I raise my chin high enough to see the cashier's face, but low enough mine isn't fully exposed.

A grin carves on my mouth when the petite frame of Mary Walker pops into my peripheral vision. Her glistening blue eyes stare into mine, her excitement building with every step I take.

"Hey." Grinning broadly, she fiddles with the hem of her floral skirt. "I knew it was you."

Mary was in Ava and Jorgie's grade at school. Since she was born ten weeks premature, she's always been a tiny little thing, looking much younger than her real age. Her older brother, Mitchell, was a good friend of mine in high school. We lost contact when his life took a ride down a steep hill while mine hit a brick wall.

"How are you doing, Mary?" I ask while accepting the crumpled-up notes she's holding out and shoving them into my jeans pocket.

Her smile broadens, both shocked and happy that I remember her. "Good," she replies quietly. "If you're in town long, come on over to the house one day. Mitchy would love to see you."

With twisted lips, I nod. "I will. I'll try and get there later this week."

She smiles even bigger. With a dip of my chin, I bid farewell to Mary before walking out of the gas station, not missing the extra sets of eyes I gained from our brief exchange.

After sliding into my car, I crank the ignition, loving the rush of adrenaline the healthy roar of a motor always gives me. As I pull onto the road, I roll the window back down, needing the crispness in the air to calm the mad beat of my heart.

One mile is all I have left to travel.

The town is quiet, not surprising since it's late on Christmas Day.

As I pull down a familiar street, my eyes drift between familiar buildings and features. The same wrought iron lights line the edge of the cracked concrete sidewalks, where clapboard houses in a range of pastel colors, and rolling lush front yards are situated on either side.

Nothing's changed.

I release my heavy compression on the accelerator, slowly creeping closer to my childhood home. When I come to a stop in front of the two-story house, I'm not surprised when I spot a light flicking in the back right-hand corner of the property. No doubt, my mom is still packing away the dishes from the Marshall Christmas party she hosts every year.

I wonder what her reaction will be when I stroll back into her life? Will she greet me like she did the morning I turned up for family brunch? Or will she be angry for the way I left?

"There's only one way to find out," I mumble to no one.

I pull into the driveway and park behind my mom's station wagon, shocked she still drives that old piece of crap. My hand shakes when I crank open the car door and step out onto the concrete driveway. The smell of pumpkin pie and mashed potatoes filters in the air as I stride down the side of the house. My steps are fast and uninhibited, ensuring I don't allow myself to back down on my quest.

I've daydreamed about this day for years, but I never thought it would come to fruition.

As I grip the screen door handle, I will for the memories of the last time I exited these doors to slip my mind. Then, once I've sucked in a lung-filling gulp of air, I yank open the door. The old wood gives out a creak, but it's barely heard over the Christmas music playing on a radio in the middle of the kitchen counter.

As I step into the sweet-smelling space, I absorb the room.

Nothing's changed.

It is *exactly* the same.

My mom's hair, although a little grayer than I remember around the temples, is pulled back in a bun. She has a pair of pink gloves on her hands as she works her way through a pile of dirty dishes stacked at her side.

Her hips bob side to side as she sways to "Jingle Bell Rock" by Bobby Helms drifting from the speaker on the counter. Half-eaten pies and containers of food are stacked on the same counter. The refrigerator is most likely too crammed to fit in all the goodies she bakes every Christmas.

I open my mouth, preparing to speak, but my words halt in my throat when the swinging door between the kitchen and the dining room swings open, and Ava glides inside. My heart freezes along with my feet.

My god, she's even more beautiful than I remember.

Her hair is a crazy mess of ringlet curls sitting a few inches past her shoulders, and her face is fresh and unmarked. She hasn't aged a day in five years, and her body is captivating. Her lush tits are only just hidden by a dusty pink cashmere sweater that's hem sits above her rounded hips. Her stomach is smooth and flat, and although I can't see her legs through her black jeans, I'm sure they're as stellar as the rest of her. She's captivatingly beautiful, and I'm on the verge of dropping to my damn knees.

My heart freezes for the second time when a scream rips through my eardrums. My mom's focus is no longer on the dirty dishes. She's staring at me wide-eyed, her face pale and full of disbelief.

Her squeal demands Ava's attention. When she follows my mom's fretful stare, Ava slowly pivots around to face me. When her eyes lock on my face, she intakes a sharp breath and tears well in her eyes. The wine glass she's holding plummets to the floor when she clamps her gaped mouth to muffle her shocked scream. The wine glass shatters around her feet as the first tear slides down her cheek.

SEVEN
AVA

When an ear-piercing scream rattles through my core, I spin on my heels, panicked beyond comprehension at what has caused Mrs. Marshall to react in such a way. Her entire body shakes, and her face is pale, clearly in shock. She looks like she's seen a ghost. When I swing my eyes to the side, both eager and fearful to discover what has caused her unusual reaction, her response makes sense.

She is staring at a ghost—as am I.

The air is vehemently removed from my lungs when my eyes drink in a face I only see in my dreams. The shock slicks my hands with sweat, and before I can stop it, my wine glass slips from my grasp and plummets to the floor. It shatters into a million pieces at my feet, but I can't look away.

This can't be true.

It can't be him.

He's dead.

Gone.

Never coming back.

After clamping my gaped mouth to ensure the contents of my churning stomach can't escape, I snap my eyes shut and shake my head, compelling myself to wake up. I must have fallen asleep, or perhaps I'm in a food-induced coma from eating too many carbohydrates during Christmas dinner.

My breath hitches halfway between my lungs and my throat when my eyes slowly flutter open, and the man from both my nightmares and dreams still stands before me.

Even with half of his face shadowed by the brim of a baseball cap, I'd never forget that profile—his plump, delicious lips, perfectly straight nose, and eyes that captured my soul and never gave it back.

It is him.

Hugo.

The man who both loved and destroyed me.

Mrs. Marshall's shocked face doesn't lessen any as her head flings between Hugo and me. Even with tears streaming down her face, her excitement at seeing her youngest son again is evident all over her beautiful face. She graces me with a shaky smile before she dashes to Hugo. Her steps are slow and unstable, overwhelmed with the same emotions keeping my feet firmly planted on the floor.

She crashes into Hugo with so much force, a woosh of air parts his lips. As she slings her arms around his neck, a tormented sob tears from her mouth. I lower my shaky hand to my thigh and pinch it hard, urging myself to wake up.

I pinch so hard, I'll be sporting a nasty bruise in the morning, but I don't wake up.

Surely, I'm dreaming.

I have to be.

Mrs. Marshall's loud cries secure the attention of the remaining Marshall residents still clearing away the mess of a chaotic Christmas Day. Although we're all exhausted, none of us wanted to leave the burden solely on Mrs. Marshall's shoulders.

Mr. Marshall's brisk strides to his wife falter when Hugo's head lifts from his mom's neck. She accidentally knocked off his cap, fully exposing his Marshall family heirloom—his glistening baby blues.

I bite the inside of my cheek hard, battling to keep my tears at bay when Mr. Marshall's knees buckle, and he lands on the floor with a thud. Tears seep from his eyes as unbridled joy overwhelms him.

When Chase and Helen rush into the kitchen, their faces morphing from panicked to astounded in record-breaking time, I fling a handful of rogue tears off my cheeks. They help their father from the floor before greeting Hugo with the same enthusiasm their mother showed.

I stand still, numb and in shock. My brain can't comprehend the complexity of the situation, let alone command my legs to move.

The last person to enter the kitchen is Marvin. He appears more annoyed about the interruption than concerned about what caused Mrs. Marshall's screams. He props his shoulder onto the doorjamb, then swings his eyes around the room like the situation unfolding is nowhere near as heart-tugging as it is.

When, in the corner of my eye, I spot Hugo patting his brother on the back before stepping past him, I revert my attention back to the Marshall family reunion. My heart thrashes wildly against my ribs when Hugo's hooded gaze locks with mine before he prowls my way.

His eyes blaze into mine, and they render me more motionless than my shock. As they lower to absorb my body, a salacious smirk curls his lips. He looks like a cat staring at a bowl of cream, and his grin causes more than my heart to thud.

Suddenly, his pace slows before he swallows harshly. I discover the reason for the brisk change-up when I follow the direction of his gaze. His eyes are glued to the diamond dazzling in the bright overhead lighting. He's staring at my engagement ring, scorching it with as much heat as I used when Marvin popped open the box it was nestled in.

I battle not to squirm. Hugo always had an issue with jealousy.

I'm glad to see nothing's changed.

After returning his baby blues to my face, Hugo musters up a fake smirk before recommencing his long strides. The sparkle lighting up his vibrant eyes dampens when I'm unexpectedly clutched around the waist and pulled into a heated body.

"We should go, Ava," Marvin jerks me in even tighter, his grip firm enough to sting. "Our Uber has arrived." He gestures his hand to a black SUV parked behind an unfamiliar car in the driveway before using my shock to his advantage.

After guiding me past Hugo, he shoves my coat into my hands then drags my beanie over my crazy curls. Bitterly cold winds blast my face when he ushers me onto the back patio. I'm shaking intensely, but I don't know if it's from the crispness of the winter night or because I'm traumatized. It may be a combination of both. I've been hoping for this day to happen for five years, but I never thought it would actually occur.

"Ava," murmurs a voice from behind.

A voice I immediately recognize.

A voice I'll never forget.

"Keep walking, Ava," Marvin demands before he seizes my elbow and drags me toward the waiting Uber.

His eagerness for us to leave doesn't slow Hugo down. "Ava, wait." He leaps off the patio, then follows us down the concrete path. "Just give me a minute. That's all I'm asking for... a mere minute."

The plea in Hugo's tone has my eyes shooting up to Marvin, stupidly requesting permission. As his lips thin, he briskly shakes his head, denying my wordless request. He yanks open the SUV's door with aggression, snatches my coat from my hand, throws it into the Uber, then gestures for me to enter before him.

Although shocked my body instinctively jumps to obey him, the disbelief hazing my astute mind clears when Hugo mutters under his breath, "Nothing's changed. You're still letting a man tell you what to do. First your dad, now Marvin."

Something inside me snaps, and for the first time in years, it isn't my heart. When I pivot on my heel, preparing to storm toward the cause of the agony in my chest, Marvin snatches my wrist, halting my angry steps. I yank out of his belittling hold, my anger too great for him to stop me. A jolt of pain spasms up my arm, but I'm too irate to register it.

"Give me one goddamn minute!" I snarl through clenched teeth, my sneer for my second tormentor.

Marvin glares at me, but his slit eyes hold no threat.

Even if they did, nothing could stop me.

This confrontation has been years in the making.

My entire body shakes when I race Hugo's way, but I continue on, only stopping when I'm within an inch of his face. I'm so close, our chests connect with every breath we inhale. "Don't you dare judge me!" I scream like tears aren't threatening to spill down my cheeks. "You don't know what I've been through. The hell I went through." I pound my enclosed fists on his chest. "So you can't come waltzing back into the picture, acting like nothing happened. It's been five years, Hugo! Five goddamn fucking years!" As I step back, I angrily brush away a string of curls that have fallen in front of my face. "You can't come back from that amount of time and pretend it never happened."

"We have before," he argues as his remorseful eyes bounce between mine.

"We were kids." As the pain in my chest cripples me, my voice lowers to a whimper. "Stupid pathetic kids too young to know any better."

Hugo shakes his head before stepping closer to me. "The past cannot be changed, forgotten, edited, or erased. It can only be accepted."

I spread my hand across his chest, keeping him at a safe distance. "You can't change the past... but you can learn from it. I let you back in my life once. I learned from my mistake. I will *not* make it again."

With that, I pivot on my heels and race back to the idling Uber. While ignoring Marvin's obvious anger, I slide into the back seat and slam the door shut, forcing Marvin to enter the SUV from the other side.

Against the better judgment of my head, I float my eyes up from my balled fists. The pain making it hard for me to breathe amplifies when I spot Hugo fighting to get out of his brother's clutch. His expression is devasted, and the number of times he begs for the chance to explain threatens to tear my heart in two.

Marvin doesn't care, though. He enters the Uber from the opposite side, recites my address to the driver, then settles in for a lengthy bout of you-are-in-Marvin's-bad-book silence.

I don't mind. His cold shoulder will give me plenty of time to gather my skewed emotions that I'll bottle away until I'm alone and without the fear of repercussions.

EIGHT
HUGO

Everything's changed.

"Ava!" I shout as her Uber reverses out of the driveway of my childhood home.

After shrugging out of Chase's hold, I chase after her with more than words. My steps are sluggish, weighed down by the heaviness of a maimed heart. Seeing Ava cry hurts more than I could have ever imagined but knowing I'm the cause of her tears makes it ten times worse. It killed me seeing tears stream down her pale cheeks, but I want the chance to wipe them away, to beg for forgiveness. I want to explain what happened, and why I did what I did, but I didn't even get to say hello.

Or goodbye.

When the taillights of the SUV become nothing but a speckle of red on the horizon, I crouch down on the ground still misting from the heat of the engine passing over before running a shaky hand over my head. I don't know what I was expecting. I knew Ava's reaction wouldn't mirror my mom's, but I was hoping it would follow a similar path. That happy tears would flow down her face, not ones filled with heartbreak and despair.

If I were honest, I'd admit on the drive here I was kind of hoping Ava had moved on and that she was married and had a couple of kids. Because if she was happy, the guilt I've felt for the past five years wouldn't have been warranted. I was hopeful my absence only caused a slight ripple in her pond, not a tidal wave. But from the devastated look in her eyes when she banged her fists on my chest, screaming about the hell she's been living, I realized my prayers were left unanswered, just like Ava's.

It felt like a grizzly bear was clawing my chest when I noticed the giant rock on her ring finger, but that maim was nothing compared to the pain that shredded through me when Marvin clutched Ava's waist. That grizzly didn't just sink his claws into my heart, he ripped it out of my chest and shredded it to pieces. I want Ava to be happy, but that won't be possible if she's engaged to a man like Marvin. He doesn't deserve her. Not in a million years. And I won't stop until she knows that.

I'm pulled from dangerous thoughts when Chase squeezes my shoulder before he squats down in front of me. "Give her some time, Hugo. It's been a really long and now emotionally draining day."

He's preaching to the wrong person.

It's been the longest fucking day of my life.

After standing, Chase offers me his hand. Snubbing the guilt creeping into my veins that I caused my family more anguish, I accept his offer. Pain rockets through my shoulder when he yanks me from the ground with a hearty tug.

I don't relish pain, but it is a good reminder of how far I've come.

"Getting a bit soft in your old age," Chase jests when he hears the wince I failed to fully stifle.

I bite back a huff. "Something like that."

He playfully barges me before he curls his arm around my shoulder and guides me back inside a place I once thought was home but am slowly learning its foundation doesn't make it that.

The people inside it do.

"You're got to be kidding me!" My words are barely audible from the breathy chuckle escaping my lips. "It's *exactly* the same!"

With a nod, Chase laughs. "Mom didn't change a fucking thing." He dumps my overnight bag onto my childhood bed with its shamefully embarrassing camo bedspread. "Even Jorgie's room is the same."

Since it came out of Chase's mouth, it doesn't hurt hearing Jorgie's name as much as it normally would. I often forget I'm not the only one who lost Jorgie. Everyone in this house did. Ava included.

"How long has Ava been engaged?" I try to keep my tone neutral, but it smears with agitation at the end of my question. I'm still shocked as fuck that out of all the men in the world, Ava paired up with Marvin.

Chase screws up his nose. Apparently, he isn't a fan of Marvin's either. "From what Helen told me, it happened last week, but Ava hasn't officially announced it yet."

My lips quirk, pleased by his response. When Chase senses my piqued interest, he arches a brow. Although the corners of his eyes are creased with wrinkles, and his jaw is covered with a thick beard, he's still the same man who stood by my side when Hawke married Jorgie five years ago. The same Chase who dared me to eat a bee to see if it tasted like honey. He is my brother. My blood.

Feeling the same heavy sentiment in the air as me, Chase

pushes out with a deep exhale, "Fuck. I still can't believe you're here."

Air whizzes out of my nose. "You're not the only one."

"You missed so much, Hugo. *So much*... Jesus. What Ava went through. *Fuck*. You have no clue."

He's wrong there. I understand what Ava went through. Leaving her broke my heart too. Losing Jorgie gutted me, but losing Ava devastated me.

"Don't expect her to just forgive you, Hugo. It isn't that simple. You didn't just walk away, leaving her with a broken heart. You shattered her soul."

The constrictive hold strangling my heart strengthens. "I know, Chase. I live with the guilt of what I did to her every day."

When my voice cracks, he scrubs a hand over his tired eyes. "It's been a long-ass day. I'm tired. You look dog-ass tired."

I throw my head back and laugh.

He's always been direct and to the point.

"I'm heading out. If you're not busy tomorrow, come meet your nieces."

As my eyes bug out of my head, they shoot to Chase's smug face. "You have kids?"

He smirks at the high tone responsible for the neighbor's dogs' howls before saying with a nod, "Yeah. Two girls."

I stagger backward when he wiggles his ring finger in the air, flashing the platinum band wrapped around the once-empty digit. "Holy shit! You're married? Chase No-Girl-Is-Ever-Going-To-Catch-Me Marshall is married? Fuck... I've missed so much."

Chase chuckles about his high school nickname before muttering, "You have no clue how much you've missed." He slings his arm around my injured shoulder then pulls me in for a quick man hug. "No fucking clue." He inches back, his gaze unease. "See you tomorrow?"

I smirk, trying to ease his uncertainty. "I'll be there with bells on."

After throwing a punch into my chest, he ambles out of the room. I stare at the now-closed door, utterly dumbfounded. Chase was adamant no girl would ever tie him down. He often joked that's why our parents called him Chase. Because women would be chasing him across the country. Now he's married with two kids. That's fucking crazy to comprehend.

While pacing around my room, endeavoring to loosen the knot in my stomach, I rub the painful kink in my shoulder. My room looks exactly like it did the last time I was here—*when I snatched Ava's virginity.* Same bedspread and faded border. Even the pictures hanging on the wall are the same.

Being here brings up so many memories. Most are good, but there are a handful that still haunt me, and they are even more prominent when surrounded by silence. They come in hard and fast, and within seconds, it feels as if the walls of my childhood room are closing in on me.

I shake my head, begging for the images that plague my dreams to vanish. When they become too great to ignore, I snag my duffle bag off my bed, then bolt down the stairs. I can't stay here. It reminds me too much of her and the time I stole Ava's virginity.

The house is eerily quiet. Not a peep can be heard. I'm halfway out the back door when recollections of me running five years ago smack into me.

I can't do that to them again.

I can't run.

After snatching my mom's shopping list off the refrigerator, I scribble a note saying I'll be back first thing in the morning. For extra reassurance, I add my untraceable cell phone number at the bottom of the lined paper. Once I'm confident they'll know I'm not running within minutes of finding my room empty, I head out to Jorgie's baby, then veer it toward the closest motel.

Forty-five minutes tick by before I call in defeat and pull my car into the driveway of Jorgie's house. I checked every motel in town, but due to the late hour and being Christmas, every hotel, roadhouse, and inn within a twenty-mile radius is either booked up or closed.

Although memories of Jorgie are strong in her house, for the majority, they're good memories, so I'll have no issues staying here. She isn't who I was running from in my childhood room, but since it's late and I'm zonked, we'll have to keep that conversation on the back burner for another five-plus years.

Turning off the ignition, I crank open the door of Baby before walking up the cracked concrete path. After barely a wink of sleep last night and the draining events of today, I'm exhausted. I can barely stand straight.

After scrubbing my tired eyes, I run my hand along the top lip of the door, aware it's the prime spot every Marshall family member hides their spare key.

"Third pot on the left," whispers a voice to my side a short time later, scaring the living daylights out of me.

I gather my heart off the ground before shifting on my feet to face the voice. "Mrs. Mable?" I ask, my surprise evident. Nothing against Mrs. Mable, but she would have to be close to ninety, and that's on a good day.

"If you're looking for the spare key, it's under the third pot on the left," she instructs, her words whistling between her false teeth.

I lift my chin in thanks before searching through the flowerpots lining the edge of the patio. A heavy sigh leaves me when I find a shiny gold key hidden under a small pot of Japanese Yew.

"Thanks," I praise while holding the key in the air. After pushing the key into the lock, I swing my eyes to Mrs. Mable. "Why aren't they hiding the key on the door lip anymore?" Every Marshall family member does that. It's been our 'thing' for generations.

She waves her hand through the air like she's swatting a fly. "Jeez, do I look like a giraffe?"

I toss back my head and laugh. Mrs. Mable reminds me of Estelle Getty, the actress who played Sophia Petrillo in *The Golden Girls*. She's small and compact but more explosive than dynamite.

"I keep an eye on the place, make sure no one is up to any mischief," she explains, her tone a mix of bitchy and humorous. "You're not up to any mischief, are you, Hugo?"

I shake my head. *Not today, I'm not.*

"Alright, then don't let me hold you. It's almost dawn." She enters her house, only to spin around two seconds later. "And take your boots off. Their noisy stomping woke me up."

"Sorry," I apologize while struggling not to laugh about the glare she's hitting me with. It has no heat to it whatsoever. What can I say? I'm a lady's man no matter how old the lady.

I kick off my boots and dump them at the side of the patio before unlocking Jorgie's front door and slipping past the warped wood. I don't switch on any lights. I've walked these floors so many times I could recall each inch in photographic detail if asked.

My plan is to catch up on some sleep before unearthing a way to force Ava to talk to me. Until I'm given the chance to hash out the guilt that's been eating me alive the past five years, I'll once again be her shadow. Even risking the possibility she'll never want to talk to me again after my confession, I want to explain why I vanished. Maybe once she realizes I did it to protect her, she'll let go of some of the pent-up anger she's harboring toward me.

When I reach the hallway where the bedrooms veer off, I pull my long-sleeve shirt over my head. My eyelids are heavy, exhausted from being awake nearly thirty-six hours. I take a left at the end of the hall before entering the second door on the right. Although never officially given the title, this room was mine anytime I crashed at Jorgie's house.

As I make my way to the bed in the middle of the room, I unbutton the fly on my jeans and slide down the zipper. By the time I hit the end of the double mattress, I'm wearing nothing but a pair of stinky socks. The bed creaks when I plop my ass on it so I can yank off my last article of clothing.

Once they're discarded on the floor with my jeans and shirt, I tug back the thick duvet cover, then slip underneath. The coolness of a winter night is a forgotten memory when I sink into the heavenliness of a warm bed. A beautiful smell is infusing the air. It's homely. Fresh. Sweet but with a dash of manliness. The perfect combination of a man and woman's scents being intermingled during raunchy activities.

It's intoxicating, so much so it takes me several long seconds to register the heat of a body curling around mine. Regretfully, the person cozying up to me isn't as slow off the mark. They scream a loud, high-pitched squeal that pierces through my ears so fiercely I'm confident I'll sustain permanent hearing loss before they scamper out of bed.

After sending a quick prayer to God for their husband not to own a gun, I join them on what I'm hoping is gun-free, mutual territory.

When the bedroom light flicks on, through the blinding rays of the unnatural light flooding the room, I spot a blurry figure frantically racing around the room. "Where the hell is it?" she mumbles under her breath, her voice as enticing as her scent. "I swear I left it here…"

She stops talking a mere second before a steel baseball bat veers past my head. It misses my nose by a mickey whisker. An inch closer, and my head would have been knocked into the next century.

"Jesus!" I take a giant step back when the bat whizzes past my head again.

This time, it grazes the tip of my nose, but the impact isn't enough to slow down this little warrior. She continues swinging at me over and over again until the exhaustion of wielding a bat almost as big as hers stills her movements long enough for me to recognize the blur of fury behind the bat.

Ava's curls are clinging to her sweaty temples, and her chest is thrusting hard as her lungs hunt for air, but after a quick breather to regain her strength, she steps up to the plate before swinging her bat like Babe Ruth is standing out on the pitch. "If you come near me, I'll shove this bat where… where…. where the sun doesn't shine!"

Too shocked by her threat to act nonchalant for a second longer, my head flings back, and the loudest laugh I've ever cackled in my life barrels up my throat. My lungs burn when they lose the ability to fill with air, and salty blobs stream down my face. I laugh like a man who has lost his marbles because I have.

Ava could never issue a decent threat.

Clearly, nothing has changed.

Either recognizing my laughter or aware the only person in danger here is me, Ava stops swinging the bat. She props it on her barely covered leg then stares at me with wide eyes and a gaped mouth. When my sluggish brain registers that she's standing before me in nothing but a pair of tiny sleeping shorts and matching cami that doesn't have a chance in hell of hiding her perfect, cock-twitching body, my mouth snaps shut, and my eyes bug out of my head.

With a body crafted by the Almighty himself to bring men to their knees, Ava is like a bottle of fine wine. She gets better with age. Her lush tits are straining against her meager satin top, and inches upon inches of her glorious legs are peaking out the bottom of her satin shorts. Her rocking body makes my cock as hard as stone, not to mention the way her sugary sweet smell doubles the longer she rakes her eyes over my body.

I'm confident she likes what she's seeing. I've had plenty of time to work out the past five years, but the more she absorbs the tattoos covering my torso and arms, the tighter her brows pull together. Other than the squadron tattoo on my forearm, every tattoo in my collection was added *after* I vanished. They also remind me of her in some form, but for now, we'll keep that snippet of information between us.

My head slants when Ava inhales a sharp breath. Her hooded gaze is locked on something lower than my stomach but creeping up to my belly button the longer she stares. I'm once again standing before her as naked as the day as I was born and hard enough to drill through the Arctic Circle.

"Sorry," I mumble before raking my eyes across the room, seeking anything that could cover my primed and ready-to-plunge-into-Ava's-tight-pussy cock.

Cringing, I grab a ball-shrinking pink lace scatter cushion off the floor then plop it in front of my stiffened shaft. I'm not joking when I say it is the most hideous pillow I've ever seen. If Ava weren't standing across from me, practically naked, it would have made quick work of the hard-on turning my brain to mush. But even looking like I'm about to dance on a float at Mardi Gras, my dick isn't softening in the slightest. If anything, it gets harder. That probably has something to do with the smile Ava is trying to conceal.

She's even more beautiful when she smiles.

Needing to say something before I ravish the mouth of a taken woman, I mutter, "Why do our reunions always start with me being naked?"

The happy gleam on Ava's face vanishes before it's replaced with a look of a woman ready to castrate me. When she storms around the bed, reaching me in two heart-thrashing seconds, I swallow harshly.

Not all the threat scorching my veins is warranted. She isn't planning to cut off my dick with a blunt instrument. She's merely marching me out of her room like she'd rather maim my heart than ever touch my cock again.

The thought is as distressing as wondering how I'd live without a male appendage.

"Get out!" With her palms flattened against my back, she attempts to walk me to the door.

I say 'attempt' as I wouldn't budge an inch if I didn't want to. I could dig my feet in the carpet and stand my ground, but I won't. I am an intruder in her home, and I don't want her to ever believe she can't protect herself in her own domain.

That doesn't mean I won't try to talk an invitation out of her, though. "It's three in the morning—"

"I don't care," she interrupts before she doubles the strength of her pushes. "You are *not* staying here!"

"Come on, Ava. It's late, and I already checked every motel in town. They're either full or closed." A grin tugs on my lips when her pushes are strong enough for my bare feet to slip on the plush carpet pile. "Just one night. I'll be gone first thing in the morning." When her brisk steps ease along with her windless pants, I know I have her right where I want her. "Before you've even woken.

Please, Ava. I'll get down on my hands and knees if I have to." I bring out the twang I used on her when begging for her to make blueberry pancakes for us for dinner when we were younger.

It works a treat.

After dropping her hands from my back, the sound of Ava's tiny feet padding along the wooden floor of the living room resonates through my ears. While spinning around to face her, I cover my half-masted cock with my hands. I don't want to give her an excuse to renege on the offer.

Once she has gathered a sheet and blanket from the hallway cupboard and a spare pillow from her bed, Ava rejoins me in the living room. With an adorable smirk etched onto her face, she nudges her head to the teeny tiny couch next to us. I cringe. Half my body won't fit on that couch, and don't get me started on the monster dick Ava's smile has instigated.

With her brow cocked, Ava mutters, "It's either the sofa or the patio. The choice is yours."

She keeps her eyes fixated on my face, vainly trying to act unaffected by my nakedness. I'm not buying *anything* she's selling. I can see the battle in her dilated eyes. Smell it slicking her skin. But I won't call her out on it because she isn't the only one struggling. I'm fighting the same tortuous battle, but since I don't want to sleep outside in below-freezing temperatures, I keep my eyes planted on her face instead of her cock-twitching body while saying, "The sofa it is." While laying the sheet she handed me over the faded material of her dated couch, I ask, "Why are you staying here anyway? What happened to your apartment?"

I don't know what the fuck I said, but after shoving the blanket into my chest with enough force to wind me, Ava snarls at me before she storms into her room, slamming the door behind her.

NINE

HUGO

A groan rumbles up my chest as I reluctantly flutter my eyes open. The migraine pounding my temples to oblivion worsens from the blinding rays of the early morning sunshine beaming through the opened living room drapes.

While scrubbing the back of my hand over my tired eyes, I sit up. My back is kinked from sleeping on a couch harder than a rock, and my neck is out of sorts. I drift my eyes around the room, seeking the grandfather clock I heard ticking all night long. When I find it, the reason for my throbbing head is unearthed. It's not even seven.

I told Ava I'd be out of her hair before she woke, but she failed to mention she gets up before the birds. She's been bashing and crashing in the kitchen for the past forty-five minutes. I did my best to ignore the racket, yearning for more sleep, but the longer I stayed sprawled on the couch, the louder the noises emerging from the kitchen became.

While rubbing the sleep out of my eyes, I stagger toward the kitchen. My stomach grumbles when a delicious aroma fills my senses. I've only smelled one thing sweeter in my life. *Ava.* When an even more ravishing visual greets me, my eyes bug out of my head. The heaviness weighing down my eyelids is a forgotten memory as my eyes absorb every scandalous inch of Ava's body.

She's wearing an old, faded Columbus State University shirt, and her hair is pulled up, sitting in a messy bun on top of her head, exposing her long and delicate neck.

As my heart rate kicks up, I angle my head to the side then dip down low. A disappointed growl emits from my lips when I realize she's wearing pants–*barely!* If I hadn't bent my knees, I would have continued believing her teeny tiny denim shorts were panties.

After propping my shoulder on the doorjamb, I drink her in with the dedication she deserves. It's been years since I've been enthralled by such a stimulating visual. "How Does It Feel" by D'Angelo is playing out of a speaker on the two-seater table at the side of the room, and Ava has her back to me since she's facing the upright oven. She has a spatula in one hand and a tea towel in the other.

When the song hits the chorus, her hips swing. She naturally seduces me without even trying. My cock jumps when she grips the counter before she bobs down to do a seductive twerk. Only Ava could make twerking look sexy.

The same can be said for the Gangnam dance she did years ago.

Even after spotting a massive pile of pancakes cooling at her right, I can't tear my eyes away from the sexy curves of her ass peeking out the bottom of her tiny shorts. She dances with such ease and grace. I'm not surprised—she's always been innately sexy.

Nothing's changed.

I scrape my hand along my unshaven jaw when the visual becomes too enticing not to spark a reaction from me. Upon hearing the scrub of a desperate man, Ava's spine snaps straight before she spins on her heels to face me. With a massive grin stretched across her adorable face, her eyes run over my covered body. Since I didn't want another naked incident, I slept in my jeans and a long-sleeve shirt. Now do you understand why my sleep was shit?

When Ava's eyes eventually return to my face, I chew on my bottom lip. Her nipples are budded against her shirt, her eyes are wide and exposed, and the spark of lust is blazing in her beautiful eyes. She's famished, but her hunger has nothing to do with food.

"How did you sleep?" she asks, her voice sugary sweet.

"Good." *I spent the entire night dreaming of you.* "You?"

As her teeth rake her lower lip, she shrugs. "Could've been better."

When she prances toward the refrigerator, swings open the door then dips her lower half inside, my heart rate kicks up a notch. I have many fond memories of us in a refrigerator. I lick my lips when she emerges from the chilly box with a can of whipped cream and a seductive grin two seconds later.

With her eyes locked on my face, she walks to the massive stack of freshly prepared blueberry pancakes on her right. "Cream or syrup?" Her voice drips with sexiness like hot lava erupting from a volcano.

"Syrup," I answer, my throat groggy complements to my suddenly dry mouth.

Smiling, Ava places the whipped cream onto the counter before opening the cupboard above her head. My cock, now hard, strains against my jeans zipper when she struggles to reach the maple syrup on the top shelf. I push off the counter, head her way, then arch over her back. I can easily reach the syrup, but I take my time, pretending I can't so I can relish her closeness for a few seconds.

"Thank you," she says when I eventually hand her the syrup, her voice as sweet as her scent wafting in my nostrils.

After slipping under my arm, she moves to the far side of the kitchen, taking the stack of pancakes with her. Even with her standing at the other side of the room, the kitchen is too small not to feel the sexual energy zapping between us. It's electrifying and has my cock hardening more.

Ava slathers the pancakes with syrup, ensuring every inch is covered in the sugary goodness I love before she pops her thumb into her mouth to lick off the excess stickiness. When a moan tumbles out of her lips, the hardness of my cock turns lethal.

I've never been so hard.

Nothing's changed.

Not a single fucking thing.

It wouldn't matter if a year had passed or a hundred, Ava will always be the girl who'll knock me on my ass. Although I will admit I'm surprised by her quick change in behavior overnight, but I am loving her newfound playfulness.

"Hungry?" she asks, her tone is laced with sexual undertone.

"Fuck, yes." *For you.*

My eyes drift between the stack of pancakes balancing precariously in her hand and her soft, pouty lips.

I know which goodie I want to taste first.

There is *no* contest.

My eyes rocket to Ava's when she asks, "What do you want to taste first?"

I swear she can read my mind, but just in case she can't, I ask, "I have a choice?"

She bites her lower lip before she nods.

"You," I answer without pause for thought.

Her eyes spark with fervor as a smile curves her lips. "Who said I'm on the menu?"

I run the back of my fingers down her flushed cheeks. "These."

She always blushes when she's turned on.

As her throat works hard to swallow, the fire in her eyes dampens. "Well, I'm not... *yet*. But these are." Her eyes dart down to the massive stack of mouthwatering goodness in her hands.

Her lips tug high as she outstretches her arm, offering the pancakes to me. My mouth salivates. It's been years since I've tasted anything as good as Ava's pancakes.

A disbelieving gasp whizzes out of my mouth when she releases her grip on her end of the plate before I've secured my end. As the pancakes plummet toward the floor, time slows to a snail's pace. I scramble, trying in vain to save them before they land in the trash bin I'm standing next to, but I'm too late.

The pancakes are history.

Ava's hand darts up to cover her gaped mouth. "Oh no."

"It's okay, we can save a few of them," I assure her. Although they've landed in the bin, the top ten aren't touching anything that resembles rubbish, giving me the all-clear to salvage them. "The top few haven't touched anything gross."

"Oh..." With an evil smile I've never seen her wear, Ava dumps a bowl of empty eggshells onto the untouched pancakes. "Can they still be saved?" Her voice no longer has the sugary sweetness it had earlier. It is mean and unhinged.

My brows meet my hairline. *What did the poor defenseless pancakes ever do to her?*

When my wide-with-shock eyes lift from the destroyed lumps of carbohydrate goodness to Ava, gone is the little sex kitten who was prowling around the kitchen earlier, replaced by a lady whose heart must have been carved by an expert ice sculptor. Because only someone with an icy heart would sound so cold when warning, "I'm going to take a shower. You better be gone by the time I get out. If not, I *will* call the police."

Oh my god. I can't believe I did that. I've never been so rude, but I bet Jorgie is proud that I've finally grown a backbone. It might have taken twenty-nine years, but late is better than never.

I barely slept a wink all night. I couldn't comprehend that the man who snatched my ability to enjoy a restful night was in my living room, sleeping on my rock-hard couch. I've dreamed of nights like last night, prayed that one day Hugo would suddenly reappear, but I could have never anticipated the flood of emotions that would return along with him.

At first, I was shocked. I didn't believe what my eyes were relaying. I thought it was a cruel, twisted joke. It was only when the fog cleared did reality dawn. Hugo isn't dead. He's far from it. So where the hell has he been the past five years? And why did he wait so long before emerging again? He would have had to have known what his mother was going through. He saw firsthand the pain she endured when she lost Jorgie and her grandson, so how could he put her through that again?

How could he do that to me?

That's when my anger surfaced. It festered and boiled all night, overheating my body with more fury than I've ever felt. I'm furious Hugo was so selfish that he could do that to his own mother. I, at least, got a goodbye. Mrs. Marshall didn't even get that.

Hugo took the coward's way out. He left his family. Me. *Us.*

It was *his* choice, so he doesn't get to waltz back into my life acting like nothing's changed.

Everything has changed.

A callous grin tugs on my lips when I slip out of the denim shorts I rustled from the back of my walk-in closet this morning. Hugo has always been a legs man, and even though his physical characteristics have changed from the man I once knew, his insides are *exactly* the same. The shell of an egg can be painted any color you like, but the inside will forever be a heartless yolk.

Aware Hugo loves legs nearly as much as he does blueberry pancakes, I fathomed a little ploy to get back at him.

Was it childish? Yes.

What is over the top? Yes.

Would I do it again? Yes! In a heartbeat.

The look on his face when his beloved pancakes toppled in the bin was priceless. Totally worth the hour I slaved over the open-flamed cooktop to make them.

Still grinning, I yank my shirt over my head then step into the steam-filled shower. To regain some of my composure, I take my time in the shower, lathering and pampering my exhausted body. I plan to wash out Hugo's re-entrance in my life as easily as he rid me of his years ago, but within seconds, he pops back into my head.

While running the washcloth over my body, images of my run-in with him last night hog my thoughts. Although covered with more tattoos than my eyes could ever absorb, his body is panty-drenching good. Ripples of hard muscles, smooth planes of colorful skin, and his cock—*my god*—I thought my imagination had gotten the better of me the past five years. I hadn't. *Jesus.* If I were a cartoon, my eyes would have sprung out of my head.

My body. Well, a lot has changed there in the past five years. My boobs no longer sit where they should, their perkiness dwindling away with my youth. My thighs are larger, and my stomach is anything but smooth. We couldn't be more opposite if we tried. Hugo is hard, colorful, and accentuated, whereas I'm squidgy, plain, and boring.

Hold on. Why am I even comparing us? Hugo is a nobody. He's the equivalent of a barfly buzzing in and out of my life as he sees fit.

Not anymore.

I'm putting my foot down.

This isn't just about me anymore.

After a long, hot shower, I exit the bathroom. The house is eerily quiet, only the grandfather clock pendulum swinging in the distance can be heard.

Hugo must have heeded my warning.

Good, because it wasn't an idle threat.

I walk into the laundry room then slip out the back door. The rusty-hinged gate separating the land between my house and Mrs. Mable's gives out a small squeak when I open it. The gate was Mrs. Mable's idea. She figured it would save me scaling her fence if I ever felt the need to once again add fertilizer to her award-winning rose garden.

While stumbling out the worst apology of my life, my cheeks inflamed. I'd never been more embarrassed. Although I was joking about adopting Mrs. Mable as a grandmother at Jorgie's wedding, she has become exactly that. She's a bundle of mischief who keeps my life interesting.

I would have loved to have introduced her to Patty, but unfortunately, his gigantic heart gave out a few weeks after Hugo disappeared.

It really has been a shit few years.

When Mrs. Mable hears the glass sliding door on her back patio opening, she walks out of the kitchen, drying a china teacup. Her lips purse as her rheumy eyes roam over my face. Her gaze is full of suspicion, and it piques my curiosity.

Arching a brow, I return her ardent stare. When her rascally expression registers as familiar, my jaw drops. "I'm revoking your key holder privileges." I stare into her smitten gaze. "You told *Hugo* where the spare key was, didn't you?" A squeak pops from my lips when I say *his* name.

Mrs. Mable doesn't deny my claim. Not a word seeps from her lips. It wouldn't matter if she did refute my allegation, though. The truth is projected by her wholesome eyes.

After placing the china cup into the display cabinet, Ms. Mabel shifts on her feet to face me. "I thought you could use a night of fun. Get your knickers out of the twist they've been in the past five years."

"Knickers?"

Her silver ringlets bounce in her brisk movements when she *pffts* me. "I'm British. Can't you hear my accent?"

My eyes bulge. Her tone couldn't be more Southern if she tried. She sounds like Reese Witherspoon after smoking three packs a day.

Ignoring my wide-mouthed expression, she continues, "But I gather from the way you waddled in here like you have a stick stuck up your bottom that my ploy didn't work? What was it? The tattoos? Or are you not a fan of his shorter hair?"

A snarl forms on my lips as my eyes narrow. It doesn't bother Ms. Mable. Not in the slightest. She pats her translucent, wrinkled-covered hand on my forearm, then says with a whistled breath, "Don't pretend you weren't interested in what he was hiding under his clothing. That boy... oh, he could crank my engine anytime he likes."

My cheeks get a rush of blood behind them. Although this type of jeering is nothing new for Mrs. Mable, I've never been one to air my dirty laundry in public.

"So, what was it?" She eyes me curiously. "The tattoos or the hair?"

Thankfully, I'm saved from answering her highly inappropriate question when a little pair of arms wrap around my leg. "Hi, Mommy."

I crouch down to scoop him into my arms. "Hi, baby. I missed you so much." I plant a sloppy kiss on his cheek before asking, "Were you a good boy for Grandma?"

His expressive eyes enlarge before he nods. "Uh-huh. We stayed awake until it was *really* late watching cartoons." He turns his eyes to Mrs. Mable. "Well, I stayed up. Grandma fell asleep. *Again.*" Air hits my cheeks when he huffs dramatically.

I snort when Mrs. Mable waves her hand in the air, shooing off Joel's tease. I'm not worried about their late-night adventures. Anything past eight is late to Joel.

After running my fingers through his thick afro curls, fixing them into place, I set him back onto his feet then put on his jacket. He eyes me curiously, staring at me like he's seeing me for the first time.

"You look pretty, Mommy," he mumbles a short time later. "Did you have fun at the p-party?" I smile when he stutters over the word 'party.'

My eyes shoot up to Mrs. Mable when she fails to cover her snickers with a fake cough. Once I'm certain her snickering has been reined in, I reply, "It was very interesting." I clasp Joel's hand in mine before standing from my crouched position. "Thank you for watching him."

"It was my pleasure, sweetie. Anytime," replies Mrs. Mable.

She has said on many occasions that Joel keeps her young. She loves babysitting him. Although I make sure her hearing aid batteries have been replenished before she watches him, I'll never hesitate leaving Joel with her. They have a unique bond that grows stronger with every moment they spend together, so I refuse to let her age create an unnecessary barrier between them.

After thanking Mrs. Mable with a kiss on the cheek, Joel and I exit the back sliding door.

"What did you want to do today?" I ask while opening the gate so he can enter our home before me. "I was thinking Netflix and a pizza?"

Joel screws up his nose and gags.

"No?" I say with a shake of my head and pursed lips.

"We had pizza last night. Grandma likes olives and anchovies." His face pales like he's about to be sick.

I laugh. "Okay, so no pizza. What about—"

"Pancakes!" he pipes up, his voice high as excitement takes hold of his vocal cords.

I grimace. "I'm sorry, honey, Mommy used all the eggs this morning." *Teaching a bad man a valuable lesson.*

Joel's lower lip drops into a pout.

"But I can duck down to the store this afternoon, and we can have pancakes for dinner."

Joel's eyes bulge. "Really?"

I smile and nod. "Really."

As we walk through the back entrance of our home, Joel shares the story of how Mrs. Mable fell asleep with her mouth open. "She was drooling too. It was gross—" He stops talking before his head lifts in slow motion. The more his neck tilts back, the larger his mouth gapes. "Who are you?" he asks once his head is fully cranked back.

My head swings to the side so fast my neck screams in protest.

There standing before us in all his six-foot-five glory is Hugo.

Shit.

ELEVEN
HUGO

My eyes dart between Ava and the little boy standing at her side, clutching her hand. I stare at him. Not a general stare—I stare, stare, absorbing every little feature of his adorable face—big plump lips, smooth unblemished skin, a crazy mess of ringlet hair on top of his head, and the biggest pair of blue eyes I've ever seen.

When they register as familiar, I take a giant step back, utterly flabbergasted.

Holy shit. It can't be.

The little boy's eyes run the length of my body from the tips of my toes to the top of my head. When they reach their final destination, his jaw slackens. I'm not surprised by the little pegs of white standing perfectly straight in his mouth. His mom is a dentist, after all.

"Who are you?" he asks, his voice as adorable as his handsome face.

Ava flinches before her head rockets to the side. Her eyes travel the same path the little boy's just did, but when she reaches my head, her mouth doesn't gape open in surprise, but her eyes sure do. After mustering a fake smile onto her ashen face, she bobs down in front of the boy I'd guess to be four. "Sweetie, go into your room. I'll be there in a minute."

"But, Mom—"

"No arguing. Go!" Ava's voice is stern and authoritative, a tone I've never heard her use.

The boy's hands ball and he screws up his nose, but with a loud huff, he does as requested. He storms down the hall like a bat of hell yelling, "You're not being fair!" before he slams his bedroom door shut.

The picture frames lining the hallway rattle from the force he used to close his door, and Ava balks. She appears as shocked as me. I don't understand how. She's not the one finding out he's fathered a child years after the fact.

After running her hands down the front of her white-washed jeans, she stands from her crouched position. When I step closer to her, desperate to discover why she didn't tell me about my son last night, she holds her hand out in front of her body, demanding for me to stop.

When I do, her moisture-glistening eyes lock with mine. "He isn't—"

"Don't you dare," I interrupt, my words sterner than I was expecting. "I *know* he is my son."

He's the perfect mixture of both Ava and me. My hair coloring, her curls. My eyes, her lips. His nose is a combination of us both. He's my son, and nothing she could say would change my mind on that. Even if I wasn't looking at an exact replica of my eyes, I can feel it in my bones. He has my blood pumping through his veins.

He is *my* son.

As my eyes bounce between Ava's, I ask, "Why didn't you tell me?"

Her head flings back as she laughs. It isn't the beautiful, soulful giggle I'm used to hearing. It is a laugh that expresses how much she's hurting. It's crammed with pain, and it breaks my heart just hearing it.

Once her laughter settles down, she returns her eyes front and center, then fans her hands across her hips. "And exactly how was I supposed to tell you? Put an ad in every newspaper in the state... or perhaps the entire country since I didn't know where you had gone?" She glides her hands through the air, dramatically expressing herself like a fight promoter holding a press conference. "Naïve virgin fucks high school crush in his childhood bedroom, stupidly forgot to check if he's wearing protection, falls pregnant the very first time she has sex. If this sounds like someone you know, please call 555-I'm-a-naïve-idiot!"

Ice-cold fear grips my heart when tears flood her eyes. I bridge the gap between us, wanting to offer her comfort, but she angrily shakes her head before she takes a giant step backward. My heart hammers from the dejected look in her eyes. She appears broken. Utterly heartbroken.

After stuffing her hands into the pockets of her jeans, her gaze strays to her feet.

"Babe."

Her eyes snap up to mine so fast they replicate balls in a pinball machine. "Don't call me that," she sneers, her words dangerously low. "You lost the right to call me a nickname, *any name*, when you left me pregnant and heartbroken."

"If I'd known—"

"If you didn't run, you would have known! You would have!" she yells. "But you ran. You were a coward who ran!"

The pounding of my heart increases, but I remain quiet, unable to negate her truthful statement. I was a coward who left, but if I had known she was pregnant, I would have...

Fuck, I don't know what I would have done.

When Ava's angry voice bellows around us, she intertwines her fingers, then gathers her composure, not wanting to startle her son... *our son.* I stare into her heartbroken eyes when she steps closer to me. Her legs shake with every stride she takes, and her eyes are packed with hot, salty tears threatening to spill at any moment.

"Hugo..." She scrunches her brows. "Is that even your name anymore?" Even though she's asking a question, she continues talking as if she didn't. "Maybe you changed it. What is it now? Slade, Jesse... oh, I know! You're the *asshole* who has five seconds to get the hell out of *my* house before I call the police and tell them a *stranger* is standing in the middle of my home."

"I get it, you're pissed."

"I'm not pissed, Hugo, or whatever the *fuck* your name is now. I'm *way* beyond pissed. You have no clue what I've been through the past five years. I walked through the gates of hell to keep our son fed, to keep him looked after, but because of you, I nearly lost everything! And now, just as everything is *finally* panning out after an *exhausting* five years, you waltz back into the picture, throwing a wrench into the works. I'm not the stupid and naïve Ava you remember. I refuse to let you ruin everything I've worked so hard for... *again.*"

Her words crack as the first lot of tears splash down her cheeks. I take a step closer to her, aspiring to stop her tears. Each one that falls down her beautiful face adds more cracks to my already decimated heart.

"*Please* leave," she begs, her pleading eyes on mine.

The constrictive hold on my heart tightens. "He's my son, Ava. I can't leave him. I can't leave *you.*"

More tears flood her cheeks. "*Please*, I'm begging you. I'll fall onto my knees if I have to." The squeeze on my heart turns deadly when she locks her dispirited eyes with mine. "If you cared for me at all, if you ever loved me, you'll walk away. *Please* don't drag our son through the hell we've both walked through."

My heart is a massive mess of confusion, torn between wanting to ease her pain and officially meeting my son.

Ava's lips quiver as a fresh batch of tears streams down her face. "If you can't do it for me, then do it for him. He doesn't deserve to be thrown into this mess. *Please*, Hugo, I'm begging you."

As hard as it is for me to do, I immediately walk away.

TWELVE

AVA

When Hugo slips out my front door, my knees buckle, and I crumble to the floor with a howl. After gathering my legs close to my chest, I sob uncontrollably. I cry for all the years we missed, my son who never had a chance to know his dad, and from the sheer pain that washed over Hugo's face when I begged him to leave. My words cut him deep, but I'm angry, and rightfully so.

I went through hell the past five years. I lost my best friend, my soulmate, and a man who was like a grandfather to me within a matter of months. It was one horrific blow after another.

With everything going on, it took me a while to realize my churning stomach each morning and late afternoon wasn't grief. It was a baby, a baby I'd created with Hugo. Even after six pregnancy tests, I still didn't believe it. I was pregnant.

After attending an appointment with Dr. Tagget, it was clear I had fallen pregnant the first time Hugo and I were together.

That night, I was so caught up in the moment, I didn't consider checking if Hugo had used protection. I never filled the birth control prescription my local gynecologist gave me. I didn't see the necessity since I wasn't sexually active, and my periods were as regular as clockwork.

At first, I saw our baby as a blessing, a final gift from Jorgie and Hugo. It was only when I discovered I was due two months before I officially took my position at Gardner and Sons did my opinion change. Although Mrs. Gardner is a lovely lady, she's also a businesswoman. Like any rational businesswoman, she handled my situation respectfully while assuring her business wasn't negatively impacted by it, which meant my partnership offer was given to another intern, leaving me unemployed and heavily pregnant.

In my seventh month of pregnancy, I sold my apartment on Hamilton Street. The impressive nest egg I was ecstatic about growing was put toward my hefty tuition debt. Although my payment chewed a sizable portion off my debt, I was still left with an outstanding balance.

For two weeks following the sale of my home, I stayed at Mrs. Marshall's house. Although it has always felt like home to me, the house had too many memories of Jorgie and Hugo, and my restless sleep worsened during my time there.

After a heartfelt discussion, Mrs. Marshall suggested I move into Jorgie's place. It took days of deliberations before I agreed, and even then, it was only on one condition. I wouldn't use the master bedroom. That room belonged to Jorgie and Hawke. I didn't feel comfortable sleeping in there.

A few weeks after I moved in, Marvin started sniffing around. He would turn up with bags of fancy restaurant food any pregnant lady would salivate over and sneakily paid my heating bill when I got a little behind on a payment. He asked what I was planning on doing once the baby was born and reminded me that just because I was becoming a mom didn't mean I had to give up my career. I could have both if I wanted.

I'll admit, I was shocked. Marvin had never been a positive

man, but he was the only one encouraging me not to give up on my dreams.

Over the next few weeks, the reasoning behind his interest was exposed. Marvin and Hugo are as opposite as they come. Hugo is a tall brute of a man. Marvin is waif-thin and of average height. Hugo favors females with rich, ethnic skin and dark features. Marvin prefers blondes with fair skin and blue eyes.

Hugo has a large cock.

Marvin doesn't.

Although Marvin loves blonde bombshells, his father is a proud African American man, and he wanted his son to follow in his footsteps. During my vulnerable state, Marvin convinced me that aligning with him could benefit us both. He said if I agreed to pretend to be his girlfriend, he would assure my position at his family practice was waiting for me after giving birth. He benefited from our situation by getting his dad off his back about settling down and getting married. He was convinced it was a win-win situation for us both.

It was... until twelve months ago. Marvin didn't want to pretend anymore. He wanted us to be a real-life couple. I was hesitant to say the least. Joel knew of Marvin, but their contact was severely lacking. Neither was interested in getting to know the other.

When I voiced my concerns, Marvin was quick to remind me how he guided me through the storm and that without him, I would have had nothing. After swearing his indiscretions would end and promising to put more effort into building a relationship with Joel, Marvin and I became an official couple nine months ago.

Nothing changed.

Our relationship followed the exact path as the previous four years. Marvin's indiscretions never ended. Not that I mind. It keeps his focus off me. He continued to live in his apartment on

Pinter. I remained in my house, and he's never spent an ounce of time attempting to establish a relationship with Joel. That's why I was so shocked when he proposed. Neither of us is ready for marriage. We're barely a couple, let alone ready to walk down the aisle.

Although Marvin is an asshole, and he irks the living hell out of me, I would have been lost without him. He did save me. So, like all things in life, I accept the good with the bad. People believe Marvin is using me, but I've used him just as much. Simply put we're as bad as each other.

When Joel rushes out of his bedroom and charges down the hall, I lift my head from my knees. His little face is lit up, and his eyes are wide and excited. "I knew it!" he squeals loudly as his eyes bounce in all directions. "It's him, isn't it? The daddy in the pictures. *My* daddy."

When he fails to locate Hugo in the foyer, he runs into the kitchen. My heart squeezes painfully when he emerges from the kitchen not even two seconds later. The excitement on his face has dampened, and his shoulders are slumped and hanging low. He looks utterly devastated. "Where did he go?"

I gesture for him to come sit with me by outstretching my arms. Tears pool in his eyes as he slowly trudges toward me. When he sits on my lap, I run my fingers through his thick hair before pressing a kiss on his sweat-beaded forehead. After peering down at the photo frame he's clutching in his hand, he locks his tear-drenched eyes with mine. My heart breaks when I glance into his beautiful eyes. They're identical to his dad's in every single way.

"Was it him?"

Fresh tears spring in my eyes when I glance down at the photograph he's offering me. It's a picture Mrs. Marshall snapped of Hugo and me dancing at Jorgie's wedding. It was taken mere seconds before Marvin interrupted us, requesting to dance with his date.

I'm not ashamed to admit that nothing but love is projecting out of me in this picture. I loved Hugo for years, and Mrs. Marshall's image captured that.

"Yes, sweetheart, it was him," I answer, my voice shuddering from the brutal pounding of my heart. Although I could lie and say Hugo isn't his dad, I've never been one for deceit. If you tell a lie once, all your truths become questionable.

Joel inhales a sharp breath. Hope is all over his face. "Is he coming back?"

His eyes bore into mine, begging for me to say yes. I drag my hand across his forehead to gather the beads of sweat dotted there. His heart is beating so fast I feel his pulse raging through his temples. "I don't know, sweetheart." I run my index finger under his eyes, removing a few stray tears seeping free. "Maybe he'll be back?"

His tears dry in an instant, and they remind me that his eyes are like his father's in another way. They can see straight through to my soul. He knows I'll do everything in my power to ease his pain.

Even breaking my own heart.

THIRTEEN
AVA

I don't need to see Hugo to know he's here. I can sense his presence without needing to physically see him. We round the corner of the Marshall family residence, moving toward the back patio where the monthly Marshall brunch is held. To celebrate Hugo's return, Mrs. Marshall organized a special invitation-only brunch. I've never missed a Marshall brunch the past six years, and today won't be an exception. I have many treasured memories from the Marshall family brunch. I even went into labor at one.

Joel spots Hugo before me. His grip on my hand firms, and a dimpled blemished grin stretches across his face. I've never hidden his dad's identity from him. I shared photos and stories of Hugo with him many times over the past four years. He even has the Marshall last name. No matter how often Marvin begged for me to pretend Joel was his biological child, it was *never* going to happen. The Marshall family has suffered enough loss to last a lifetime. I refused to add another name to their already extensive list. Hugo is Joel's father, and no amount of hurt or anger will *ever* change that fact.

After exhaling a deep breath, I drift my eyes to Marvin. "I'll be back in a minute." Marvin slits his eyes as his jaw gains a tick. "Please don't create a scene." I stop his callous words before they can escape his lips. "He needs this." I gesture my head to Joel, who hasn't taken his eyes off Hugo.

Marvin aggressively crosses his arms in front of his chest, but thankfully, he continues giving me the silent treatment. The thrum of Joel's pulse jolts up my arm as we walk to Hugo, hand in hand. His excited smile enlarges with every step we take.

Hugo is flanked by two gorgeous blondes, but for the first time in my life, my claws are sheathed. His nieces, Katie and Angie, Chase's two-year-old twin daughters, are climbing over him like he's their personal play fort. They're as smitten as every female when awarded Hugo's attention.

When Hugo notices me approaching with Joel, he wrangles them off his jean-covered thighs and hands them to Chase. His eyes are still crammed with the despair he wore two days ago when I begged him to leave, but with every step we take toward him, it lessens, and a new glimmer brightens them.

As we come to a stop in front of him, I muster a small smile to feign that my heart isn't hammering against my ribs. "Hugo, this is your son, Joel Marshall," I introduce.

Hugo intakes a sharp breath, clearly shocked by my introduction.

I swing Joel's arm into the air, trying to settle the nerves trembling through his little body before continuing with my introduction, "Joel, this is your dad."

With a smile I've never seen him wear, Hugo crouches down in front of Joel before offering him his hand to shake. My heart swells when Joel swats his hand away before he wraps his arms around his neck to hug him fiercely.

He's always believed actions speak louder than words.

Joel's quick movements cause Hugo to stumble to his knees, and his jeans get soaked with dirty sludge and leftover snow, but the biggest laugh also erupts from his throat. It does weird things to my insides. Things Marvin has not once attempted to replicate.

"You're a strong little thing," Hugo mutters to himself before pulling Joel in nearer to his chest.

Tears threaten to fall when Joel curls his hand around mine while still holding Hugo's, undoubtedly proving he will tether us together for eternity. When I see nothing but sheer joy beaming from Joel's expressive eyes, I bite the inside of my cheek, hopeful it will keep my tears at bay. My simplest decision granted him so much joy. That, in itself, is worth years of heartache.

Once I've swallowed to make sure my voice doesn't croak with emotion, I say to Hugo, "Perhaps after brunch, you could take Joel somewhere? Get to know him a little better."

Even though my tears remain locked away, my swallow did nothing. My rickety voice gives away the emotions flooding me. I prayed for years for this exact moment, and I can't believe it's finally coming true.

Joel's eyes rocket to Hugo. His mouth is ajar, and his pupils are as large as saucers. "Will you?"

A vast smile etches on Hugo's handsome face before he curtly nods. Unable to control his excitement for a second longer, Joel throws his fists into the air and squeals an ear-piercing scream. His reaction verifies that my decision to include Hugo in his life was the right choice to make. He wants his dad in his life more than anything.

After running his hand over Joel's crazy, ringlet curls, Hugo's baby blues lock with mine. "*Thank you*," he mouths. The gratefulness in his eyes adds strength to his simple statement.

I smile and nod, confident I'd do anything in the world to guarantee Joel's happiness. Even if it means I have to side with the man who broke my heart and shattered my soul.

"I'll be just over there if you need me," I inform Joel while pointing to Marvin standing at the side, scrutinizing our exchange with crossed arms and a poignant stare.

"Okay." Joel bands his arms around my thigh. "I love you, Mommy."

"I love you too." I run my fingers through his ruffled hair, fixing it into place before pivoting on my heels and walking away.

I won't lie, it is one of the hardest things I've ever done. My heart thrashes against my chest, and my eyes are brimming with wetness, but the decisions I make aren't just based on what I want anymore. Every decision affects Joel as well. He wants this, and he deserves it. Every child has the right to have their father in their life. I just hope Hugo doesn't break his heart. If he does, it won't matter how much I still love him, I will never forgive him. That is unforgivable.

"This wasn't part of our agreement," Marvin sneers the instant I stand beside him.

I intertwine my fingers and pivot around. A smile tugs on my lips when I spot Joel showing Hugo the hidden finger trick Mrs. Mable has been teaching him since he was old enough to sit. It's nothing more than cupping your hands together and sticking your middle finger out and wriggling it around, but Joel thinks it's magic.

"Joel was never part of our deal, Marvin. Not once," I retort while keeping my eyes on Joel and Hugo as they move to the back deck. "He is *my* son, and any decision I make regarding him falls solely on *my* shoulders."

The hairs on the nape of my neck prickle when Marvin leans into my side and snarls. "When Hugo vanishes for another five years and shatters *your* son's heart, don't come crying to me."

After throwing a garden chair out of his way, he storms down the driveway. I want to say this is the first time he's thrown a tantrum like a child but, unfortunately, it isn't. Perhaps that's why he and Joel don't see eye to eye. Marvin sees Joel as a competitor instead of an ally. If he were smart, he'd realize my son is the key to obtaining my heart. Gaining his approval is the biggest hurdle any man will need to jump over to secure my devotion. His failure to realize that proves he doesn't know me at all.

Marvin slides into his red BMW convertible, throws the gear-stick into reverse, then pulls out of the driveway like a bat out of hell. Tires squeal, and the smell of burning rubber filters through the air when I return my eyes to the jubilant setting. Marvin's little spectacle has gained me a handful of spectators, including Hugo. His eyes have narrowed, and even from this distance, I can see his jaw muscle ticking, but thankfully, Joel is too enamored with him to be paying any attention to Marvin.

When an arm unexpectedly wraps around my shoulders, I jump. I don't need to look up to know who's embracing me. Her baked cookies and honeysuckle smell are all the indication I need.

"Sorry about that," I apologize after raising my eyes to Mrs. Marshall's face.

"It's fine, Ava. I have five grandbabies. Believe me, I've handled much worse tantrums."

A giggle bubbles in my chest. Joel could give any kid a run for his money when it comes to chucking a tantrum—until three weeks ago. I never laughed so hard when he threw a wobbly in the middle of a department store because he wanted a new Spiderman toy. When I suggested he should wait until after Christmas, he dropped to the floor, kicked his legs, and wailed like a baby.

That isn't the funny part of my story.

When Mrs. Marshall replicated his tantrum, howling sobs and all, I lost it. I had never laughed so hard in my life. A nearly sixty-year-old lady thrashing her fists against the tiled floor in the middle of a bustling department store was more than I could bear.

Her weird tactics worked, though. In an instant, Joel's tantrum stopped. His tear-soaked face popped off the floor, and he glared at his grandma, open-mouthed and wide-eyed. He looked utterly mortified, and he's never chucked a tantrum since that day.

"Maybe we should test your logic on curbing tantrums on Marvin?" I suggest, my lips pursing as I vainly try to portray I'm not embarrassed by Marvin's childish antics. In reality, I'm humiliated.

Mrs. Marshall smiles a deviant grin. "The only thing that boy needs is a good walloping."

I laugh. Marvin is the reason I raise Joel with morals. I do not want him to grow up to be a spoiled brat like Marvin. Although Joel will always be my baby, there's a big difference between coddling a child and letting them be a brat. The biggest difference between Joel and Marvin is that Joel knows the difference between right and wrong. Marvin doesn't.

Mrs. Marshall firms her grip on my shoulder. "I'm so proud of you, Ava," she whispers, her words full of admiration.

I peer into her glistening eyes, confused by the sudden shift in our conversation and her praise. She's never been one to hold back praise, but it's been a few months since she's been so frank.

Actually, the last time she was forthright was when she urged me to reconsider my partnership with Marvin. Although she said she would support me in any decision I made, I saw the disappointment in her wholesome eyes when I informed her of my decision.

"I'm proud you're not holding Joel against Hugo," she explains to my bemused expression. "You have every right to be angry at Hugo. Hell, I'm still peeved at him, but you're handling this situation with grace and dignity. Like a true lady. That makes me *very* proud of you. Not just today, but every day."

My nose tingles as fresh tears well in my eyes, but since I can't articulate how much her words mean to me, I return her embrace with an extra squeeze.

"Where the hell are you?" I mutter while lifting a plastic sheet off a half-assembled desk.

My eyes frantically dart around the space, trying in vain to locate my handbag. My cell phone has been shrilling into the room for the past two minutes, but I can't locate it under the mess.

"Check the boxes near the door," suggests Belinda before she points to a three-stack of moving boxes near the front entrance door.

The volume of my cell phone's annoying ringtone increases as I urgently step to the boxes.

"There you are!" I scold while yanking my handbag out of the top box.

My heart rate kicks up a gear when I peer down at the screen and notice it is Hugo calling.

"Hello," I greet him after pressing the phone into my ear.

"Hey, where are you?" Hugo replies. No matter how many times I've heard his deep voice the past three days, it still causes goosebumps to surface on my skin anytime I hear it. "We've been knocking on your front door for the past five minutes."

My eyes scan the mess, seeking a time-telling contraption. When my hunt comes up empty, I peer out a small tear in the newspaper taped around a window.

Shit, it's dark outside.

"I'm so sorry. I lost track of time. The plumber was a moron, and between his stupidity and—"

I stop talking when Hugo's deep chuckle sounds down the line. "It's fine, Ava. I'm more than happy to keep Joel for a few more hours if you're busy."

My heart clenches when I consider his offer. I've missed Joel so much the past three days, but I've taken a step back from my somewhat overbearing parenting to give him and Hugo time to become acquainted with each other.

For the past three days, every morning, bright and early, Hugo arrives and collects Joel. They've visited the Central Park Zoo, saw a Knicks game, and even took a day trip to Liberty Island. Although I feel like I'm missing my right arm, Joel needs this time just as much as Hugo does.

Any concerns I have of Hugo breaking Joel's heart are diminishing as the days go on. Joel has never been so happy. He even wakes up smiling, so I'm confident in saying that in an extremely short period of time, Joel has fallen in love with Hugo.

I can't blame him. Hugo is a lovable guy. I fell in love with him in days too.

Although I'm still harboring anger at Hugo for the way he left, I can't help but feel joy when I see the way Joel's face lights up around him. When I collected Hugo's death certificate two years ago, I never thought I'd see them standing side by side. That makes it a precious memory I'll treasure for a lifetime and proves what I've always known—Joel is the key to my heart.

"Could you bring Joel here?" My voice is low to ensure Hugo won't hear the sentimental tears dying to be released.

"Sure," he answers in less than a heartbeat. "Where are you at?"

Just from the change in his tone, I know he's detected the unease in my voice. He's always been able to read me. More often than not, he knew my response before I even formed one.

After reciting the address to Hugo, I throw my cell phone into the box and rush into the crammed bathroom. Belinda, the receptionist from Gardner and Sons and my friend, laughs at my frantic dash but does nothing to help me.

I grimace when I catch sight of my disheveled reflection in the mirror. I have smudge marks all over my face, my hair is a wild, frizzy mess from the scattering of snow I scurried through earlier today, and my eyes display my lack of sleep the past five years.

I look wretched.

After wetting a napkin in the grime-covered sink, I run it over my face. It isn't that I'm trying to impress Hugo, I just don't want him to think I'm a slob.

Oh, who am I kidding?

I've been waking up before the sun rises the past three days just to ensure I'm presentable before Hugo arrives. It's stupid, and I don't have the faintest idea why I keep torturing myself, but no matter how many times I reprimand myself, I continue to do it.

Hugo has seen me at my worst.

No amount of makeup will change that fact.

Huffing, I throw the napkin into the bin and pivot on my heels.

"You look fine. You have that artsy look going on." Belinda chuckles when she spots my scowl.

I stick my tongue out at her snickering face before setting to work.

By the time Hugo and Joel arrive thirty minutes later, I'm

covered with a dense layer of sweat and splatters of paint and am way behind schedule.

"Mommy!" Joel charges across the room, sidestepping numerous boxes on his way.

"Hi, baby." When he throws his arms around my legs and burrows his face into my stomach, I crouch down to return his embrace. "Did you have fun today?"

He nods excitedly, his elation increasing when he spots Belinda standing in the corner of the room. His eyes expand as he licks his lips. He loves Belinda because she sneakily hands him jellybeans when she thinks I'm not looking.

"Go on," I say while nudging my head to Belinda. "But don't eat too many jellybeans as we haven't had dinner yet. And you must brush your teeth once you've finished."

After flashing me his adorable grin, Joel hotfoots it to Belinda. His fast steps slow when Belinda says, "I'm sorry, Joel, I'm all out of candy." His lip drops into a pout as tears form in his eyes. "But there's an ice cream store half a block down."

As his eyes bulge, Joel's downcast head rockets up. He loves ice cream nearly as much as he loves pancakes.

When Belinda diverts her focus to me, seeking permission, I nod. Joel jumps into the air, throwing his fists up high before he drags Belinda out of the office without bothering to farewell Hugo or me.

While rubbing a kink in my neck, I head to the other side of the room. After dumping a rolling brush into a bucket of water, I shift on my feet to face Hugo. His brows are furrowed together tightly, and his vibrant eyes are absorbing the room. "What is this place?" he asks.

I bite the inside of my cheek, battling to keep my smile hidden while moving to the middle of the room. An immature giggle bubbles in my chest when I pull a plastic protective sheet off the dental chair, and Hugo's face fills with fret. Anyone would swear I told him I'm going to extract his teeth without any pain relief.

As quick as a flash of lightning sparks a darkened sky, the worry marring Hugo's face vanishes, and his eyes get a renewed spark. "Ava, is this your practice?"

My chest swells, honored by the pride in his tone.

Smiling, I nod. "I've been tucking away money the past few years. It's nothing flashy, but it's mine."

While Joel has been busy with Hugo, I've occupied my time setting up my new practice. When I walked into this office space six months ago, it took a lot of imagination to visualize the space as anything, let alone a dental practice. It was filthy, roach-infested, and small, but with a bit of vision and a hefty loan from the local bank manager, I'm slowly transforming it from a rundown dump to a small but clean practice. I'll be living off my credit cards for the next twelve months as I build my patient list, but it will be worth the sacrifice to have my own practice.

Not to mention being out of Marvin's clutches.

My pulse quickens when I lock my eyes with Hugo's twinkling baby blues. A venerable smile is stretched across his face, and his eyes are sparked with admiration. "You did it," he praises proudly.

I cringe. His praise is far too early. "Not yet, but I'm trying." As my eyes float around the half-painted walls and boxes of furniture waiting to be assembled, I mutter, "I've got a long way to go. My doors are supposed to be opening in the new year, but with how far behind I am, I might have to delay it."

Hugo removes his thick coat and throws it over a half-assembled office chair. "Where do you want me to start?" he offers while rolling up his shirt sleeves.

I wave my hand in front of my body, shooing off his offer as if it is a fly. "It's fine. I'm sure you have more important things to do."

He arches his brow before peering down at me with pleading

eyes. "Let me do this. Please, Ava. Not just for you but Joel as well."

My breathing quickens when I return his stare. It isn't just Joel who has fallen in love. Hugo is also smitten with him.

"Please, Ava," he pleads again. "Give me a chance to make up for some of the wrongs I've done."

"Are you sure you're not busy?" I'm hesitant. With everything going on with Marvin, I'm apprehensive about accepting assistance.

When Hugo grins a heart-fluttering smile before nodding, I dart my eyes around the space. I'm not just endeavoring to find a chore to assign him, but I'm also struggling to ignore the ludicrous surge of excitement dashing to my core from his panty-wetting smile.

Even angrier than the Hulk stuck in a beehive, my body reacts to him as if he owns me.

That, in itself, is a truly terrifying notion.

"There's so much to be done," I mumble, pretending I'm not at all affected by his heart-stopping grin. Regretfully, the jittering of my voice gives away my deceit.

"The quicker you assign me a task, the quicker we can get out of here," Hugo replies to my quiet ramblings, his smile enlarging. The sexual innuendo laced in his reply proves he isn't buying my act of decorum, and he's loving every single squirm he's forcing out of me.

After sneering at his heckling face, I ask, "Can you paint?"

My question wipes his smirk straight off his face, which also saves my panties from a complete massacre.

"I'm bent."

With a groan, I flop onto an office chair Hugo has just finished assembling. For the past six hours, Hugo and I have painted and assembled furniture. We had a quick break when Belinda and Joel returned from the ice cream parlor carrying a bundle of greasy cheeseburgers and fries.

An hour later, when Joel became bored spinning in an office chair Belinda assembled, she offered to take him home for a bath and to put him in bed. Eager to continue charging forward with my plan for my own practice, I readily agreed.

Even though Hugo and I have been working tirelessly the entire time, we've talked a lot for the past six hours. Like all parents concerned about the welfare of their child, most of our conversation revolved around Joel. It hasn't been tight or restrictive. It's been free-flowing and easy.

Like it's always been between us.

Thankfully, our chosen topic of discussion has meant we've avoided most of the sexual sparks that forever ignite in each other's presence. Although I'll always be attracted to Hugo, I'm trying to look at him as the father of my child and not an old flame.

Let me tell you it's been an uphill battle.

Age has been kind to Hugo. *Very kind.*

Hugo plops his backside onto the floor and chuckles. "Bent?"

I nod. "Yeah, bent. Tired. Exhausted. *Bent.*"

He laughs even louder. "*Bent* is when you're under the influence of alcohol or drugs. I was so *bent* after that party."

My brows scrunch as I shake my head. "No, it isn't! It means you're tired." *Doesn't it?*

Most of my adult time is spent hanging out with a four-year-old, so I'm a little out of the loop.

Hugo's brows become lost in his hair as he ogles me with a mocking grin carved on his face.

"Whatever," I mumble several heart-clutching seconds later

before snagging a paint brush out of a bucket of water and flinging it across the room.

My mouth gapes when my throw has perfect aim. The paintbrush hits Hugo smack bang on his left cheek. It smears half of his face with the vibrant sun yellow paint now lining the examination room walls of my office.

"I'm so sorry!" My words come out in a shudder since my entire body is shaking with laughter.

"Oh, yeah, you *will* be sorry," Hugo replies before he launches for me.

Squealing, I dart to the other side of the room. A ragged grunt expels from my lips when Hugo wraps his arm around my waist and tackles me to the floor. I roll onto my side and try to scamper across the floor on my hands and knees. I'm too old for a tickling attack.

Hugo snags my ankle and yanks it back. I tumble onto my stomach, laughing too hard to register the pain of crashing onto the rigid floor. The plastic sheets we laid to protect the newly-installed wooden floorboards crinkle under my body when Hugo drags me backward.

Partway there, I kick out of his hold, roll onto all fours, then scramble onto my knees, mimicking his position. Even with my insides dancing like a stripper on crack, I force a stern mask to slip over my face. I can't let him know I'm loving his playfulness. *I haven't mucked around like this in years.*

"Don't you dare tickle me." I wave my index finger in the air like I did when I disciplined Joel for eating an entire box of frosty flakes in one serving last week.

A grin stretches across Hugo's face as he waggles his brows. We kneel across from each other, staring but not speaking for several long seconds. Our chests thrusting up and down as we endeavor to fill our lungs with air is the only audible noise heard as we undertake a sweat mustache-provoking stare down.

I should bow out of the fight immediately.

His eyes are his biggest ally in repairing the damage he inflicted on my heart. They truly feel like they can see through to my soul.

"What happens if I do?" Hugo asks a short time later, drawing my focus back to his plump lips. "What happens if I tickle you?"

I swallow to relieve my parched throat from the seductive purr of his voice before saying, "I'll... I'll..." *Come on, brain!* When a crass grin morphs onto his lips, I say without a stutter, "I'll use this against you."

All the color drains from Hugo's face when I yank the drill off the dentist chair we're kneeling next to. His widened eyes dart between the functioning drill vibrating in my hand and my leering face.

I've got him right where I want him.

Before my very eyes, the fretful mask Hugo is wearing slips off his face. "It will be worth it," he says with a wink before diving at me.

I don't get the chance to react. I'm pinned to the floor by his large frame and subjected to his tortuous, tickling fingers in less than a second. I squeal a window-shattering scream when his hands unleash a torrent of tickles on my ribs and stomach. Tears stream down my flushed cheeks as I buck and wail against him, but no matter how hard I fight, a woman of my size is no match for a beast of a man like Hugo.

"Mercy!" I try to scream, but I can barely breathe, let alone speak. "Mercy! Mercy!" I scream again.

If he doesn't stop soon, I'll pee my damn pants.

When Hugo finally hears my roaring pleas, he rolls off me. I suck in a deep breath. My heart is beating wildly against my chest, my cheeks are sore from the giant grin I've been wearing all night, and my throat is hoarse from the childish laughter that tore from my lips. It feels like we've stepped back in time thirteen years, and we're once again two teens lying on the floor in the middle of Jorgie's bedroom.

Oh, what I'd give to really step back in time.

My examination room falls into eerie silence. It is so quiet you could hear a pin drop.

Unexpectedly, one of the most wonderful sounds in the world thunders through my ears, startling the living daylights out of me. Hugo's head is thrown back, and he's laughing. Not a small, brief chuckle but a full-hearted laugh that shreds through my soul and heals some of the cracks in my damaged heart.

Just hearing his boisterous chuckle spurs on my own laughter. Before I can stop myself, giggles bubble up my chest and erupt from my mouth. Upon hearing my hearty giggles, Hugo laughs even louder. And thus begins the vicious cycle of belly-crunching laughter.

We lay next to each other cackling loudly until we don't even know why we're laughing.

Then we laugh some more.

By the time Hugo wipes the tears from his cheeks and scrambles off the floor, my stomach is riddled with cramps, and I've laughed more the past twenty minutes than I have the past twelve months.

A smile stretches across my face when Hugo thrusts out his hand, offering to assist me off the floor. After settling my erratically beating heart, I accept his offer. A girly squeal emits from my lips from his strengthened tug on my arm. My nipples bud, and a husky moan topples from my mouth when my chest crashes into the hard ridges of his pec muscles.

The shift of air between us is so great, they would feel it all the way in the city.

As Hugo stares down at me, flicking his gaze between my lips and my eyes, I drink in the features I missed assessing the past five years. Other than the small wrinkles in the corners of his eyes when he smiles, he hasn't aged a day in half a decade. His eyes are youthful and full of life. They're identical to Joel's in every way.

Identical to the little boy who had to grow up without a father the first four years of his life.

With my heart a confused mess, I maneuver out of Hugo's embrace. I feel his eyes tracking me, but he remains quiet as I gather my bag and cell phone from the newly assembled reception desk in the foyer of my office.

"Can I give you a ride home?" he offers when he realizes I've had enough antics for one night.

I shake my head. "No, I'm fine. I have my car."

I continue gathering my stuff, not trusting myself to spin around. When I look into Hugo's eyes, they make me want to pretend the last five years never happened. They want me to act like he isn't the man who shattered my heart and left me broken. I'd give anything to stare up at him in awe like Joel does and pretend nothing else in the world matters more than gaining his attention, but that isn't real life. I'm not a sixteen-year-old girl gushing over her high school crush. I'm also not a twenty-four-year-old virgin seducing a man into her bed. I am a mom who will do everything in her power to ensure her son's heart is protected.

That my *heart is protected.*

My plans go to shit when Hugo mutters, "You don't have your car here, Ava. Remember?" When I pivot to face him, my brash movements cause a rush of dizziness to cluster in my sleep-deprived brain. "You asked Belinda to take your car, so Joel had a car seat," he explains to my confused face.

Shit, I completely forgot.

"Come on." Hugo gestures to the door. "It's only a lift, Ava, nothing more than a friend offering another friend a ride home."

He can say that. He isn't the one who's snuggled into a pillow drenched in his aftershave the past five years just for a few measly hours of sleep. I've been struggling the past six hours to ignore his intoxicating woodsy smell, and that was in the space of an office. Imagine how impossible it will be in the small confines of a car?

Before I can answer Hugo's suggestion, the annoying shrill of a cell phone breaks the quiet. The fretful mask that slipped off Hugo's face thirty minutes ago settles back into place when he realizes the noise is resonating from his jeans pocket. As he digs his hand into his pocket to retrieve an outdated silver cell, his brows furrow.

With twisted lips, he flips open the phone and presses it against his ear. "Boss," he greets, his tone packed with apprehension. "Alright. When?"

His eyes snap to mine. They're filled with guilt. I shift my focus to my newly decorated office, pretending my heart isn't hammering my ribs from the devastated look crossing his face.

When he finishes his phone call, he moves to stand in front of me. My eyes travel up his body from his paint-splattered boots to the week-old stubble on his chin. After exhaling a nerve-cleansing breath, my eyes finalize their journey, landing on his Marshall family heirlooms—his glistening baby blues.

"I have to go... my job... my boss needs me." His words sound as tormented as he looks.

Snubbing the tears pricking in my eyes, I fake a smile and nod. "When do you have to go?" I query, my voice quivering.

Hugo rubs a kink in the back of his neck before announcing, "Now."

My heart plummets into my stomach as quickly as the first tears escape my eyes.

"I'll be back, Ava. I promise you, I'll be back." When he steps closer, engulfing me with his delicious scent, my tears flow even more quickly. He bands his arms around my shoulders and pulls me into his thrusting chest. His heart is beating so fast, it pulverizes my eardrum. "I'll be back. Nothing could keep me away from Joel. *From you.*"

The truth in his eyes when he peers down at me weakens the stranglehold crippling my heart. After assuring me for several long seconds that he'll be back using nothing but his eyes, he runs the back of his fingers across my cheeks, removing my tears in one quick sweep. Once my face is free of any moisture, he lifts his sorrow-filled eyes to mine. "I know it's late, but can I please say goodbye to Joel?" he requests, his voice on the verge of begging.

More tears spill when I nod.

The drive back to my home is somber. The mood is most certainly void of our earlier playfulness. Even the shock that Hugo is driving Jorgie's *Baby* hasn't fully registered. I assumed it was still rusting in the back garage at the Marshall's residence.

When Hugo pulls into the driveway, the shake of my hands engulfs my whole body. I walk up to the front door with a mute Hugo in tow. If I didn't hear his feet stomping, I would have assumed he was still in his car. That's how quiet he is.

When I stuff the key into the lock and swing open the door, Hugo asks, "Where does Marvin live?" His face is fettered with confusion. I would say it is an adorable confusion if he didn't look so torn.

My eyes stray to my shoes as I mutter, "Marvin still lives in his apartment on Pinter."

"You're engaged, but you don't live together?" I can't tell if he's humored by my response or disgusted.

Either way, I say, "It's complicated." I enter the foyer, then nudge my head to the hallway like he doesn't know the floorplan of this home like the back of his hand. "First door on the left."

He grins a tight smile before walking down the hall. His strides are long but heavy.

After seeing Belinda off, I hesitantly walk down the hallway. A small sheen of light from Joel's room is illuminating the hall, no doubt the nightlight he sleeps with is on. Ever since Chase read him *Der Struwwelpeter,* he's requested to sleep with the light on.

When I reach Joel's room, I prop my shoulder on the wall just outside the doorjamb then prick my ears.

"Are you coming back?" Joel's voice is groggy from being awoken so late.

The mattress springs creak before I hear, "Yeah, buddy, I'll be back soon."

I smile when Joel asks, "Will you bring me back a present? When Uncle Chase went to Disney World, he brought me back a present."

Hugo laughs a breathy chuckle. "I'm sure I can wrangle up something. What do you like?"

Nothing but hope resonates in Joel's voice when he asks, "Do they sell candy where you're going?"

"I wouldn't live there if they didn't."

When the room falls into silence, I sneak a peek. My heart squeezes when I realize what has caused the quietness. Joel's little arms are flung around Hugo's neck. He's squeezing him tight. Hugo is embracing him just as robustly. When Joel releases Hugo from his embrace, Hugo's face strains with remorse. He doesn't want to leave Joel any more than I don't want him to go.

"I'll see you soon, buddy," Hugo assures him before standing from the bed.

Joel nods and dives back into his bed. After tucking him in and placing a kiss on his forehead, Hugo reluctantly leaves his room. Tears burn my eyes when I see the confounded look crossing his face.

"He isn't going anywhere," I comfort him, willing to say anything to ease the uncertainty clouding his usually alluring eyes. "He will be waiting for you when you come back."

Although words cost nothing, sometimes they're the most valuable thing you can give a person.

After a nod, Hugo places a kiss on the side of my mouth. Try as I may, I can't ignore the quiver of his lips against mine. "I'll see you soon," he mutters before he spins on his heel, races for the door, and exits without so much as a backward glance.

FIFTEEN
HUGO

"You take Hugo, or you don't go, Isabelle."

As my eyes bounce between Isaac and Izzy, I consider if I've been transported to a different universe. When I left Ravenshoe, they were announcing their engagement and blissfully in love. Now, they stand across from each other as if they're strangers.

Trust me, after the five days I've just endured, I'm more than aware that a lot can happen in a short span of time, but I'm still surprised to return to this. Izzy and Isaac are solid. They remind me a lot of Hawke and Jorgie, so I know they'll get through the latest debacle, but it makes me wonder what happened the past couple of days to tilt the axis of their relationship so viciously.

My last five days have been surreal.

I have a son.

A precious little boy who captured my soul in under a second.

Just glancing into his eyes heals wounds I never thought would mend. I'm not biased when I say Joel is perfect. He's perfect in every single way. It isn't surprising considering who his mom is. Joel has so much of Ava in him. The way he screws up his nose when he's thinking, his crazy curly hair, and how his eyes see straight through to my soul. But I also see some of my qualities in him as well.

His love of sweets for one. That's the only thing the poor guy lucked out in by having Ava as his mother. I laughed hysterically when he told me Ava sings him the 'Brush the Teeth' nursery rhyme every morning and night to ensure he brushes his teeth for the recommended timeframe. He also disclosed that she limits the amount of sugar he consumes. When he argues, declaring she isn't fair, Ava says she doesn't need his praise because his teeth will thank her when he's older.

My attention reverts from reminiscing when Izzy exits Isaac's office. Her face is gaunt, and her eyes are full of tears. I trail quietly behind her, still reeling too much from my own emotions to handle more. Izzy moves around the master suite of the home she shares with Isaac, hastily gathering a small bag of bare necessities.

"Is that it?" I ask when she hands me the overnight bag.

When she nods, relief engulfs me. From how light she has packed, my hope our trip to Tiburon will be a short one increases. Isaac was vague on the phone last night. He simply requested for me to accompany Izzy to her hometown. He didn't give any stipulations on how long we will be away or why we were going. He merely said he "needed me."

After everything he has done for me the past five years, I couldn't deny his request.

My heart was maimed leaving Joel and Ava. It was one of the hardest things I've ever endured, but it's only a matter of time before I see them again. I'll never be parted from them for an extended period ever again. I just need to steer Isaac and Izzy through their latest crisis, then I'll sit down and work out how to balance both my loyalty to Isaac and my family.

"Alright. I'll meet you in the foyer. Roger will take us to the airport," I advise Izzy before pivoting on my heels and rushing down the stairs.

My steps are eager because the quicker we get to Tiburon, the faster I'll return to my family.

By the time the private jet Isaac hires touches down in Tiburon, I'm a wreck. I haven't slept in over thirty-six hours. I assumed the sleep I missed during my nine-hour car trip from Rochdale to Ravenshoe would be corrected during the flight over.

It wasn't.

Anytime I closed my eyes, Ava's tear-stained face haunted me. Only halfway across the country did it hit me why the image taunted me so much. If she reacted so fearfully with me promising to return, how many times did I cause her to cry the past five years? The thought riddles me with guilt. I hate that I've caused her so much heartache.

The message I left on Ava's voicemail the day I vanished is as solid now as it was back then. I still love her. I always have, and I always will. I just hope one day she can find it in her heart to forgive me. Not just for vanishing without a trace but for breaking her heart.

My eyes float up from the eat-in kitchen floor when Izzy says, "You can put your bag in the spare room. It's the third door on the right."

I nod before ambling down the hall. Photo frames ranging in size are scattered on the walls. They're all pictures of Izzy at various stages of her life from a freckle-faced little girl to a stunning teen all dolled up for a school dance. In most of the photos, she has her arm wrapped around a large brute of a man. He's nearly as tall as me but double my weight. The camera's flash bounces off his shiny head, but even looking like a trained killer, nothing but admiration beams out of Izzy's eyes as she stares up at him.

After dumping my bag onto the double bed in the middle of the room, I drop my eyes to my watch. It is a little after five local time, so it's close to eight at Rochdale. Almost Joel's bedtime. While swallowing the lump in my throat, I pull out my cell phone and dial Jorgie's old home number I have memorized, hoping Ava's number is the same. I push the phone in close to my ear, ensuring I can hear her over the mad beat of my heart.

"Hey, you've reached Ava and Joel. We're not home right now so leave a message after the beep," Ava and Joel say in sync.

A grin tugs on my lips from the corniness of their message. "Hey, it's me... umm... Hugo. Joel's dad." *Jesus, I sound like a moron.* "Just wanted to say goodnight to Joel. Goodnight, buddy, I hope you had a good day. And to let you know I'm thinking of you... both of you. Bye."

I'm pulling the phone away from my ear when it dawns on me what I said. My phone smacks me up the side of my head when I push it back to my ear with urgency. "Not goodbye. I'll see you so —" I stop talking when a loud clink sounds over the line. "Hey, you're home."

"Yes, they are," advises a male voice I don't immediately recognize. "Home with me, where they belong."

My teeth grit when I recognize the condescending tone shrieking down the line. *Marvin.*

"Leave my family alone, Hugo," he sneers like he has a say in the matter.

"They're not *your* family," I snap back. "Joel is *my* son. He has *my* blood." *And Ava owns my heart.*

"Joel may have your blood running through his veins, but I'm the man who raised him, fed him, and clothed him. Without me, he wouldn't even have a roof over his head."

Fury blackens my veins, but even fuming mad, I can't negate his claims. I haven't been there for Joel, but that's only because I didn't know he existed. If I did, I would have done everything in my power to ensure he was looked after. To ensure he didn't have to endure the pain Ava and I went through the past five years.

"Put Ava on the phone." My words are rough as a surge of emotions flood into me. "I want to talk to Ava."

Marvin acts as if my tone wasn't demanding. "Do everyone a favor, Hugo. Stay away. That will be the kindest thing you could ever do for your son."

When he disconnects our call, I throw my phone onto a bed then run my hand over my head. Even if everything he's saying is true, I can't give them up. It isn't possible. It was hard enough staying away from Ava for the past five years. Many times, I jumped into my car and headed to Rochdale. I was dying to see her again, but I was also desperate to learn if she was safe and protected.

I never made it any further than the 'Welcome to Rochdale' sign four miles out, though. I couldn't risk her life for my own selfish reasons, and I also didn't want to see the pain in her eyes knowing I was the one who put it there. So, with a heavy heart, I turned around and steered my car back to Ravenshoe, back to the town that sheltered me during my roughest storm.

I've often quoted that your home isn't where you were born and raised. It is where your family is. For the past five years, Ravenshoe has been my family, but not anymore. The woman who owns my heart lives in Rochdale as does the boy who captured my soul in under a second.

My already high heart rate jumps up a notch when I peer out

the window. A shadowy figure is moving throughout a room at the back of the property, and I am meant to be protecting Izzy.

Shit!

After housing the firearm Isaac asked me to get a couple of weeks back into the waistband of my jeans, I rush in the direction I saw the figure.

"Izzy," I call out when I enter the backyard.

The furious beat of my heart lessens when her girlie voice emerges from an office attached to the side of the house. When I sprint into the moldy-smelling space, my eyes scope the premises, ensuring it's free of any threats.

It is. Other than stacks of ruined boxes, Izzy is the only living thing inside the demountable building.

"What is this room?" I ask, pacing deeper into the space.

Dark hair whizzes off Izzy's face when she huffs. "Years of hard work wasted. My Uncle Tobias never relied on computers. He said they were too risky. I guess he never met a cracked roof tile before."

When she rolls her eyes while dragging a stack of sagging boxes across the room, I chuckle under my breath. I've never been a fan of computers either. I prefer communicating in person than over the internet. I used to think that was a good thing. Now, I'm not so sure. Perhaps if I hadn't been so stubborn, I would have discovered Joel's existence years ago.

Hours pass in an instant when I aid Izzy in saving years of her uncle's FBI paperwork. I've never had a fondness for law enforcement officers, but the way Izzy speaks about her uncle tilts the pendulum in his favor. My lack of respect for law enforcement wasn't engrained in me until my sister's death. I made a mistake five years ago when grief overruled my moral compass, but in my defense, I did try to handle the situation legally. It was only when it failed that my anger got the better of me.

A giggle spills from Izzy's lips when my stomach grumbles. I'm not surprised by its reaction. I haven't eaten anything since the cheeseburgers Joel and Ava's friend brought back last night.

"I'll climb onto the roof tomorrow morning and patch the hole the best I can, but you might need to get a professional out to look at it."

Izzy smiles. "Thanks. I guess I should feed you then, to make sure you don't fade away before tomorrow morning."

I laugh. Given the chance to meet, Izzy and Ava would get on like a house on fire. Both can make me laugh even when my mood is woeful. My stomach is still cramping from how much I laughed in Ava's office. I can't believe how immature I acted last night. I'm nearly thirty years old, but that didn't stop me from tackling Ava to the floor and tickling her until she begged me to stop.

It's been years since I fooled around like that. I'm not surprised, though. Only Ava can make it seem as if I've stepped back in time. Anytime I'm around her, I'm once again a teenage boy chasing his high school crush.

"I don't think there's much chance of me fading away." My tone is playful as the memories of last night drastically improve my mood.

"Just give me a chance to get the box I originally came in here for and then I'll order us some pizza from Maria's," Izzy advises while heading for a stack of shelves housing document boxes.

When she walks back toward me with a box marked Oo1P15, I slant my head to the side and stare at her. It isn't the box gaining my attention, it's the fretful mask slipped over her face causing my greatest concern.

Remaining quiet, I follow Izzy into the main house. Her steps are nowhere near as spirited as they were earlier.

"I'll order in some pizza, then I'm going to take a quick shower."

Not waiting for me to reply, she steps into the hallway. As I prepare myself a coffee, my eyes continuously glance over at the box responsible for her dour mood. I tell myself it's nothing, that she will be open and honest with me when she's ready, but no matter how hard I try to keep my focus off the box, my eyes remain fixated on it.

Unable to assuage my curiosity for a second longer, I set down my half-empty mug of coffee and amble toward the box. After darting my eyes to the hallway to ensure the coast is clear, I lift the box's flap. Air vehemently escapes my lungs when my eyes zoom in on the first photo in the box.

Him.

I toss off the lid with force, sending it flying across the kitchen floor. My hand shakes when I snatch the photo from the top of the pile as a million thoughts fill my head. The most concerning—*why is Izzy investigating the man who killed my sister?*

As I scour through a ton of photos and handwritten records, my concern grows. Numerous photos of Isaac are stored in this box, taken around the age he was when I first met him. Does that mean what I think it does? Is Izzy investigating Isaac? And why would she do this? Why can't she just leave it alone? What's done is done. It can't be taken back.

Before my head can formulate a single answer to my millions of questions, a shocked voice at my side says, "What are you doing? You can't go through that. Those files are highly confidential."

"Confidential?" I sneer, glaring at Izzy as she storms across the room. "You're invading his privacy, and you're worried about confidentiality. Is this why you came here? Searching for answers to questions he can't answer yet?" *Questions he shouldn't have to answer.*

Izzy snatches up the articles and images spread across the table. Her face is pale, and her eyes are welling with tears, but it won't stop my interrogation. "If you want answers, you should have kept asking, not go behind his back and investigate him." *Furthermore, he doesn't deserve your interrogation. I do.*

"I'm not investigating him," she retaliates.

"Then what do you call it, Izzy? You're looking into his past, digging through his *personal* life—"

"I'm not prying into his personal life!"

I slam a surveillance photo of Isaac onto the wooden tabletop. "You're not prying into his personal life, hey, then what the fuck is this?" I yell, no longer able to harbor my anger. Isaac has sheltered and defended me for years, all to have the woman he loves investigate him like he's a criminal. "He isn't a criminal, but you're treating him as if he is one and not the man you've agreed to marry."

A tear rolls down Izzy's cheek, calming my anger. I inhale a deep breath and count backward from ten. A trick Avery encouraged me to do when my anger is spiraling out of control.

"Ten seconds can be the difference between a lifetime of mistakes or a lifetime of memories," she has often quoted.

Battling against her tears, Izzy snaps her eyes shut before her hand slips into the back pocket of her jeans. I eye her curiously when she removes a folded-up piece of glossy paper. After carefully unfolding it, she hands it to me. The blood surging through my body has turned potent, but the fear in Izzy's eyes is what has me most on edge.

I understand why when my eyes drop to the piece of paper. It feels like a freight train crashes into me. As I struggle to reel in my shock, I bounce my eyes between the photos of Isaac and his girl-friend before her untimely demise sprawled over the table and the image in my hand of a girl who looks eerily similar to Isaac's deceased girlfriend.

No way, it can't be.

"This can't be true," I mutter, my tone quickly shifting from angry to sympathetic.

"It is," Izzy mumbles, her voice groggy. "This file proves it is. Ophelia is alive, and she's been living in Tiburon the entire time."

She matches up the photos side by side, proving without a doubt that the lady in the new photo is the same girl photographed with Isaac six years ago. Everything is similar—her face, her eyes, and even a small mole in the corner of her neck.

"I gathered she was here because that's Old St. Hilary's Church on Esperanza Street in the background. It is a well-loved landmark in Tiburon."

My eyes lift to Izzy. She isn't devastated to discover the secret Isaac's been hiding the past five years. She's gutted because she thinks she is losing him.

"Jesus Christ," I mumble under my breath. "Does Isaac know about any of this?"

Izzy bites on her lip and shakes her head. "No, I wanted to come and see for myself. I couldn't risk hurting him if it wasn't true. If it wasn't really her."

"If it is her, are you planning on telling him?"

She lifts the newest image of Ophelia off the dining table before faintly nodding. Her defeated expression slams a heavy weight into my chest. "What can I do to make this easier on you?"

New tears form in her already drenched eyes as she replies, "Just remind me that he loves me. And that I'm doing this to ease his pain."

SIXTEEN
HUGO

I climb the stairs of a private jet with Izzy cradled in my arms. She hasn't stopped crying since we left a pharmacy nearly thirty minutes ago. I've always been a communicator, but I'm too shocked at the events that transpired today to configure a response.

The hunch Izzy was running with was solid. She found Ophelia—Isaac's girlfriend who was killed in an 'accident' well over five years ago is alive and well. As if that isn't shocking enough, Ophelia has a child, a boy who would only be a year or two older than Joel.

Isaac could be a father, and he doesn't even know it.

I'm honestly at a loss on how he will react. Isaac protects every member of his empire as if they're his family—his blood—so imagine how great his response will be to discovering he has a child?

A few hours into the flight, Izzy's tears finally dry, and her head lifts to me. "How old do you think Ophelia's son is?"

I want to lie. I want to tell her there isn't a possibility Ophelia's son is Isaac's, but I can't. I can't deceive her like that. I'm not a deceitful person, so I mutter, "Five or six."

Her hand shakes as she takes a sip from a bottle of water. "So the dates could add up? He could be Isaac's son?" She tries to put on a brave front, but she isn't fooling anyone. Her eyes are extremely expressive. I can read her like a book.

I sit in the spare seat next to her before wrapping my arm around her shoulders and pulling her into my chest. A whimper escapes her lips, but other than that, she accepts my comfort. It reminds me of the time I comforted Jorgie in my parents' kitchen weeks before her death and reminds me some things you don't have to fight to achieve.

"You can't fight fate, Izzy, but that doesn't mean you should give up. Isaac gave you that engagement ring as a promise." I peer down at the dark gray and purple gemstone on her finger. "He's never spoken those words to another woman before, so that alone shows your importance to him. You need to have faith that things will work out the way they're meant to."

As do I. I fought my attraction to Ava for years, using any pathetic excuse I could find. She was my sister's best friend. My parents treated her like a daughter. I didn't want to settle down. Only now do I realize why it has only ever been her occupying my thoughts.

She was the first girl I ever lusted over, the first girl I ever asked out, and the first girl I've ever loved. My very existence begins and ends with her, and I'm going to make sure she's fully aware of that. Even though she's wearing another man's ring and has agreed to be his wife, I'll fight to my very last breath. I'll never give up.

After watching Isaac participate in a charity UFC match, I understand why he is feared by his rivals. The smile he wore in the cage didn't reflect the viciousness of his attack. I'm considering changing his nickname from Boss to the Smiling Assassin.

"Are you alright?" I ask Izzy while punching in the security code for Isaac's private residence. I've been here a handful of times, but I've not once been invited inside.

Keeping her gaze fixated on the arched window of Isaac's house, she faintly murmurs, "Yes."

When I pull to the side of the driveway, I turn off the engine, then grasp the door handle latch, preparing to exit. My escape plan is foiled when Izzy places her hand on my knee. "I want to talk to Isaac alone," she advises, her words weak. "He's a private man and wouldn't appreciate an audience."

Her uncle should be proud. She has grown up to be an admirable woman. Even with her heart breaking, her priorities remain on protecting Isaac. She harbors so many of Ava's qualities. Even though I left her heartbroken, she's been nothing but encouraging of my relationship with Joel.

For that, I'll be forever indebted to her.

"Alright. I'll wait here until Isaac arrives, then I'll head out. But if you need anything, Izzy, you have my number."

She nods before leaning over to press a kiss on my cheek. "Thanks, Hugo, for everything."

Not long after she's peeled out of my car, the headlights of Isaac's Bugatti illuminate the driveway. When he notices Izzy standing at the entrance of his house, he tries to keep his face passive. He fails miserably. Just like the night I introduced Hawke to Jorgie, anytime Isaac and Izzy are together, the dynamic between them is explosive—like fireworks in a blackened sky.

Once Isaac joins Izzy on the porch of his home, I jump into my Chevelle and tear out of the driveway. My mind is jumbled. I'm torn between driving back to Rochdale now or grabbing a few hours of sleep.

"You won't do anyone any good if you end up wrapped around a telephone pole," I mutter to myself.

My excessive speed down the winding roads of Isaac's estate slows when I notice a blue BMW parked on the edge of Isaac's property line. A snarl forms on my lips when my car's headlights light up the number plate on the BMW. *Blondie.*

What the fuck is he doing here?

When I pull in behind Blondie's BMW, he climbs out of the driver's seat. I don't know what it is, but something about him sets me on edge. I can't tell if it stems from the way he looks at Izzy when he thinks no one is looking, or if it is the cloud of secrets his wholesome eyes are concealing, but no matter how well he portrays the image of a humble Boy Scout, I ain't buying the shit he's selling.

I can't comprehend why Izzy can't see the darkness invading his eyes. To me, it is as obvious as the sun hanging in the sky, but Izzy seems oblivious to it.

Blondie is hiding something, and I plan on exposing his deepest, darkest secrets.

"What are you doing here, Blondie?" I ask, pacing toward him.

I've nicknamed Brandon Blondie. It isn't his blond hair that has given him the title. It is the fact I don't believe Brandon is his real name. Hunter, Isaac's head of security, is one of the world's best hackers. Not Adrian Lamo on a good day. He's Adrian Lamo on his best day. After completing a search on Brandon that Philip Marlowe would have been proud of, Hunter couldn't find a trace of information on him. Not a single smidge.

Brandon is even more of an illusion than I am.

From experience, I know only men with something to hide keep their information locked up tighter than Fort Knox. That's why I know Brandon is hiding something, and it isn't his fascination with Izzy.

That's even more obvious than the sun shining in the sky.

"Are you sniffing around hoping Isaac left out a bone?"

He smirks, misconstruing my statement as a joke. I wasn't joking.

He fidgets on the spot, kicking dust up from the loose gravel when he notices my furious wrath. "I just want to make sure Izzy is alright," he replies while peering sheepishly into my eyes.

"Then why not go knock on the door like a real man?"

He laughs and shakes his head. "Been there. Done that." I stare into his eyes, confused by his statement. "I've tried numerous times to see Izzy since she left the hospital. My attempts were always denied... by Isaac."

I'm not surprised by his confession. I thought the jealousy that plagued me with Ava was fierce. It is nothing compared to the jealousy Isaac has when it comes to men getting close to Izzy. I can't say I blame him. From the gleam Brandon's eyes get when Izzy is in his vicinity, I have no doubt he'd trample anyone in his way if Izzy were ever placed back on the market.

"Izzy is fine. She's with Isaac, where she belongs," I inform him before pivoting on my heels and ambling back to my car.

My brisk strides halt when Brandon mutters, "Even with Ophelia being alive?"

The beat of my heart kicks up as I turn around to face him. His face is washed with confusion, and his brows are furrowed tightly.

"How do you know about that?"

His pupils enlarge as his throat works hard to swallow.

"You gave Izzy the photo, didn't you? You thought it was your way in. The key to breaking up Isaac and Izzy."

Brandon's lips form a snarl, and he shakes his head.

"Bullshit," I retaliate, moving to stand in front of him, wanting to look him in the eyes as I call him out as the weasel he is. "You weaseled your way into Izzy's life by pretending you're her friend, all so you could undermine her relationship with Isaac. I've got news for you, you can't fight fate, so I suggest you give up while you're ahead."

"I'm her friend," he responds, his tone surprisingly strong. "Everything I've done is because I'm trying to protect her."

"She doesn't need your protection," I roar when I spot the all-familiar gleam in his eyes. "She has Isaac. She has me. She doesn't need you. So go jump on your white horse and find another damsel in distress to save because Izzy doesn't need saving."

I count down to ten as I walk back to my car.

If I don't control my anger, I'll burst.

"Are you going to protect her like you did Gemma?" Brandon shouts, his voice crammed with anger.

I freeze when Gemma's name rips from his mouth. Surely, I didn't hear him right. My pulse is blaring in my ears, so I must be mistaken. *I have to be.*

When I spin around to face him, I have no doubt he said what I thought he said. The look of fear in his eyes is all the indication I need to know he's aware of the night that still haunts my dreams...

"If only you liked white chocolate," Gemma gabbles while plopping her backside onto the barstool next to me.

My chuckle rumbles over the music blasting out of the jukebox in the corner of the room. I've spent most of my night with members of my squadron at a dime-a-dozen watering hole in the middle of a town we are stationed at. Although rundown, Cantina Vault is a buzzing hive of activity. Line dancers and regular nightclub patrons share the floor space. Air Force officers from second lieu-

tenants to brigadier generals are spread as far as the eye can see, and the beer is the coldest I've ever guzzled.

What more could a man ask for?

I toss down half a bottle of beer before turning my eyes to Gemma. Gemma is the first female lieutenant in my squadron. Her wittiness and willingness to give anything a shot meant we became close friends in a short period of time, but in all honesty, when I was first introduced to her, I was concerned about how she'd cope with the rough conditions we'd immersed ourselves in. It wasn't that I was a chauvinistic asshole. I was just raised by my father to protect my mother and sisters, so I assumed it would take me a bit of time to adjust to Gemma being a fellow officer and not my little sister who needed protecting.

The adjustment didn't take as long as I was predicting. It lasted all of a week—the time it took for me to walk in on Gemma showering in the male latrine. The boiler in the female dorm broke so Gemma ducked in our latrine, expecting my squadron to be longer at our TI drill than we were.

After raking my eyes down her naked body, any worries about treating her like my sisters flew right out the window. Although she's a little on the short side and couldn't weigh more than a pile of feathers, Gemma is gorgeous. No doubt about it—cascading blonde hair falling to her shoulders in a satin waterfall, rich, prominent green eyes that dazzle even in the poor overhead lighting, and perfect unblemished skin, except for the smallest mass of freckles sprinkling her tiny nose.

She's beautiful—a prime example of both looks and personality—but even being hot enough to cause my dick to stir, nothing has ever happened between us. Gemma likes to say it's because she has the wrong skin coloring, but it isn't that. There has only ever been one girl I want to jump the friendship line for—Ava. So as much as Gemma's offer is tempting, I've never taken her up on it.

I angle my body to the side, tilting closer to Gemma. "Who said I'm not a fan of white chocolate?"

She drifts her glistening eyes from the diverse gathering of people cavorting on the crammed dance floor to me. She cocks her brow before pulling her I'm-not-buying-the-shit-you're-selling look she regularly uses when dealing with her male counterparts in the Air Force. "How long have we been stationed together? Nearly ten months?" she queries with her lips pursed.

I nod, agreeing with her assessment.

"In that whole time I've not once seen you share the love with your fairer companions."

I laugh. It's the only plausible reaction to her absurd misconception. For one, the week before we deployed, I had a very compelling meeting with one of Gemma's sorority sisters from Alaska. Two, any time we go out, Gemma spends her night dancing like the floor is on fire, too busy to pay attention to my female companions. And third, but not at all the least, just from the impish glimmer in her eyes, I can tell she's full of shit. She has eyes like Jorgie. I can see straight through to her soul.

"Jealousy has never looked so good," I quip, my tone doused with smugness.

Gemma's head snaps to mine. "Jealous? Please! You had your opportunity... you lost it. No second chances around here," she remarks while wiggling her index finger in front of my face.

I chuckle at her sassiness before taking a swig of my beer.

Malted liquid sprays out of my mouth, dousing the wooden countertop and Gemma's face when she says, "I also snuck a peek at the photo you hide in your footlocker. Ava is very beautiful. I can understand your fascination."

My heart freezes at the mention of Ava's name, but thankfully, my outward appearance gives no indication to the treachery of my heart.

"I'd like to say this is the first time I've had beer sprayed in my face but, unfortunately, it isn't," Gemma mutters before dabbing her face with a midnight black napkin. Once my beer has been removed, she lifts her expressive eyes to me. "Ava is in San Diego, not on the moon. You know that magic tin can we're flying home in on Monday? They have similar ones that can fly you to any destination of your choice. San Diego included."

I smirk against the rim of my beer before taking a mouth-filling gulp. "You sound like my sister, Jorgie."

Gemma smiles broadly. "I need to meet this Jorgie. She sounds a little too good to be true," she jests before placing an order with a bartender for a virgin margarita.

"Loose lips sink ships," I mutter to myself.

I learned the meaning of that saying the weekend following Warrior Week. That week of training should be called Hell Week. We slept in tents, ate funky combinations of beans and rice, and practiced war-like conditions, but it wasn't the unappetizing setting or the less-than-stellar accommodations that gave it the coveted title of Hell Week. It was TI Drill Sergeant Cody Spencer.

He was the hardest, bare-knuckled, and bloody drill sergeant I'd ever encountered. After a week in his presence, I could barely crawl, let alone walk. Deciding we needed to celebrate surviving our trip to hell and back, our regiment went out to a local salsa bar.

After celebrating as if it was Cinco de Mayo, my lips become as loose as the salsa dancers' hips. One slip-up during a game of twenty questions saw me mentioning my high school crush's name. Ever since that night, Ava's name is mentioned at every celebration.

I slam down the remainder of my beer then signal to the bartender for another. My squadron only has two days remaining in Afghanistan until we return home from our second stint. We're guzzling down drinks like we're not paying fifteen dollars for a can of bootleg beer, but when you're celebrating a successful end of our *tour without any causalities to your unit, you'll happily pay the premium price because you can't put a value on that. It is priceless.*

"Why aren't you out there dancing?" I ask Gemma when I notice the direction of her gaze. Her glistening eyes are absorbing the hot, sweaty bodies mingling on the dance floor.

Her nose screws up. "Grabby McGee is being extra grabby tonight."

My eyes rocket to the dance floor. Madden McGee is a fucking sleaze, and that's putting it nicely. He was born and bred with Air Force blood pumping through his veins. His uncles, grandfather, and brothers all served in the same Air Force squadron. Although his predecessors honored his family name, Madden has done nothing but tarnish it. He ignores any instructions given by his superiors, he treats the female members of his squadron as if they're inferior, and he has his nose so far up his ass, he thinks his shit doesn't stink. He's the type of guy who gives Air Force officers a bad name. I also have a knack for reading people, and I didn't like him from the moment I met him.

I drift my eyes back to Gemma. "Do you want me to talk to him?"

"No." She dramatically draws out the short word. "I can handle Grabby McGee."

A smirk tugs on my lips. After seeing the way she handled Warrior Week, I have no doubt she can handle a worm of a man like Madden.

After accepting her virgin margarita from the bartender, Gemma hip-bumps me before making her way to a handful of female squadron members mingling at the side of the dance space. "Come find me when you're ready to go."

After a handful of beers, I decide to call it a night and head back to base. I straighten my spine, extending to my full height so I can seek Gemma in the crowd of people cavorting on the dance floor. Although we aren't a couple, we always arrive and leave together when we go out drinking.

When my search fails to locate her shiny blonde locks, I head for the bar. A bartender with inky black hair and a neck tattoo stops wiping the counter and ambles toward me.

"Have you seen Gemma? Blonde hair, green eyes, around this tall," I ask, holding my hand across my chest. "She's been ordering virgin margaritas all night."

He smiles. "White floral dress?"

"That's the one."

Gemma is the only girl who can pull off a floral dress in a war-torn country.

He stops drying a glass and gestures his head to the entrance door. "She left a few minutes ago."

My brows furrow. "She left?" Skepticism radiates from my voice. Normally, I have to drag Gemma out of any bars we visit.

"Thanks."

I tap my knuckles onto the wooden bar top before spinning on my heels. As I walk to the double swinging doors, the churns of my stomach ramp up as the feeling of something not being quite right overwhelms me.

My steps to the door become urgent, only hindered by the beer sloshing in my twisted stomach. When I emerge out the double wooden doors, humid air hits me in the face, making my stomach churn even more. I crank my neck to the right before drifting to the left. A handful of late-night, drunk partygoers are scattered on the sidewalk, but Gemma is nowhere in sight.

My head shifts to the side when a young blond-haired man stumbles out of the alleyway. His face is ashen and his pupils wide.

I lift my chin in greeting as I eye him with curiosity. I've never seen a kid look so rattled before, even after serving in Afghanistan for two years. The blond kid's eyes stare into mine as his chest thrusts upward. He's struggling to secure a full breath.

His eyes snap to the side at the same time a faint whimper overtakes the hum of music pumping out of the bar. My head rockets in the direction he's peering at lightning speed. When I spot what has his attention, I freeze and take a step backward. I'm winded as if I've been sucker-punched in the gut.

The shock of what I'm witnessing quickly converts to fury as the scene unfolds in front of me. I charge down the alleyway, my steps no longer impeded by the alcohol I drank. The blood rushing through my veins turns potent, blackened by the fury scorching it.

"Get off!" My deep angry snarl bounces off the stained brick walls. "Stop it! Stop it! Get off!"

Blinded by rage, I grab the first man I see and throw him against the trash can he is standing next to. His head connects hard with the steel edge, sending a stream of blood running down the side of his face. He stands, dazed and confused. While holding his wounded head in his hand, he staggers down the alleyway.

I storm toward a group of men, dragging them away from a pair of fear-filled green eyes staring up at me, pleading for me to save her. A man I've seen before but have misplaced his name stops in front of me. He cracks his knuckles and sneers at me like I'm the one in the wrong.

I have news for him.

A bone being fractured bellows through the eerie quietness when my clenched fist connects hard with his jaw. When he falls to the ground, I grab another man, and then another. I unleash hit after hit in a haze of rage. Even outnumbered, fear never approaches me. I'm running on adrenaline, too enraged to stop the anger burning me from the inside out.

My sweat-drenched shirt clings to my chest when I fist the shirt of another man.

"Stop, Hugo. It's me. It's Brody," says a voice quieter than a mouse.

My wildly swinging fist freezes mid-air, inches from a terrified face. The face of the man who stumbled out of the alley mere minutes ago stares up at me, terrified and confused. My clouded eyes dart up and down the alley. When I find it empty of the men who were here ten minutes ago, I unclench my fist. My chest rises and falls as my body fights to rein in my usually carefree composure.

Any sense of normality vanishes when a painful sob shreds through my ears. My eyes dart down to Gemma, huddled against a brick wall. The roughness of the brickwork scratches her skin as she scrambles across the cracked, stained pavement. The strap of her dress is broken, her knees are bloody and bruised, and black lines of mascara are running down her pale cheeks.

As her frantic eyes scan the area, her entire body shakes. Ignoring the trembling that has overtaken my hands, I remove my blood-stained shirt.

"Don't touch me. I don't want you to touch me."

"It's okay," I assure her. "I won't touch you."

I crouch down in front of her to carefully drape my shirt over her shaking body. She stares up at me, wide-eyed and in shock, but not another word escapes her quivering lips. I return her stare, allowing my eyes to issue the words my mouth refuses to produce—my apologies for what she went through while also relaying that I won't hurt her.

When the sounds of sirens approach, Gemma leaps forward and digs her nails into my arm. She clutches onto me for dear life like I'm her safety shield...

I've never forgotten the terrified sobs that tore from her throat that night and having Brandon remind me of them sees me lunging for him. I grab the scruff of his shirt before he can react, then haul him to within an inch of my face. The mad beat of his heart pounds my clenched fist pinning him to his car.

"Who are you?" My voice fails to conceal the shivers havocking my body as a flurry of memories delve into me.

Brandon's eyes dance between mine but not a word parts his mouth.

"Who are you?" I scream again after tightening my grip on his shirt.

He stares into my eyes while stammering out, "My n-name is Brandon James—"

My teeth grit, furious he's trying to play me for a fool.

"McGee," he adds on.

The air is vehemently removed from my lungs. I roam my eyes over his face, studying him in precise detail—same eyes, defined nose, and wonky smile. It was just his blond hair leading me astray.

I take a step backward, overwhelmed by a surge of emotions pummeling into me at once. "You're Grabby McGee's brother?"

Fury unlike anything I've ever felt makes it hard for me to breathe when Brandon nods. I yank him forward before slamming him back with vicious force. Metal crunching echoes in the quietness of the night, but even with his back slamming into his car with brutal strength, Brandon's face remains staunch. It gives no indication to the pain rocketing through his body.

"Do you know who I am?" I ask, my words a vicious snarl.

Brandon's nostrils flare as he inhales a quick, sharp breath. "Yes," he mutters, his chin quivering.

My stomach tenses when it faces an emotional blow. Every secret I've fought to keep hidden is about to become exposed.

My panic doesn't last long. It is soon replaced with anger—anger that I was ever forced to keep such a secret to begin with.

When fury scorches through me, it burns my chest with its

ferocious heat. "Do you know what they did?" I ask, my eyes blazing as my lungs feel.

Heat scorches my veins. I'm spiraling out of control as a range of reactions crash into me—anger, remorse, devastation. They all hammer into me and almost send me sprawling onto my ass.

When Brandon remains quiet, I scream, "Do you know what they did to me!"

"Yes," he replies, his head jerking in a nod.

My entire body trembles and my nostrils flare as anger burns me alive. But Brandon just stares.

"I'm nothing like them," he assures a short time later, his eyes dancing between mine. "I didn't change my name because I didn't want people to know who my father is. I changed it because I'm ashamed of it. I'm ashamed of them."

He stares at me, begging for me to believe him. I know what he's saying is true. Even with his eyes hazed by sorrow, I can see the truth relayed by them. I can feel his shame—his remorse—but it doesn't lessen my anger.

I want to lay my fists into him.

I want to make him suffer the way Gemma suffered.

The way *I* suffered, but then, I'd be just as much a coward as they were.

So instead, I release my grip on his shirt then stalk to my car.

SEVENTEEN
HUGO

With my head pounding as fitfully as my heart, I stumble out of my room. My confrontation with Brandon last night turned my mood woeful. Instead of remembering the lessons Avery taught me over the past five years, I once again sought the aid of a liquor bottle to guide me through the storm. I was desperate, doing anything I could to wash away the memories asphyxiating the joyful mood I'd been in the past four days. I wanted the grim memories that haunt my dreams to vanish.

Normally, I could only achieve that with a bottle. Last night, alcohol did nothing. The only people with the ability to stop my nightmares were seven hundred miles away. Just looking into Ava's eyes can appease any storm brewing on the horizon.

Noticing my stagger, Hawke opens a bottle of whiskey and pours two glasses before he slides one across the marble counter to me. The inexpensive brown liquor sloshes over the rim, landing on the glistening countertop.

"Hair of the dog?" I mutter while securing the glass in my hand.

Hawke arches his brow. Every man knows there's only one cure for a hangover—keep drinking.

The bitter-tasting bile sitting in the back of my throat washes into my stomach when I down the whiskey in quick succession. I grimace when the familiar burn scorches my throat before it settles in my churning stomach. Hawke props his elbows onto the kitchen counter. His change in position allows me to see the time on the microwave. It is nearly five in the afternoon.

My brows hit my hairline.

I slept for over twelve hours.

Hawke peers at me with uncertain eyes. "I wasn't expecting you back so early. Didn't go as you hoped?"

By the time he walked through the front door of my apartment last night, I was well past tipsy. Assuming I was drowning my sorrows about my trip to Rochdale, he gathered a second bottle of whiskey from the bar and joined my silent commiserations.

We didn't talk. We just sat, side by side, staring into space, drinking in silence.

"Rochdale was good." I rub at my temples, praying for the pounding drilling my skull into the next century to settle so I can get back on the road. *Back to my family.* "Actually, Rochdale was more than good. It was fucking great."

Hawke's eyes shoot to mine. His brow is arched, and his expression is even more uncertain than the glint in his eyes.

"I have a son," I enlighten him. Even having a hangover that rivals all hangovers, I can't stop an ecstatic smile stretching across my face. Joel has captured my soul even more quickly than Ava stole my heart.

Hawke's eyes bulge as he looks at me in utter shock. "Who's the mom?"

My brain screams blue murder when I throw my head back

and laugh. It bounces off the laminated cabinets and ricochets into my ears.

Hawke doesn't see the hilarity of the situation. His brows are stitched, and his lips are screwed. He looks utterly confused.

"Who do you think?" I ask once my laughter dies down.

"I don't know, that's why I'm asking," he replies, his tone deadly serious.

When I waggle my brows and smile, clarity forms in his baffled eyes.

"Ava?" His voice is super-alto.

I bite on my lower lip and nod. If I'd slapped Hawke in the face with a cold fish, it wouldn't have shocked him more.

I slant my head and eye him curiously when his eyes get a spark in them I haven't seen since the day he married Jorgie. "She was right." He crosses his arms in front of his chest. "Jorgie always said you and Ava were destined to be together. Your son proves it. You can't—"

"Fight fate," I fill in, smiling.

Hawke nods and smiles before his eyes get a glossy sheen to them. A tingling sensation scratches my throat when he locks his glistening eyes with mine. "I'm really happy for you, man."

I won't lie. My eyes are welling with tears. He may have only said six little words, but his eyes are expressing much more than his mouth ever could. His normally unreadable eyes expose fragments of a Hawke I haven't seen in years. The pre-heartbroken Hawke.

"Thanks."

After coughing to clear his voice of any hindrance, he says, "I'm going to squeeze in a workout at the gym before heading to Nick and Jenni's. I'm on night watch." He smacks me on the back before ambling to the door. Just before he exits, he cranks his head back and peers at me. His mouth is carved in a lopsided grin, and his eyes are sparked with mischief. "You should consider heading to the gym yourself." He waggles his brows. "Get some testosterone pumping through your veins. I don't want you to run the risk of waking up in the morning with a vagina since you're getting all sentimental and shit."

When I catch sight of his shit-eating grin, I pick up an apple from the fruit bowl in the middle of the counter and peg it at his head. He chuckles before darting out the front door. I snarl when my throw narrowly misses his head. It slams into the mirror hanging in the entryway, shattering it into tiny shards.

Darn it. The last thing I need is seven years of bad luck.

After showering to wash off the funk of a heavy night of drinking, I clean up the shards of glass in the foyer. Half of me was tempted to leave it for Catherine's arrival tomorrow afternoon, but my laziness only lasted as long as it took for me to remember a quote my mom has always said. *A real man knows how to respect a woman. Because he knows the feeling if someone would disrespect his mother.*

While picking up the last shards of glass, my eyes catch sight of a white envelope on the entryway table. My heart smashes against my ribs. It isn't the fact I don't get any mail delivered to my home address that's piquing my interest. It's the fact it has my full name scribbled on the envelope. My full *deceased* name—Hugo Joel Marshall.

After snatching the lightweight envelope off the table, I rip it open and upend the contents onto the table. My eyes scan the official-looking document before I've even gathered it in my hands. The more I speed-read the paper, the more my blood boils.

I shove the document under my arm, snatch my keys and cell

phone out of the crystal bowl on the entryway table, then race to the elevator at the end of my hallway. When the elevator dash-board announces the elevator car is still in the lobby, I push open the fire escape door and sprint down the stairs.

By the time I make it to my car, I'm sweating profusely and shaking. Neither is from the effects of running down thirty flights of stairs.

I jump into my car, crank the ignition, then reverse out of my parking space. Burning rubber and gasoline infiltrate my nostrils as I throw *Baby* into gear and fly out of the underground garage, narrowly missing a blue BMW entering. I don't miss Brandon's curious glance as my car whizzes by, but I've got more important matters to deal with right now than him and his guilty conscience.

While drifting my eyes between the road and my phone, I dial Ava's cell phone. Ignoring the shake in my hands, I press the phone against my ear.

"Hey, you've reached Ava. Leave a message."

"Ava, please don't do this. Please don't take my son away from me." I snap my eyes to the paperwork sitting on the passenger seat. "I know I hurt you and broke your heart. I know you may never forgive me, but please don't do this. I need him. *I need you.* I'll do anything you want, anything at all, but I can't sign those forms, Ava. I can't give him up. I can't give *you* up."

I continue pleading into her voicemail until a message comes over the line saying her voicemail is full. After snapping my untraceable cell phone shut, I throw it onto the forms requesting that I sign away my parental rights to Joel. They want me to relin-quish full custody to Ava and Marvin. No request for child support has been included and no visitation rights were stipulated.

As if that weren't already a low blow, the last page gutted me. It's requesting a paternity test to prove Joel is my son. I know he is.

I've never doubted it from the moment I laid my eyes on him, but now Ava is trying to deny it.

It doesn't make any sense. I can't comprehend why her perspective has altered so greatly the past two days. She said Joel would be there waiting for me when I came back, that he wasn't going anywhere, but this paperwork says different.

Approximately two hundred miles outside of Ravenshoe, my untraceable cell phone rings. Not bothering to look at the screen, I flick it open and push it against my ear. "Ava, please—"

"Who's Ava?" Hunter's voice is laced with mockery.

"Hunter, I don't have time. I'm—"

My words stop when he says, "Izzy needs you."

"What's going on?"

"Travis called to say she arrived at the Dungeon an hour ago. She's fairly intoxicated."

I smirk. *Sounds like something Izzy would do.* "Where's Isaac?"

After Izzy was cleared of murder charges, Isaac gave me the month off, clearly stipulating Izzy wasn't going to leave his sight until he "had his fill." Reading his coded statement for what it was, I was more than happy to take a leave of absence from my position.

It's my first official vacation in nearly five years.

"Isaac is in Tiburon," Hunter replies while scrubbing his hand along his scruffy beard. "I don't know when he's coming back. I've been trying his cell phones all day. They keep going straight to his voicemail."

My brow arches. Isaac is never unreachable. His cells are an extension of his body.

"Can you send Roger to keep an eye on her? He's as boring as bat shit, but he's good at his job. He'll make sure Izzy stays out of mischief."

"Can't," Hunter retorts. "He's at Vegas helping Parker secure Isaac's asset."

My eyes squint when a semi-trailer comes over the horizon, blinding me with its high beams.

After flashing my lights at the truck driver and flipping him the bird, I say, "What about you?"

Hunter sheepishly chuckles. It is a laugh I only hear when he's in trouble or causing it. "I'm a little *indisposed* right now."

He's not the only one.

"I'm two hundred miles out."

Normally, I wouldn't hesitate, but it'll take me at least three hours to get to Izzy. Someone else on Isaac's team might be closer.

"That's means you're fifteen hundred miles closer to Izzy than me. I've tried everyone, but being New Year's Eve, I'm running out of options. Besides, you're the only man Isaac trusts with Izzy."

Muffled voices sound down the line before Hunter says, "I got to go. Can you do this or not, Hugo?"

My eyes flick to the clock on my dashboard, displaying it is a little after nine. Even if I continue my trip, I won't reach Rochdale until three in the morning. I don't think Ava would appreciate me rocking up to her door that early, and I don't need more nails banged into my coffin by pissing her off.

"I'll do it," I say while pulling my car to the side of the road. "But you fucking owe me, Hunter."

He chuckles. "I'll add it to the long list of favors."

Not giving me a chance to reply, he disconnects the call.

By the time I turn onto the street the Dungeon nightclub is on, I'm exhausted and beyond pissed. I promised Isaac I'd always protect Izzy, and I will, but her timing couldn't be more fucked.

I pull my Chevelle to the curb at the front of the club and peel out of my car. Travis, the bouncer, greets me with a dip of his head as I storm toward him. "Cormack sent a town car to collect Cate," he advises. "That only leaves you Izzy to deal with."

I roll my eyes before entering the door he's holding open for me. The intoxicating scent of alcohol infused with sweat smacks me in the face when I enter the main section of the Dungeon. It's crammed to the rafters with patrons enjoying the end of another year.

A year that packed more punch than I was prepared for.

I extend to my full height, seeking Izzy amongst the crowd. The quicker I get her out of here, the faster I can get back onto the road.

My brows furrow when I spot Izzy dancing with a man with sandy blond hair. He either has a death wish or isn't a local because no man in this town is brave enough to talk to Izzy, let alone dance with her.

"He has a death wish," I mutter after pacing closer to Izzy.

Not only is Izzy wearing a dress that leaves *nothing* to the imagination, but he's also grinding up on her like Robin Thicke ground against Miley Cyrus at the MTV Video Music Awards.

Isaac is going to kill him.

As the final minute of the year counts down on the clock shackled to the ceiling, I barge my way through the mass of sweating bodies cavorting on the dance floor. Just as the cheer of "Forty-eight" seeps from Izzy's mouth, I seize her elbow and drag her to the edge of the dance floor.

"What the hell are you doing, Izzy?" I ask, staring into

massively dilated eyes that expose the extent of her intoxication. She's *well* past tipsy.

"What does it look like I'm doing? I'm dancing," she replies, her slur not impeding her sassy attitude.

When she attempts to stumble away, I grab her wrist. "Dancing? You're not dancing. You're provoking Isaac, trying to force his hand."

She snarls, baring teeth before she shakes her head. Beads of sweat fling off her drenched nape and land on the floor. "You don't know what you're talking about. He left, Hugo. He walked straight out of the house without a backward glance. He left me. So, I'm free to do *whatever* I please."

Whatever or whomever?

With the determination of the ninja she is, she squirms out of my grip and stumbles back to her blond dance partner. I count backward to ten, trying to keep a grip on the anger bristling my spine. Once I have a small sense of rationality, I step in front of Izzy, halting her wobbly steps.

"Bullshit, Izzy. You, yourself, had to see if the claims were true, but you don't expect Isaac to react the same? You're using that guy all because you want to antagonize Isaac. All because you want to force him to react."

Her face scrunches as she shakes her head, denying my statement.

"If it isn't that, then why are you going to all this effort? What is the purpose? A free drink? A grope on the dance floor? A stupid midnight kiss?"

"Yes!" Her loud voice projects over the music blaring out of the speakers. "Because that is probably what he's doing to her right now. He's probably kissing *her* right now!"

"That's what you want? A kiss? All this heartache for a pathetic kiss on New Year's Eve?"

Anger blackens my blood. I could lose *everything* because she wants a stupid midnight kiss. My son, the woman who owns my heart, I could lose them both because she's acting like a selfish little brat who didn't get every item on her Christmas wish list.

If she wants a stupid midnight kiss, I'll give her a fucking kiss.

I snag Izzy's wrist and pull her back to me. Her nipples pebble when her chest crashes into mine, and her gasp flutters my mouth with a fruity cocktail scent when I press my mouth against hers. I run my tongue along the seam of her lips before plunging it inside her warm and inviting mouth. After weaving my fingers through her hair, I increase the intensity of our kiss.

I kiss the living hell out of her.

I don't hold anything back.

I give it my all.

When she pulls away from my embrace, her lust-filled eyes dart between mine as she runs the back of her hand over her red, swollen lips. "Isaac will kill you," she mutters as tears well in her eyes.

I smirk and nod. "Yeah, well, at least I know what I'm getting myself into. That dumb fuck had no clue you were in the process of signing his death certificate."

I know Isaac. I know him better than he thinks I do. He won't let anyone come between him and Izzy. Just like I'm no longer willing to let anyone come between my family and me.

That's why I kissed Izzy.

She is my one-way ticket home.

EIGHTEEN
HUGO

I feel Isaac's presence before I see him. His anger is so paramount I could feel it all the way from my guest bedroom. After pulling a shirt over my head, I round the corner of the hallway and enter the main living area. I dump my duffle bag near the entryway before lifting my downcast head. Isaac is standing in the middle of the sunken living room. His back is facing me, and his fists are clenched and hanging at his sides. I don't need to see his face to know he's aware of the kiss Izzy and I shared. Not only can I feel his anger vibrating out of him, but he also knows everything, especially when it comes to Izzy.

Sensing my presence, he spins on his heels to face me. I take a step backward when I see his despondent expression. His eyes are darker than I remember and his jaw more set. The veins in his neck thrum as his thinly slit eyes roam my face. He looks like he wants to kill me. Rightfully so, he should.

After exhaling a deep breath, I enter the living room. My steps are hesitant, weighed down by the guilt my shoulders are carrying. I place the keys to my apartment and Chevelle onto the wrought iron and glass coffee table in the middle of the room. Although my *Baby* was initially Jorgie's car, it was nothing but worthless scrap metal before Isaac had it rebuilt, so it belongs to him.

I slip my hand into the back pocket of my jeans to remove my wallet. Isaac watches me like a hawk, but he doesn't speak a word. He doesn't need to. His eyes relay his disappointment and anger. *My firing.*

When I remove the first check he gave me in the limousine over five years ago, Isaac's eyes drop to my hands. After everything he did for my family and me, no matter how tempting the figure written down was, I couldn't bring myself to cash it.

After placing the check next to the keys, I dip my chin in farewell then head for the door, cowardly walking away without saying goodbye since my mouth is refusing to relinquish any words.

Isaac's hand shoots out to seize my arm. He grips my arm tight enough to display his strength but not enough to warrant me to react. I wouldn't anyway. I deserve any punishment he wants to dish.

His nostrils flare as his eyes burn into mine. They sear my soul with their furious heat. Nothing but pain reflects in his uniquely colored eyes. They issue more punishment than any fists or words ever could. My betrayal cut him deep, and his eyes are his battle wounds.

My brows furrow when he releases me from his grip and strides toward the master suite of my apartment, his steps fast and efficient. I expected a much harsher punishment.

Once he enters the main bedroom, I slip out the front door of my apartment and walk down the hallway, not once looking back on my old life.

Hugo Jones is now dead.

My brows meet my hairline when I discover Hunter's Dodge

Challenger SRT Hellcat parked at the curb of my building. The passenger window glides down before his scruff-covered face pops into the frame. "Get in," he says, his tone rough.

When I slip into the passenger seat, he flattens his foot on the accelerator, showcasing his car's 707 horsepower motor. After cracking sixty miles per hour in under three seconds, he flicks his eyes between the road and me. Even with a thick beard covering his jaw, I can't miss the twinge besetting his jawline.

When we reach the T intersection at Tivot, his eyes lock with mine. "Airport or train station?"

I smirk and shake my head. "How do you know I'm leaving?" *More like running.*

"Come on, Hugo. Don't treat me like I'm stupid." He runs his hand along his beard. "You knew he'd be watching."

He's always watching.

When Hunter takes a left without signaling, a motorist beeps and curses. "You couldn't have just quit? You had to force Isaac to fire you. It was a stupid move, Hugo. You know what he's like with Izzy. You're lucky you're still breathing."

"I have a son," I blurt out, no longer able to stand his disappointment.

Hunter may be my supervisor, but he's also my friend. That's a hard title for any man to achieve when you've spent the last five years as a ghost.

Hunter remains quiet for the next five miles. His brows are knitted tightly, and his eyelids are twitching, but his lips remain rigid.

After a beat, he says, "Why didn't you tell Isaac that?"

"You don't think he has enough on his plate? He's been dragged through the trenches this past month." My tone is rough from the guilt strangling my vocal cords.

"So you thought you'd add to it?"

My eyes rocket to Hunter's. He stares at me, exposing what I already know. I just added more drama to Isaac's already drama-filled life.

Fuck!

"I don't work well under pressure," I mumble while dragging my hand over my head. "I tend to charge first, ask questions later."

Hunter pulls his car into the curb at the front of the domestic terminal at Ravenshoe Airport before he clicks the locks into place, trapping me in the car with him. "Take a week. Sort your shit out with your family, then come back here and wade through the shit you just dumped."

I shake my head. "Can't."

"Why not?" he interrupts, his tone clipped.

"I can't do both. My family is over seven hundred miles away. I already missed four years of my son's life. I'm not willing to miss anymore."

"So you want to be a dad?"

I nod.

"A good dad?"

I nod again.

"Then lead by example, Hugo. Show your son how to do the right thing. You owe Isaac—"

"You don't think I know what I owe him?" My question booms around Hunter's car. "I know what I owe him. I owe him *everything,* but I owe my family more."

His hard-hearted eyes stare into mine. "There's no reason you can't have both. Be a man. Talk to Isaac. Don't thank him for everything he's done for you by messing around with the only good thing he has in his life."

Emotions pummel me. I owe Isaac the world. Without him, I'd be dead, but I won't have a life worth living without my family. *Without Ava.* I barely survived the past five years without her, but now, knowing what I'm missing, I can't live without her and Joel. I can't give them up.

"Besides, how are you supposed to care for your son if you don't have a job? You're a ghost. A phantom. No one will hire a dead man."

Shit! I didn't even consider that.

How can I entice Ava away from a man who has more money than sense with a dwindling bank account and no employment prospects? Ava doesn't love Marvin. She doesn't look at him the way she used to look at me, not in the slightest, but she's stuck between a rock and a hard place, struggling between putting her heart before the welfare of her son. *Our son.*

I understand her dilemma. It's why I stupidly kissed Izzy. When I first considered the insanity, it was out of anger. I was furious her childish antics were risking my chances of seeing my son, but the instant I pressed my lips against hers, it dawned on me that Isaac would be watching. *He's always watching.* So instead of manning up and talking to him, I took the coward's way out. I did what he hates. I forced his arm.

Kissing Izzy was my way out. She was my golden ticket home.

I will admit it, I was shocked as hell when she kissed me back, but after a sleepless night, I realize why. She was hurting. She believed Isaac had left her for Ophelia, and she wanted him to experience the pain she was feeling.

It worked. I've never seen Isaac look so dejected, and I never want to see that look again. Not on Isaac's face and not on Ava's.

I'll make this right for both of them.

I have to.

Noticing my defiant stance weakening, Hunter continues with his campaign, "Take a week, then come back, and we'll talk it out like real men. There's no reason you can't have both your family and your Ravenshoe family."

My lips twist. "That sounds like an ideal situation, but Isaac won't—"

"Don't worry about Isaac, I've got him covered," Hunter interrupts, his tone cocky.

I arch my brow. "Who the fuck are you, and where's the real Hunter Kane? No one has Isaac *covered.*" When I stare into Hunter's shimmering eyes, the *real* reality hits. "Who has your dick wrapped around their little finger?" I ask, my tone not matching the heaviness of our conversation.

It can't be helped. Hunter's longest relationship is the length of time it takes him to fuck her and walk her to the door. He's never had a girlfriend. Not once, but I can't misread the glimmer in his eyes. It's the same gleam my eyes get every time I see Ava.

I chuckle when Hunter leans over, unlocks the passenger door, then barges me in the shoulder, shoving me out of his car. A winded grunt escapes my lips when my backside crashes onto the sidewalk. Even with a jolt of pain rocketing through my shoulder, a broad grin still etches onto my face.

"Are you in *love?*" I draw out my last word in a long, husky drawl.

Hunter snags my duffle bag from the back seat of his car and throws it into my chest, winding me with his brutal force. "Get your ass back here in a week," he says sternly while glaring at me.

I smile, loving that I've finally discovered his weak spot. It's taken me over four years to find it.

"Is it true what they say about beards? Can you smell her hours later?"

Hunter's teeth grit before he throws open the driver's side door and peels out of his car. I scramble off the ground and hotfoot it to the airport's entrance. A leering grin is stretched across my face, and I am feeling the most carefree I've felt since tackling Ava to the floor three days ago.

Realizing he has no chance of catching my long strides, Hunter returns to his car and leans on the front quarter panel. "I'll see you in a week," he says, his tone displaying it is a *demand*, not a *request*.

I jerk up my chin. "I'll be back."

Just as I enter the airport's automatic double doors, Hunter calls my name. Tilting my torso out, I stare at his chortling face.

"You have a week, Hugo. Can you woo her in a week?"

A cocky grin pops onto my face as I reply, "I've done it in less."

NINETEEN
AVA

"The wheels on the bus go round and round, round and rou—" Joel's cheerful song stops halfway down the sidewalk, closely followed by his rushed footsteps. After adjusting the heavy bag of groceries on my hip, I lower my eyes to him. His eyes are opened wide, a broad grin is stretched across his face, and his pulse is raging through our joined hands. "Daddy!" he yells at the top of his lungs before he releases his grip on my hand and charges toward our house.

My breath snags halfway to my lungs when I follow his sprint across the snow-covered ground. Hugo is standing on the patio, grinning about Joel's boisterous welcome.

He came back.

He must be freezing in low-riding jeans and a long-sleeve shirt. We had a fresh sprinkling of snow overnight. It covered the ground with a thick layer of sleet.

When Joel is halfway down the path, Hugo pushes off the patio and strides toward him. His steps are long and urgent. Tears pool in my eyes when he scoops Joel up in his arms and spins him around and around on the concrete path. Joel has missed him so much the past three days, obviously as much as Hugo has been missing him.

Warmth blooms across my chest when Joel's beautiful giggle bellows out of him. Nothing in the world is as infectious as his giggles.

I take that back.

There's nothing more beautiful than Hugo and Joel laughing together. Their laugh is very similar, except Hugo's is deeper and rumbling. *Core-shattering.*

After setting Joel back on his feet, Hugo gathers his knocked-off beanie from the ground and pops it back onto his head. "Hey, buddy, I've missed you so much," he says while adjusting Joel's coat's collar to protect his neck from the chilly winter wind.

Hugo's eyes lift to mine when I join them on the sidewalk. "Hey," he greets me, his voice softer and somewhat reserved.

"Hey. You're back sooner than I expected."

He smiles a tight grin before nodding. "Here, let me take that." He gathers the grocery bag from my hip before spinning to face my home.

"Thanks," I say, grateful to lighten the load.

When I walk to the front door, Hugo and Joel follow behind me, hand in hand. After pushing the key into the lock, I sweep the door open then gesture for them to enter. When Joel goes to walk inside, Hugo gently pulls him back until he is once again standing beside him.

Confused, Joel's brows stitch before he cranks his neck to peer at his dad.

"Remember?" Hugo says before he nudges his head sneakily to me.

Joel's face lights up before he eagerly nods, then my heart

melts when he says, "L-Ladies first," his little voice stutters in excitement.

"Why, thank you, kind gentlemen."

When I sashay into the foyer like I'm a crowned princess, Joel laughs hysterically. "You're silly, Mommy."

His laughter switches to an excited squeal when he notices a wrapped present sitting on a duffle bag on the porch. From the shape alone, I can easily perceive it's a football.

Joel's eyes shoot to Hugo. When Hugo nods, shredded wrapping paper flies in all directions, then two seconds later, Joel holds the football close to his chest like it's the Heisman Trophy instead of a regular leather stitched football. "Can we play?"

Hugo shifts his eyes to me, wordlessly seeking permission.

I smile and nod. "Go get changed into some yard clothes first."

"Okay," Joel replies before running into his room.

When he disappears down the corridor, Hugo chuckles. "Does he ever walk?"

I laugh. "No, he doesn't."

Hugo shadows me into the kitchen. After he sets down the bag of groceries on the counter, I pack away the perishable items into the refrigerator. When he props his hip on the counter and silently watches me, I eye him curiously, surprised by his quietness. Although his happiness at seeing Joel again is beaming out of him, there's something clouding his eyes, dulling their usual spark.

"Are you okay?" I query, no longer able to harbor my curiosity.

Hugo has always been a communicator. He's never had trouble expressing himself, but something is bothering him, and his reserved composure is setting my nerves on edge.

Hugo tilts his torso out of the kitchen, twists his neck, then peers down the hall. Once he's confident the coast is clear, he returns his anxious eyes to me. My heart wildly beats when I see the unease in his usually mischievous eyes.

I place the carton of eggs on the table in the middle of the kitchen then pad closer to him. I want to comfort him, but I'm a little lost as to how I can when he whispers, "I've already missed so much time with him, Ava. Please don't make me miss anymore."

My brows furrow as quickly as my heart slithers into my gut. I am utterly confused by his statement.

"I'll do anything you want to prove I won't break his heart. That I won't break it... *again*. I just need you to give me a chance," he vows as his begging eyes add strength to his request.

Although appreciative of the utmost certainty in his eyes, I am still lost. "I don't understand what you're saying."

Hugo rubs a kink in the back of his neck before attempting to settle my confusion. "The paperwork you sent me."

My brows shoot into my hair. "I didn't send you any paperwork." I shake my head before eyeing him dubiously. "I don't even know your address."

As his Adam's apple bobs up and down, his eyes bounce between mine. After a couple of seconds of quiet deliberations, he walks to his duffle bag dumped in the entryway. He yanks down the zipper before pulling out a white envelope, then he heads back my way. He grips the envelope so tightly it gets a crinkle down the middle. I can't miss the shake of his hand when he passes it to me.

My heart whacks my ribs as I lift the flap and pull out a four-page document. The more my eyes scan the official-looking letter, the larger my pupils dilate. I'd never send him such a document. I could never be so cruel.

With my blood boiling, I snatch the envelope off the counter and roam my eyes over the sender's address. Steam billows from my ears when the address registers as familiar.

That son of a bitch!

While rushing into the hallway to gather my purse and keys, I ask Hugo, "Can you watch Joel?"

My eyes shift to my cell phone on the entryway table. Normally, I'd take it with me everywhere I go, but ever since the "ghost" dropped it into the toilet bowl, it hasn't been working. It fritzed at the exact same moment my answering machine went missing.

Hugo shadows me as I race from the hallway to the garage. I'm so angry, my thighs shake with every step I take.

When I reach the side of my car, Hugo halts my frantic pace by grabbing the tops of my arms. His confused eyes dance between mine, his concern growing by the minute.

"I didn't send you those forms," I vow while returning his docile stare. "I'd *never* take your son away from you." He intakes a quick breath, seemingly astonished by my admission. "But I can't fix this unless you let me go, so can you please watch Joel?"

His eyes bounce between mine for several long seconds before he eventually nods. Happy he trusts me, I press a kiss to the edge of his mouth then dive into the driver's seat of my car. Hugo's eyes bulge when my heavy compression on the accelerator causes my tires to skid out of control on the ice-covered driveway. Hating that I've scared him, I remove my foot from the accelerator, inhale a deep, nerve-clearing breath, then try again with more patience this time around.

The panic marring Hugo's handsome face eases when I reverse out of the driveway without incident.

When I enter the bustling main street of Rochdale, my eyes dart in all directions, seeking the first parking spot. I pull into an empty space across from my office building, not caring it's marked as handicapped.

After tossing off my seat belt, I make a beeline to the dental practice I've worked at for the past five years. The freezing air blowing in from the west does nothing to dampen the fiery rage burning me alive. When I throw open the glass door and rush into the building, Belinda's head lifts from her computer monitor. I smile a tight grin before darting down the hall. Not bothering to knock, I storm into Marvin's office.

My breathing shallows, shell-shocked about the scene I've stumbled into. Oddly, my first response is relief. You'd think walking in on my fiancé during a sexual act would have my claws hackled and ready to pounce, but all I feel is pure relief.

Sweet, heavenly relief.

When Marvin's head lifts to the door, he balks, then takes a step backward. The half-dressed blonde sprawled on his desk whimpers from his loss of contact.

I roll my eyes. *Nothing on Marvin's body deserves that type of response.*

"Where are you going, sweetie?" Her sickly-sweet voice makes her sound like a porn star in the middle of a film production.

Marvin's eyes dart between the blonde and me, his panic growing with every second that ticks by. "This isn't what it looks like," he stammers out once he fixates his eyes with mine.

I raise my hand into the air, cutting off his pathetic excuse. Following Marvin's fretful gaze, the blonde shifts her head to the side. Her eyes widen, and her throat works hard to swallow when she notices me standing in the doorway. Her response exposes that she's aware of who I am and what my significance in Marvin's life is. In my book, that makes her as guilty as Marvin.

With a bitchy smirk, she scampers off the desk, then yanks her skin-tight pencil skirt down her rake-thin thighs. Her stilettos shuffle on the tiled floor when she darts to the door. She stutters an apology to me on the way by, but I don't pay her any attention. My focus is solely on Marvin.

Once the unnamed blonde exits Marvin's office, I join him by his desk. I only came here for one reason, and the shock of discovering him cavorting with an unnamed blonde isn't enough to dampen the anger scorching my veins. "You had no right to intervene in my son's life. No right *at all*. Joel is *not* your son!" I yell before slamming the paternal forms he sent Hugo onto his cherry oak desk.

Marvin paces around his desk, tucking his disheveled shirt into his undone trousers on the way. "But I want him to be my son, Ava. I want to legally adopt him. For him to have my last name."

"Why?" I fire back, skepticism rife my voice. "Why would you want that? Joel knows the local dog walker better than you, and we don't even own a dog!"

When he attempts to clutch my hand, I violently yank away from him. "Don't touch me," I sneer. "I have no clue where your filthy hands have been." I take a step backward, widening the distance between us. "Why did you do it, Marvin? Why are you trying to create a rift between them? Joel wants Hugo in his life. He needs him in his life. He *loves* his father."

"I can give him way more than Hugo ever could," he argues, his jaw quivering as his anger is unleashed.

"It isn't about money or possessions. It is about love and understanding. Taking the time to give Joel the attention he needs... that he deserves."

"I give him time and attention. You're acting like I don't give him anything. Everything he has is because of me!" Marvin's angry roars bounces around his office.

I laugh a witch-like cackle, amused by his ill conceptions. "Everything *my* son has is because of *me*, not *you*. He doesn't even know you."

"Your reaction has nothing to do with me filing adoption papers and everything to do with Hugo being back in town."

I grit my teeth and shake my head. "This has nothing to do with Hugo. I might have gone along with your little game to keep you in your daddy's good graces and myself employed, but Joel was *never* part of our agreement."

"The instant you slipped that ring on your finger..." Marvin nudges his head to my engagement ring sparkling in the office lighting. "You not only became *my* property, so did Joel."

Fury unlike anything I have ever felt before scorches my veins. I step closer to Marvin, so close my heaving chest smacks into his with every breath I take. I stare him straight in the eyes, internally cursing the day I agreed to his stupid ploy. "Joel was *never* up for negotiation. He will *never* be your son. He has a dad. He doesn't need another." I rip the diamond ring off my finger and dump it on top of the paperwork. "Our agreement is over."

I dash out of his office and race down the hall. My steps are urgent because I don't want to give Marvin the satisfaction of seeing my tears. Today will be the last time he will be the cause of my tears.

Belinda's eyes dart between Marvin's lipstick-smeared face and my quickly retreating frame. Her eyes bulge when she notices my finger is void of the engagement ring I was wearing when I entered, then they silently interrogate me.

Did you really do it? Did you leave him?

When I nod, she jumps from her desk, snags her coat off the coat rack, then marches out of the office behind me.

When we reach the sidewalk outside, and I've sucked in enough air for my brain to switch back on, I glide my eyes to her. "What are you doing? I thought you said you couldn't come with me?"

I begged her for months to leave Gardner and Sons and be my receptionist at the practice I'm endeavoring to get off the ground. She said she would if she could, but she never agreed. I understood her hesitation. Who in their right mind would leave an established company for one that has more chance of collapsing than getting off the ground?

Belinda slings her arms around my shoulders. "Who needs a dental plan when you'll be working for the best dentist in the country?"

My panicked breaths are visible in the frigid air when I laugh out a shocked chuckle. "Are you sure this is what you want? You've worked at Gardner and Sons for years. There's no guarantee my practice will get off the ground, let alone be viable."

She rolls her eyes as a lewd smirk curls on her lips. "Please, Ava. Anything you set your mind to is viable."

My chest swells when nothing but admiration reflects in her glistening green eyes.

"Can you start Monday at nine?"

A squeal ripples from my lips when someone taps on my car's window, startling me half to death. Clutching my chest, I peer outside. My brows stitch together when I spot Mrs. Marshall standing next to the passenger side door, rattling the door latch. Her hair is covered with silver foils, and a hairdressing towel is wrapped around her shoulders.

Grimacing, I lean over and unlock the door. A freezing breeze blasts into the car when she opens the door and slips inside. She doesn't say anything, she just sits quietly next to me, staring straight ahead. It is only when I see the shadow of Mrs. Mable moving away from her front window does it dawn on me what has caused Mrs. Marshall's sudden arrival.

I've been sitting in my car in my driveway for the past twenty minutes, futilely trying to unjumble my confusion. I can't comprehend what's happening to me. When I stumbled into Marvin's office, all I felt was relief. I should be angry that my fiancé was having an affair. I should have stormed into the room and gouged the blonde's eyes out before running my nails down her abhorrent face.

I should have felt something, but I felt nothing.

Not anger.

Not jealousy.

Nothing.

"I'm a terrible person," I mutter to myself. "I broke off my engagement, and I don't even care."

Mrs. Marshall adjusts her position to face me. She clutches my hand in hers, then wordlessly secures my attention with her dazzling green eyes. When she gets it, she says, "Don't feel guilty for what happened, Ava. Your heart has only ever belonged to one man. Marvin knew it wasn't him, and he used that knowledge to his advantage."

"I can't just blame Marvin for our pathetic attempt at a relationship. I'm just as bad as him. I knew I'd never love him the way I loved Hugo, but instead of telling him that, I continued to lie. I dragged him down as much as he did me."

I've wanted to leave Marvin for months, but I never did. I was too scared about losing my security blanket. Although I've never allowed Marvin to financially support me, I liked the security that came with having a partner. As callous as this makes me sound, I wanted an emergency backup. For years, Marvin has been that safety net.

Mrs. Marshall screws up her nose and waves her hand in front of her face. "Please. You supported him for years, not the other way around. You stroked his gigantic ego and stood by his side while he accepted all the praise from the wonderful things you *both* achieved."

When I shake my head, she squeezes my hand tighter. "Tell me one thing that man did *solely* for you, Ava, without expecting some type of reward for it?"

I peer into her empathy-filled eyes while racking my brain, trying to think of something. I'm truly stumped. The only time Marvin and I were ever seen together as a couple was at fundraising events or work functions. We never went on dinner dates alone. He never attended a Marshall family brunch until Hugo arrived back in the picture, and I had to beg him to accompany me to the Christmas Day celebration at the Marshalls' residence this year. The only reason he agreed to go is because I agreed to continue with the ploy of us being engaged.

Upon noticing I am unable to answer her question, Mrs. Marshall cocks her brow. "Exactly. Now what has he given you?" She waves her head to Hugo zooming past the front window of my house with Joel in his arms.

Joel has his arms outstretched like he's soaring through the air. I never thought I would have the opportunity to witness this, father and son standing side by side, playing airplanes. I dreamed it would happen, but I never thought my dreams would turn into reality.

"Joel," I answer without a hesitation. "Hugo gave me Joel. The best thing that's ever happened to me."

Mrs. Marshall smiles as she squeezes my hand.

"And this." I press my palm against my madly beating heart. "He gave me his heart. It's the reason Marvin's betrayal didn't hurt because it wasn't my heart Marvin was deceiving, it was Hugo's. But even being Hugo's heart, Hugo's betrayal still *hurts*. It hurts so much. I don't know if I can get past this."

Mrs. Marshall's tear-glistening eyes lock with mine. "I'm not saying this because Hugo is my son. I'm saying this because you're my daughter, Ava, and I know you. I've watched you grow from a girl into the beautiful woman you are today." Overwhelmed by the pride radiating in her words, a tear escapes my right eye and rolls down my cheek. "If you don't give Hugo the chance to fix the mistakes he made, you'll never forgive yourself. You've wanted this for years. Every wish you've ever made the past five years was for Hugo to come home. Your wish came true. Cherish it, Ava. We learned from Jorgie's passing that we must make the most of every day we have. No one is saying you have to forgive and forget, not at all, but harboring anger will only diminish your quality of life, not improve it. Live the best life you can, as you only get one."

My face scrunches as I battle to keep my tears at bay. Everything Mrs. Marshall said is true. Every time I blew out the candles on my birthday cake or saw a shooting star, I wished for Hugo to come home. I swore I wouldn't care where he'd been or why he left, all I wanted was for him to come home and meet his son. *To come back to me.*

My wish came true, but instead of relishing having my greatest wish granted, I'm letting anger ruin a true miracle.

"Do you remember the promise you made to Joel the day you walked through those doors with him cradled in your arms for the first time?" I wipe my hand under my nose before nodding. "You kept your promise to Joel. Now it's time to keep the promise you made to yourself."

TWENTY
HUGO

"Mayday, mayday. We're experiencing catastrophic engine failure." A big boom sounds from my mouth, startling Joel flying in my arms. "Mayday, mayday, our engines are on fire. We're going down."

I jolt Joel in my arms, replicating the shuddering of an engine. A grin carves on my mouth from the hearty chuckle bellowing from his lips. "Prepare for a crash landing, select emergency fuel." My voice mimics the helicopter pilot in the movie *The Day After Tomorrow*.

Joel squeals in excitement as we race through the living room, zooming around the couches and past the antique clock. He holds his arms out like a plane and makes engine noises with his lips. When I round the rock-hard couch I slept on a week ago, our makeshift plane crashes to the floor. I roll and land on my back, ensuring Joel lands safely on my chest. Blood surges to my heart when he giggles into my chest before he wraps his arms around my torso to snuggle in close.

"That was the best game ever!" he screams at the top of his

lungs, his voice coming out in a flurry, overcome with excitement. "Can we do it again?"

I chuckle. "Yep, just give Dad a minute to recover, and we'll get this bad boy back into the air."

Joel nods against my chest before cuddling in deeper. He is as light as a feather, but my shoulder has been giving me grief the past week. I could ease the stabbing pain rocketing through my body by taking the pain relief tablets Dr. Jae prescribed, but with the box clearly warning that side effects may include dizziness, tiredness, and delayed response time, I refuse to take them. I don't want to impede my response time, especially because Ava has entrusted me to take care of Joel alone.

As we catch our breath in preparation for round two in our game of airplanes, I run my fingers through Joel's hair. The tips of his curls are damp from our exhaustive playdate. We haven't stopped mucking around since Ava left nearly an hour ago. I want to squeeze in every moment I can get. I can't make up for the time I missed, but I can make the most of the time I have left.

Joel's head pops off my chest when the front door cracks open. He inhales a quick breath before he pushes off my chest and dashes to the foyer. Ava's beautiful laugh sounds through my ears when Joel bands his arms around her thighs and squeezes her so tightly he almost knocks her over. Anyone would swear she has been gone for days, not an hour.

After scrambling off the floor, I move toward them. My long strides shorten when I notice a shimmering of wetness on Ava's cheeks. My eyes dart up to her face so I can assess her in careful detail. Red rims are circling her eyes, and her lips are cracked. Those are clear signs she's been crying. After running her fingers through Joel's hair, fixing his messy curls, she lifts her glimmering eyes to mine.

"*Are you okay?*" I mouth, not wanting to alert Joel to her distress.

She smiles and nods. "I'm good."

The crippling pain in my chest dampens when she playfully winks before crouching down to Joel's level. After adjusting the collar on his shirt, she asks, "What do you think we should have for dinner?"

Joel puckers his lips, and a serious mask slips over his face. He takes his food selections very seriously. Just like his father.

"Because I was thinking we could have... *pancakes.*" Ava's tone falsely portrays apprehension, like she's concerned Joel may not like her suggestion.

Joel's eyes bug out of his head before he jumps in the air. My insides are also bouncing around like a ho on crack, but thankfully, my outward appearance gives no indication of my excitement. I recall the last time Ava made pancakes in this house, so I can't let my excitement get away from me.

"Pancakes! Yay!" Joel squeals in an ear-piercing scream.

Ava laughs. "Do you want to help me make them?"

Joel eagerly nods.

"Alright, go wash your hands then."

I laugh when Joel pivots on his heels and charges down the hall. I swear I've never seen the kid walk.

When Ava stands from her crouched position, my eyes shift from a disappearing Joel to her. "Do you have any plans tonight?" Ignoring the mad beat of my heart, I smile and shake my head. "Did you want to stay and have some pancakes with us?"

My brow arches. Even if I missed the hidden innuendo laced in her simple question, I can't overlook the glimmer in her eyes. Ava has never been good at hiding her true intentions. She wears her heart on her sleeve, clear as day for all to see. I can also read her like an open book. To strangers it may seem as if she's asking me to stay for dinner, but her eyes are relaying much more than that.

She inhales a quick breath when I take a step closer to her, bridging the gap between us. Her eyes linger on my thrusting chest for several heart-clenching seconds before she tilts her head back. When her eyes lock with mine, the shift of air between us is so great, electricity surges through my body, sparking my heart with renewed hope. Her eyes expose that I haven't lost them yet. That I still have a chance. Not just with Joel, but her as well.

"I'd love to stay." My voice is strangled by the flood of emotions hammering me. "But I should warn you I have a slight obsession with *sweet* things. Once I taste them, I can't stop."

Her breath fans my lips when she expels a large gasp, proving she didn't miss the innuendo in my reply. I stare into her eyes, wanting to ensure she understands I'm not just here for Joel. I want her too.

We stand across from each other for several long seconds, staring but not speaking. The connection between us is as strong as it's ever been, if not stronger. *Joel makes us stronger.* I peer at the woman I've loved before she even became a woman, hopeful my eyes will express the words my mouth is refusing to relinquish.

I'm sorry. Please forgive me. I love you.

When I run the back of my fingers down her feverish cheek, removing a tear tracking down it, Ava nuzzles into my hand. I want to kiss away every tear trekking down her beautiful face. I want to fall to my knees and promise I'll never be the cause of her tears again, but before I get the chance, Joel tugs on the hem of my shirt.

I was so mesmerized by his mother's beautiful face I didn't hear him approaching. He stands between Ava and me with his head rocketing side to side. A smile curves on my mouth when he screws up his nose and gags. "Girls are gross," he mumbles while glaring at me with reprimanding eyes.

Who is this kid? I had no clue about girls until I was well into middle school. He's only four and can already read the undeniable connection between Ava and me.

"I'll show you gross," Ava threatens while shifting her squinted eyes to Joel.

When she puckers her lips and makes gaga kissy faces, Joel screams a window-shattering squeal before racing to the other side of the room. Ava is on his tail before he even makes it halfway across the living room. She tackles him to the floor, then holds him down how I normally pin her down. She smoothers his face in kisses, smooching noises and all.

Joel screams in protest, but the smile etched on his adorable face gives away his deceit. He's loving every single moment of his mom's attention. And rightfully so, he should.

"Daddy, help me," he squeals between giggles. "Save me from the girl germs!"

I throw back my head and laugh.

I don't want to be saved from Ava's girl germs.

I want to be smothered in them.

"Is he asleep?"

I nod. "Yeah, he was asleep before his head hit the pillow."

Ava laughs like I'm joking. I wasn't. The poor little guy was exhausted. After Joel and I ganged up on Ava to tickle her into submission, we went into the kitchen to prepare pancakes for dinner. Joel's excitement was beaming out of him the entire time. As was mine.

After a good dose of sugar, Joel was literally bouncing off the walls. We played a few more rounds of the airplane, then Ava gave him a bath. He didn't stop yawning the entire time I dressed him in his air fighter pajamas. Only after I promised to take him to the park tomorrow did he agree to go to bed.

I'm not going to lie, I was as smitten as the President on Inauguration Day when Joel asked me to read him a bedtime story and tuck him into bed.

We never got to read a story... *maybe next time?*

"Did you want some wine?" Ava offers while walking toward the kitchen. When my nose screws up, Ava chuckles. "Beer?"

I nod before plopping onto the rock-hard couch. My shoulder is screaming in pain. Not a faint scream, an Alex Koehler from Chelsea Grin's scream at the start of the song "Sonnet of the Wretched."

I'm still rubbing the knot in my shoulder when Ava re-enters the living room with a refilled wine glass and a bottle of beer. I drop my hand when I notice the direction of her gaze, but she's far too receptive. "What's the deal with your shoulder?" She hands me the beer before filling the spare seat next to me with her scrumptious backside. "I've noticed you rubbing it a few times tonight."

I take a swig of my beer before angling my torso to face her. If I want any chance of regaining the trust I lost when I vanished, I need to be honest with her.

About everything.

"I got shot."

When her wine traps in her throat, she wheezes and coughs before she sprays the coffee table and my shirt with red wine splatters.

"Are you alright?"

I set my beer on the coffee table so I can pat her back. She takes a few moments to recover from her coughing fit before she lifts her tear-glistening eyes to mine. I can't tell if they're welled with tears from her almost choke or because I was shot.

I soon learn it was the latter. "Shot? Like shot-with-a-gun shot?"

I nod.

"By whom? Why?" Her words come out in a hurry as a panicked mask slips over her face.

"The girl I was protecting was kidnapped. Her kidnapper didn't appreciate my presence." I shrug like it's no big deal I could have died. I'll do or say anything to remove the cloud of concern plaguing her beautiful eyes.

Ava stares at me, her eyes widening more with every second that goes by. After a beat, she mumbles, "And here I was thinking root canals and extractions were exciting."

I laugh. Only Ava would find the lightheartedness in a somber conversation. I shouldn't be surprised. She doesn't have a judgmental bone in her body. She's never judged me. Not once. Not even when she was bursting at the seams to know something would she ask. She preferred being divulged information when the informant felt comfortable sharing it. She doesn't understand the meaning of the word 'strong-armed.'

After setting her wine glass on the coffee table, Ava props her legs under her bottom and swivels to face me. "Can I see where you were shot?"

When I nod, she licks her lips, leans forward, then gently pulls down the neckline of my shirt. I grab the back of my shirt and yank it over my head. Her eyes enlarge as her throat works hard to swallow, somewhat surprised by my impromptu strip.

"I was shot in the chest, but the bullet exited my shoulder," I explain while trying my hardest not to smile like a smug prick about the lust burning in her eyes. "You won't see the wound properly with my shirt on."

I catch my eye roll halfway. I sound like a slack-jawed idiot. It's nearly as good as the fake yawn maneuver I regularly used on her when we were watching reruns of *Friends*.

Ava gasps when her eyes drift over my chest. She assesses my wound from a safe distance like she might possibly hurt me if she were to touch me. Her pulse thuds through my hand when I curl it over her hand so I can run two fingers over the wound site. When her fingertips glide over the sharpness of the stitches that still haven't dissolved, she inhales a sharp breath. Although it's healed well the past two weeks, the grittiness of the wound will never fully diminish.

"Did it hurt?"

I bite back a smirk. "Like a bitch."

Only one knock has hit me harder. Leaving her.

When Ava presses her lips on the border of the scar tissue, my stomach muscles bunch. My dick turns to stone when she mutters against the angrily stretched skin, "I should kiss it better then," before she places a second kiss on the other side of the wound.

My heart thrashes against my ribs when she lifts and locks her eyes with mine. Ava's eyes have always been expressive, and today is no exception. They're crammed to the brim with desire, and it isn't a hunger for food.

Although I want nothing more than the answer the hankering in her eyes, I can't. Not yet. So instead, I scoop up her hand, kiss her fingertips, then toss my shirt back over my head.

Feeling rejected, Ava sinks deeper into the chair as she nervously shifts her eyes around the room. I scoot across the loveseat until not an ounce of air is between us. Gripping her chin, I tilt her back until our eyes lock. "I want you. I want you more than anything. More than my next breath, but I can't have you yet."

"Why?" she whispers, her short reply incapable of hiding her rejection.

"Because I need you to know the truth, to ensure you aren't walking into this relationship blind."

She shakes her head, sending tears flinging through the air. "I'm not. My eyes are open. I know you, Hugo." When she fists my shirt, I notice her ring finger is void of the large diamond engagement ring she was wearing earlier. Upon spotting the direction of my gaze, she mutters, "It was a lapse in judgment. A mistake."

Any further words about to spill from her mouth stop when I squash my index finger to her lips. "We all make mistakes. We can't change them. We can only learn from them."

She drags her bottom lip through her teeth before nodding. Her eased response proves she does know me. She knows me better than anyone, so I can be assured she will never judge me.

She never has.

After capturing both her hands in mine, I peer into her shimmering eyes while confessing, "I've made plenty of mistakes I'm not proud of, and my very first one was in Afghanistan."

TWENTY-ONE
HUGO

Ava tries to put on a brave front, but her remorse for Gemma dims the spark in her eyes the longer my story goes, let alone the way her hand shakes when she runs it under her eyes. She wants to catch her tears before they roll down her face, but there are too many for her hands to keep up with.

"She endured so much, and it still wasn't enough. It took months for Gemma's case to make it to court, but we thought the main fight was over. Little did we know, the battle had only just begun..."

My knee bounces up and down, exposing my agitation. Leticia, the assigned DA, places her hand on top of my knee, moving the twitch from the lower half of my body to my jaw.

"There has to be something you can do?" I whisper after tilting into her side. "Interject, argue bias, something?"

Leticia shakes her head. "The accused has the right to be represented by a lawyer of his choice."

"Even when it's his father?" I interrupt, disbelief heard in my voice.

Leticia's green eyes float from a terrified Gemma getting slammed by the defense attorney in the witness stand to me. "Yes." Her answer is swift and precise, but it does little to rein in my anger.

"That's fucking bullshit. He's treating her as if she's a criminal." My angry sneer reverberates off the whitewashed walls of the courtroom.

Leticia doesn't respond to my outburst. She can't. Everything I said was true. Gemma is getting grilled by the defense attorney. The same defense attorney who is the father of her accused. He's making out that Gemma is using the courts as a way to clear her guilty conscience. He's proclaiming that she initially agreed to the 'liaison' with his client and only sought medical treatment after her 'boyfriend' caught wind of her indiscretion.

He's pretty much implying if I had failed to aid Gemma that night, no charges would have been filed against his clients because I would have been none the wiser about her 'adulterous activities.'

My eyes drift from Gemma's tear-stained face to Madden McGee and three of his fellow-accused. Madden's fingers are laced together, and a callous smirk is etched on his face. When a painful sob rumbles from Gemma's quivering lips as she denies the defense attorney's blatant lies, Madden sinks deeper into his chair. He seems pleased Gemma is so rattled.

I fist my hands into tight balls, battling the urge to wipe the smug smirk off his face with my fists. The desire turns potent when Madden's older brother leans over the wooden barrier separating them to pat him on the shoulder. It's like he's commending him on a job well done, oblivious to the fact that his brother is facing charges of aggravated battery and sexual assault.

By the time Gemma finishes giving her testimony, she's as rattled as she was the night in the alley. When she rushes out the swinging doors that separate the well of the courtroom from the *seating area, I attempt to follow her. My fast steps stop when she briskly shakes her head, wordlessly requesting solitude.*

"Give her a few minutes to calm down, Hugo," Leticia suggests after enclosing her hand over my shaking one.

I slump onto the hard wooden bench, feeling the most helpless I've ever been. I run my trembling hand through my shaggy mane while struggling to maintain enough strength for both Gemma and me. The past few months have been the most draining weeks of my life. Just getting Gemma to press charges was a hard-fought battle. She wanted to pretend it never happened. To sweep it under the rug. It was only when I asked her how she'd feel if another woman had to endure what she went through did she agree to meet with Leticia. She still had conditions, though. The main one was that no one in our squadron was to be aware of what was happening. I instantly agreed. It wasn't my news to share anyway.

"Have you had any luck finding the witness from the alley?" I ask Leticia.

She shakes her head. "No, but the Air Force isn't exactly forthcoming when I request personnel records for every enlistee called Brody. Are you sure he was in the Air Force?"

I nod. "I'm certain he's in the Air Force. I have a knack for remembering faces. He isn't in my section, but I've seen him around the base."

Leticia smiles a tight smirk. "Hopefully, he will grow a conscience and come forward."

He never did...

"The defense attorney was a real snake. He was conniving and low-handed. The moment I met him, I was on guard." I peer at Ava, who's watching me with compassion in her eyes. "I had a reason to be wary. He was a deadly snake hidden in the long grass. Not only did the jury believe him and his clients' side of the story, but he also twisted everything Gemma said on the stand." I swallow a brick in my throat before confessing something I've never told anyone, "Eight weeks after Madden McGee was cleared of all charges, I was arrested..." Ava's wet eyes dart between mine as I mutter, "... for the sexual assault of Gemma."

She sucks in a sharp breath before breathing it out with a heap of questions. "What? How? You saved her. You *protected* her, so that doesn't make any sense." She curls her hand over my shaking one like Leticia did in my story. "What happened?"

Her eyes are void of the judgment I expected to see when I shared my story, freeing me to say, "I was on my way to..."

"Keep walking, Hugo. He isn't worth the effort."

Tyrell wraps his arm around my shoulders and guides me down the hallway, straight past the snickering face of Madden McGee. We only arrived back on base earlier this week, preparing to re-deploy to Afghanistan. I had just finished a grueling workout in the gym and could hear the showers beckoning me all the way from the fitness center. The instant I spotted Madden, any thoughts on enjoying the rest of my rec time disappeared.

This is the first time I've seen him in person since a jury of our peers found him and his three co-accused not guilty of sexually assaulting Gemma. I assumed even with the jury handing over the verdict of not guilty that some type of reprimand would still be given to Madden by our superiors in the Air Force.

I was dead wrong.

Nothing happened.

Gemma's entire life was upended in an instant. She was left unemployed and on the verge of a nervous breakdown. Madden didn't suffer the slightest. He took an extended period of absence for 'personal' reasons before returning to his original rank of captain. Pictures of him riding a jet ski in the Caribbean have been circulating the dining facility most of the day, spurring on my agitation. He was vacationing in paradise while Gemma was living in hell.

My long strides down the corridor falter when Madden snickers, "If he'd been giving it to her right, she wouldn't have been looking elsewhere."

I hardly hear the laughter of the group surrounding Madden over my pulse shrilling in my ears when I pivot on my heels and charge for him. When he notices me approaching, the veins in his neck thrum, and his eyes widen. My fist cracks against his right cheek before lowering to his stomach.

I don't know how many punches I inflict before Tyrell pulls me away, but my punishment is severe enough for Madden to sport a black eye and split lip while giving his statement to the Air Force Police during his request to press charges against me.

I sit in a holding cell at Security Forces compound of our base for nearly sixteen hours before being ushered into a cold, sterile interrogation room. I'm surprised when I shuffle into the room, dragging a pair of metal shackles behind me, and discover Madden's father in the corner of the room, talking to a JAG officer.

Since when did a civilian have any input in a case involving an airman?

After removing the shackles from my hands and ankles, the JAG officer, whose name badge states "Christopher," gestures for me to sit in a wooden chair pulled up close to a steel table. He then pulls out the chair across from me and takes a seat, his eyes arrested on a document in his hand. "These types of cases are generally hard to prove. With the whole she-said-he-said notion coming into play, it falls to the jury's mood for how the verdict will swing."

My heart rate kicks up, but I continue with my fifth amendment right to remain quiet. I've already decided to plead guilty to the charges of battery against Madden, but I won't disclose that to the DA. It is in my best interests to wait it out for a plea.

When I take a seat, Christopher's eyes lift from a manila folder to me. "But in your case, it's a slam dunk. I can't lose," he states, his voice smeared with cockiness.

I give him an arrogant wink. Madden's blood on my knuckles is pretty incriminatory.

"So, instead of wasting our time dragging this through court, we're going to be kind and offer you a plea deal."

My lips twitch, fighting to suppress the smile trying to cross my face. I knew they wouldn't have brought me in here without having a pre-drawn plea agreement.

"If you sign this statement, admitting to all charges, you'll avoid doing jail time and tainting your honorable family name with mud."

My brows furrow. My mother would be proud I defended Gemma, not dishonored. The confusion on my face amplifies when Christopher slides a pre-typed statement across the table for me to sign. His abrupt movement causes the ballpoint pen to roll off the name on top of the Alford doctrine.

"Why do you have Gemma's name written in the victim field?" I query, my words as uneasy as my swirling stomach.

Christopher smirks. "The victim's name is generally placed in the victim section."

The pompousness in his tone fuels my annoyance. "Gemma is not my victim. I didn't hurt her, I protected her."

Christopher's eyes turn to Madden's father in the corner of the room. The shrewd look that crosses Mr. McGee's face is only there for the tiniest second, but I don't miss it. It's cunning and judicious.

The churning of my stomach ramps up when my eyes return to the document, and I speed-read the charges against me.

"I want a lawyer," I request as my eyes snap up from the document accusing me of the sexual assault and battery of Gemma. "I'm not speaking another word until I have a lawyer present."

Madden's father pushes off the wall. He reaches the table in *three long strides. "Even the best lawyer in the state won't be able to help you." His tone is a deep rumble that bounces off the stark white walls and bellows into my ears. "They have your DNA and skin fibers in Gemma's rape kit. Your blood was even discovered under her fingernails."*

"Because I protected her!" I stand from my chair, toppling it over. "You're not pinning your son's crime on me because I taught him a lesson. Maybe if you'd spent more time with him as a child instead of hobnobbing with golf buddies, he would have learned the difference between right and wrong, but I guess lining your expensive threads with money was more important than raising your son with morals."

Before I have the chance to react, Mr. McGee grabs my shirt and pulls me to within an inch of his face. I stare into the eyes of a snake with flaring nostrils. My body shudders with fury, but I don't back down. He raised a monster, and I'm not scared to tell him of that.

"Your son is a rapist," *I sneer, staring into his bleak, desolate eyes. "And a fucking coward..."*

I turn my eyes to Ava, who is watching me sympathetically. "I plead guilty to the sexual assault of Gemma three weeks later."

Her eyes widen before darting between mine. "What! Why, Hugo? Gemma would have never testified against you. You saved her, so she would have done the same for you."

"She tried, but Madden's father offered to chair with the DA. He twisted everything Gemma said during her testimony. He even made out to the jury that the time I walked in on Gemma showering in the male latrine was what started my 'obsession' with her."

I run my hand down my tired face, scrubbing away my tiredness while also wishing I could erase the memories that haunt my dreams just as easily. Once I exhaled a deep breath, I continue my confession. "I've always had a knack for reading people, so I could tell the jury was believing the lies the DA was spilling. Even with Gemma testifying on my behalf, they were going to find me guilty. So, to save my family name being tarnished, I requested a plea."

Ava smiles a tight grin as she curls her hand over mine. She doesn't speak. She doesn't need to. The compassion in her eyes is all the comfort I need.

"On the agreement that the nature of my charges remained undisclosed, I plead guilty to the sexual assault on Gemma and for battery in the second degree on Madden. I was issued a criminal record, stripped of my ranking, and dishonorably discharged from my position within twenty-four hours of signing the plea bargain."

After brushing away a tear on her cheek, Ava crawls across the minimal space left between us. Air whizzes out of my lips when she straddles my hips, wraps her arms around my torso, then squashes her ear over my heart. I won't lie. Even with a morose mood suffocating my usual persona, I smile. I love having her in my arms again.

A length of silence crosses between us. It isn't awkward. It's more comforting than anything.

"What happened to Gemma?" Ava queries a short time later, her voice low and filled with concern.

I run my hand down the ringlets hanging halfway down her back while answering, "She never returned to her position after the incident in the alleyway. We stayed in contact sporadically six months after I was discharged, then I reunited with you, and everything went a little crazy."

Her head pops off my chest so her eyes can bounce between mine. A grin tugs on my lips when I notice the corners of her mouth are drooped downward.

"A good type of crazy." I pinch her chin, then angle her head up. "Those weeks we had together were the only thing keeping me going the past five years. Without them, I don't know how I would have survived." I pause before correcting, *"If* I would have survived."

She chews on her bottom lip as she struggles to keep her tears at bay before confessing, "Me too. Our memories, then finding out I was expecting Joel were the only things forcing me to get out of bed each morning."

I drag my index finger across her cheek, capturing a tear rolling down her pale face while saying, "Please don't cry." I've seen enough tears seep from her eyes to last me a lifetime. "I'm so sorry, Ava. For everything I did, for everything I put you—"

My words stop when a delicious pair of lips press against mine. Ava's mouth steals both my words and my ability to think. When she drags her tongue along the crest of my lips, soundlessly requesting for my mouth to open, it immediately obeys. When she slips her tongue inside my mouth then entangles it with mine, a rough groan tears from my throat.

She tastes even better than I remember.

After wrapping my arms around her waist, I draw her in close. I don't want even an ounce of air between us. The husky moan that spills from her lips hardens my cock even more. It makes me desperate. After weaving my fingers through her crazy curls, I swivel my tongue around her mouth, tasting and savoring every inch.

I kiss her like a man starved of her taste because I am. It's been years since I've sampled anything as sweet as Ava's mouth, and it's better than it has ever been.

Ava kisses me back with a sense of urgency like she's afraid she'll open her eyes and discover she's dreaming. To ensure her that will *never* happen, I rub my hard cock against the seam of her sweatpants. Moaning, she glides her hands under my shirt. The bumps in my midsection bunch when she runs her fingertips over them, then they harden with anticipation when she drops her hand to my belt.

As she works the leather material through the loops of my jeans then lowers the zipper, I bite, kiss, and lick her. I nibble on her jaw, suck her delicate neck, and grope her tits that grew more mouthwatering when she became a mother.

By the time Ava curls her hand around my erect cock, precum is pooling on the tip, and her panties are slipped to the side. I'm ready to drive home, but before I can, a little voice asks, "What are you doing?"

My hand rockets out of Hugo's jeans like I've been scorched by an open flame instead of his thick cock. I stare at Hugo's smiling eyes for several terrifying seconds before I slowly filter mine to the side. Joel is standing at the end of the couch. His sock monkey is in one hand and an empty glass is in the other. He looks confused, but I'm at a loss on how to respond.

Although I was in a 'relationship' with Marvin for the past nine months, Joel never walked into a situation like this. Excluding kissing Chase and Mr. Marshall goodbye on the cheek, he's never witnessed me kiss another man, let alone participate in anything as graphic as the sexual activity I was about to undertake.

God, imagine if he was five minutes later?

Joel rubs sleep out of his eyes while saying with a yawn, "I'm thirsty. Daddy forgot to fill my glass of water."

"I'm sorry, buddy. I didn't realize you still woke during the night." The leering grin on Hugo's face doubles my confusion. Is he apologizing for forgetting to fill Joel's glass of water or reprimanding him for interrupting us?

There's one thing I am certain of, though, I need to get off Hugo's lap before I forget I'm a mother. Just the vibration of his deep voice through my aching-with-need core is surging my libido to a never-before-reached level.

"Let's get you a drink, then it's back to bed, mister."

A grin tugs on my lips when Hugo conceals his erection with a pillow after I slide off his lap. Mercifully, Joel shadows me into the kitchen. His steps are sluggish and slow, exposing that tiredness is the sole cause of the crinkle between his brows—thank goodness.

I fill his glass to the very brim to ensure he won't require another refill, then guide him back to bed. Nothing against my son —I love him more than anything in the world—but it's been years since I've been this horny. Hugo's enthralling kiss has an orgasm sitting precariously on the edge of an extremely steep cliff. Keen is an understatement for how eager I am to get back to my make-out session on the couch.

After detouring to the living room to give Hugo a hug goodnight, Joel climbs into his bed and snuggles into the pillow. His glass of water remains untouched. I switch on his night light, carefully close his door, then briskly saunter back to the living room. My fervent steps falter when I reach the end of the corridor and notice Hugo standing in the entryway, putting on his shoes.

When he hears my rejected groan, his eyes lock with mine. "I better get going." He tugs on his last shoe. "It's late, and you've got work tomorrow, and Joel has pre-school."

After shelving my rejection for a more appropriate time, I enter the kitchen to gather the Tupperware container full of pancakes I set aside for him earlier. A grin furls on Hugo's kiss-swollen lips when he spots the container in my hand.

"There's only one thing sweeter than your blueberry pancakes." His baby blues lift to my face. "You."

I have no chance of concealing the grin stretching across my face, so I set it free. After accepting the container from my hand, Hugo runs the back of his fingers down my inflamed cheeks. I try not to nuzzle into his embrace, but the urge is too great for me to restrain. I'm drawn to him like a moth to a flame.

"I really enjoyed tonight." He peers at me with smoldering eyes and a carefree grin. "Can we do it again?"

He chuckles when I nod like a loser. I swear, nothing has changed. I'm once again rolling over begging for my stomach to be scratched. I can't help it. It won't matter how much time passes, when Hugo is in my presence, I'm the braces-wearing teen flabbergasted by her high school crush.

Everything Mrs. Marshall said this afternoon was true. Hugo has owned my heart longer than I have, and even having my heart torn from my chest and stomped on when he left, nothing will ever change the fact he is my one true love.

"How long are you back for?" I query, my words juddering as nerves dangle on my vocal cords.

When I open my front door, goosebumps prickle my spine as cold air blasts through the crack of the door, but a new type of coldness freezes my heart when Hugo answers, "A week. I have some stuff I have to go back and sort out." Upon noticing my despondent expression, he cradles my cheek with his warm hand. His palm is so large, it almost covers my entire face. "I promise you I am doing everything I can to ensure I'm not away from you or Joel too long." He lifts his gaze from my lips that are still tingling from our kiss to my tear-welling eyes. "I never want to be away from either of you ever again." His chest thrusts up and down as he stares at me with beseeching eyes. "If I could take it back, Ava, I would. If I could take away your pain, make it disappear—"

"The past cannot be changed, forgotten, edited, or erased. It can only be accepted," I interrupt, quoting what he said to me over five years ago.

It was the mantra I repeated every time he dropped Joel off last week when I feared he may not arrive the next morning as promised, but his expression alone guarantees my fears will never transpire.

Hugo places the Tupperware container onto the entryway table before running his thumbs over my cheeks to remove my tears. "Accept the past, embrace the present, and believe in the future," he recites while staring into my moisture-filled eyes.

The coldness of the crisp winter night is a forgotten memory when we undertake a mesmerizing stare-down. As always, the dynamic between us is electrifying. It sparks the air with enough heat to make it feel as if we're in the middle of summer. Hugo's eyes, which darkened during his confession about Gemma, get a familiar sparkle as fragments of the teenage boy who stole my heart at the tender age of sixteen emerges from the dark shadows crippling his usually carefree composure.

"I'll make this work," he vows, glancing into my eyes. "*Us* work." The saltiness of my tears flavors our kiss when he presses his plump lips to my mouth then mutters, "I'll see you tomorrow?"

Smiling, I nod. "I wouldn't miss it for the world."

With my heart beating out a tune it hasn't played for years, I watch Hugo slip into a rental car and drive away through the peep hole of my front door. He was adamant he wasn't leaving the front porch until he heard the deadbolt click into place.

Once his taillights disappear, I lean my back against the door and suck in a big breath. I've known Hugo more than half my life, but I've never seen him be as open as he was tonight. He was raw and unguarded. *Honest.* He's always been a communicator, but as he matures, his actions are outspeaking his words. The love he displays to Joel—*to me*—is greater than I could have ever imagined. I've always said there's no love greater than the love a mother has for her child. I'm starting to think that saying also applies to father's.

I stop grinning like a loon when a little voice pops up for the second time tonight. "Can I have a brother?"

Slanting my head to the side, I peer down the hallway where the voice came from. Joel is leaning on the wall outside his bedroom. His eyes are heavy, and he's yawning. If he didn't occasionally blink, I would assume he's sleepwalking.

"I don't want a sister. Angie and Katie are so *annoying*. Please, Mommy, can I please have a brother?"

A grin curls on my lips from the tired slur of his words. He sounds like the four-year-old he is. I'm not biased when I say Joel is a genius. He speaks well above his age, reads better than any six-year-old I know, and slaughters me anytime we play Monopoly. It is only moments like these do I realize his true age. He's a sweet little boy who has confused his nursery rhymes, believing it is the girls made out of snips, snails, and puppy dog tails.

"How about we discuss the possibility of siblings after a few hours of sleep?" *And a few glasses of wine.*

"Siblings?" Joel mutters, trying on the new word for size.

"Siblings is a term for brothers and sisters," I explain while gathering him in my arms.

My heart warms when he slings his arms around my neck and nuzzles into my chest. I love him more than anything, but it was only when he was born did I realize the love you have for your partner is entirely different than the love you have for your child. Although both are as consuming as the other, they're unique and beautiful in their own way.

When I lay Joel in his bed, his twinkling eyes lift to mine. His brows are stitched together, and his lips are pursed. "Does that mean I can have more than one?"

"More than one what?" I query while tucking him in nice and firm, ensuring he can't escape for a third time this evening.

"Siblings." He rubs his eyes with his balled fist. "You said 'siblings' not 'sibling.'"

I laugh. There's no greater innocence in the world than that of a child. Not even a twenty-four-year-old virgin.

I grimace when Joel says, "I want five brothers."

After pressing a kiss onto his forehead, I switch on the night light on his bedside table before ambling toward the door. I'm knackered. Not just physically but emotionally as well. The past week has been a hazy blur of confusion. Hell, the past five years have been one devastating blow after another, but it feels like everything changed in a matter of hours. Tonight, my mind is the clearest it has ever been.

It is remarkable how much can change in a couple of hours and how one man can alter my perspective of life so greatly.

"Mommy," Joel whimpers when I reach his door.

I crank my neck back to look at him.

"I love Daddy," he whispers through a yawn before cuddling into his pillow.

A vast grin etches on my face. "So do I, sweetheart, so do I," I mutter to no one.

TWENTY-THREE
HUGO

After dumping my duffle bag onto the floor, I shift my focus to Ava and Joel. Joel's arms are wrapped around his mother's thigh, and his big blue eyes are peering up at me, wordlessly pleading for me to stay.

I don't want to leave my family. Leaving them is one of the hardest things I've ever done, but I need to settle the tension between Isaac and me. I want to explain my foolhardiness to him so I can leave his empire honorably. I've already left one position dishonorably in my life. I will not do it again, especially not with a man of utmost importance to me.

Once I've settled the dust between Isaac and me, the heavy burden weighing down my shoulders will lift, and I'll be free to begin a new chapter in my life. A phase surrounded by my family.

I've spent every waking moment with Ava and Joel this past week. I was not willing to miss a single minute. Most of the second half of my week was spent in a blur of playdates and fatherly duties with Joel while Ava settled into her new practice, but the past two days have been a little more subdued as the countdown to my return to Ravenshoe crept upon us.

Although neither Joel nor Ava have verbalized their concerns about me returning to Ravenshoe, I've seen a shift in their personas the last two days. I'll often discover Ava watching my interactions with Joel with a misting of tears in her eyes, and for the past forty-eight hours, Joel hasn't let me leave his side. He even went as far as requesting me to sleep on his bedroom floor.

A grin tugs on my lips when Ava rolls her eyes when I noogie Joel's head, messing up the curls she just finished wrangling into order.

"I'll see you soon, buddy," I assure him before crouching down to Joel's level. The heaviness weighing down my chest increases when I spot the little tears prickling in the corners of his eyes.

"Yes, Daddy," he replies, his words coming out in a whimper.

I band my arms around his trembling shoulders then pull him into my chest. The pain in my heart turns lethal when his little sobs sound through my ears. I draw him in tighter before vowing, "I'll be back soon. I promise, Joel." Willing to say anything to ease his concern, I murmur, "We've got all that practice to do before try-outs."

His quivering lips tremor against my neck when he nods his little head. It breaks my heart knowing I'm the cause of his tears. Every tear directly impacts me. "Don't tell Mommy, but I snuck a few packets of candy into your sock drawer," I whisper into his ear.

In an instant, his head shoots off my neck, and his eyes dart between mine. When he spots the truth beaming from mine, a vast grin stretches across his face, and his tears rapidly dry. I return his smile while wiping away the rogue tears on his pale cheeks.

After giving him a final head noogie, I rise from my crouched position then shift on my feet to face Ava. For Joel's sake, she's putting on a brave front. She's acting as if she isn't upset about my departure. When she initially offered to drive me to the airport, I declined. Not because I didn't want to spend every moment with her and Joel, but because I can't stand the thought of leaving her at the airport crying.

The memories of her walking away from me in this exact airport still agitate me. I thought those six years would be our longest separation.

How wrong was I?

Only after Ava assured me she wouldn't cry did I agree for her to drop me off.

I curl my arms around her shoulders then pull her into my thrusting chest. "It's different this time, Ava. We were young back then, just kids. Nothing could keep me away from you now. Not a single thing," I say, intuiting that the memories of that day are also steamrolling into her.

She runs her sleeve's cuff under her eyes before nodding.

Desperate to help her keep her promise, I mutter, "Don't tell Joel, but you might want to check his sock drawer when you get home. I may have gotten a little excited with the amount of candy I left in there." A winded grunt puffs out of my mouth when she elbows me in the ribs, but the weight on my chest eases when I see the grin she can't hide. "Leave him a couple of packets?" I plead, my words barely a whisper to ensure Joel doesn't overhear our conversation.

I hit Ava with a frisky wink when she gently nods. After snagging my duffle bag off the floor, I place a kiss on Joel's head before pressing one to the edge of Ava's lips. The battle not to slip my tongue inside her sweet and inviting mouth is tortuous. The ball-clenching kiss we shared a week ago has been the only kiss we've shared.

Don't construe my confession the wrong way. I'm more than interested in devouring every inch of Ava, but when Joel interrupted us with an expression of shock on his face, I recalled Ava was only engaged mere hours before our kiss. Marvin will never be a hard act to follow, but I don't want to be the rebound guy. Once Ava becomes mine, there will be no going back—*ever*—so I need to make sure she has time to properly evaluate what she wants because I know as well as the next man, rushed decisions can result in dire consequences.

When the final boarding call for my flight sounds over the speakers, I shift my eyes between Ava and Joel. "I'll see you soon?"

I smile when they nod their heads in sync. Even with it feeling like a knife is being stabbed into my chest, I spin on my heels and walk to my departure gate.

I need to do this.

I need to make things right with Isaac.

Then I'll have a clear conscience to move onto the next stage of my life.

The flight back to Ravenshoe is thankfully uneventful and void of the nail-biting I experienced when I flew to Tiburon with Izzy last week. I can't believe it's only been a little over a week since that day.

So much has changed since then.

Upon exiting the domestic terminal, I spot Hunter's Hellcat parked illegally in a loading zone at the side. He's sitting behind the steering wheel, either oblivious to the police officer filling in a citation for his illegal park or he doesn't care.

"I'll be there in thirty. You better get that little red number out," Hunter murmurs as I crank open the passenger door of his car and slide into the dark gray leather seat. "I'll call you back in a few," he states into his cell phone, his tone sterner than earlier.

After snapping his untraceable cell shut, he throws it into the middle console of his car and turns his eyes to me.

"Who was that?" I ask, not bothering to hide the innuendo in my voice.

He tries to conceal his grin behind his scruffy beard, but I can't miss it. Even if I could, the blaze firing in his eyes is all the indication I need to know that his heart is flipping in his chest.

"You'll meet her in a few."

He snatches the parking ticket out of the officer's hand then tears out of the loading zone. When we reach the highway, he scrunches up the parking fine and tosses it onto the pavement whizzing by. Once his window glides back into place, his eyes drift to me. He eyes me with curiosity but remains silent.

My brows stitch together when he leans over to sniff my jaw.

"Hmm... sweet," he mutters while curtly nodding. When I adjust my position to place much-needed distance between me and his out-of-character awkwardness, he grins and winks before jutting his chin out. "Your turn." I eye him with even more curiosity than earlier. "You want to know if a beard captures a woman's scent. Check." He thrusts his beard-covered chin out further.

When I punch him in the bicep, his chuckle booms around the interior of his car. He rubs the area, feigning injury before slanting his chin back in and returning his eyes to the road. After inhaling deeply through his nose, he mutters, "Never smelled anything so delicious."

I'm about to argue that there's no sweeter scent in the world than Ava's until I remember what is one man's meat is another man's poison. A man may see one woman as a precious diamond, whereas another may only see her as a dirty stone stuck in a rock.

Although I'm certain Ava is the sexiest woman alive and the sweetest smelling, it isn't my place to convince Hunter. Actually,

I'd prefer it if more men were unaware of the fact. Then I may have a chance of keeping my inane jealousy that only Ava incites intact.

"Does Isaac know I'm back?" I ask, endeavoring to return my focus to the task at hand.

The quicker I fix things between us, the faster I'll return to my family.

Hunter nods. "Yeah, he requested your assistance with a task this morning."

My brow arches. "What task?" I query, my words juddering. "Digging my own grave?"

Hunter chuckles. "Come on, you know as well as the rest of us, Isaac doesn't mind getting his hands a little dirty if he needs to, so if he wanted your grave dug, it would have already been done."

I smirk and nod. "True."

Hunter shifts his eyes between the road and me. "His asset is arriving this morning. You were an integral part of securing her. He wants you there to see Izzy's reaction."

"I don't deserve any credit for what Isaac did. He put up the money and pushed his empire into dangerous territory to secure her. All I did was recognize a pair of distinctive eyes."

"Yeah, but a lesser man wouldn't have cared what happened to her. You knew Isaac. You knew he would have responded to your discovery. If you didn't care about him or Izzy, you would have just hidden that little girl's existence to save your own ass. You didn't. That deserves credit."

I grunt. It is the only plausible reaction I can give. Although some would see my decision as loyalty to Isaac, I've been anything but loyal. Neither Hunter nor I have been totally forthright with Isaac for the past three months. After Isaac ran into Izzy at the airport, he requested Hunter to gather any information he could on her. Hunter did as requested. He just failed to disclose *every-thing* he found on Izzy.

Although I will admit, it took Hunter a lot of effort to unearth the real Isabelle Brahn from the deep pile of rubble Brandon hid her under. But since Hunter is the best hacker in the world, he eventually found a channel.

Both Hunter and I saw a change in Isaac the day he met Izzy. We knew without a doubt she was his Achilles heel. So that night, we made a plan. Izzy had a month. If she didn't disclose her true identity to Isaac within that month of them being a couple, we would out her.

Isaac was arrested before we got the chance.

My palms sweat when Hunter pulls his Hellcat into the front entrance of Isaac's property and enters the security code into the black security panel. The beat of my heart climbs astronomically when he guides his car up the driveway and parks in front of the double French doors.

"You coming?" I ask when Hunter's seat belt remains latched.

When he smirks and shakes his head, my pupils widen, and a brick lodges in my throat.

Upon spotting my panicked expression, Hunter chuckles. "This is the first time I've seen you scared."

With a roll of my eyes, I slam the passenger door shut. Hunter laughs before he tears out of the driveway, leaving nothing but dust and the scent of burning gasoline in his wake. I'll be honest, I am shitting bricks. Before, I never had a reason to fear Isaac. I had nothing to lose, so I wasn't worried about retribution when I taunted him. Now, I have *everything* to lose.

After running my sweaty palms down the front of my jeans, I walk up the small flight of stairs to the front door. Before I can grab the gold engraved door handle, the French doors swing open.

Isaac's dark eyes stare into mine for numerous stomach-churning seconds before they lower to my long-sleeve shirt and ripped jeans.

"There's a spare suit in the guest bedroom." He gestures his head to one of the numerous rooms in his private residence.

Unsurprisingly, his tone is clipped and stern. Surprisingly, this is the first time he's spoken to me as if I'm a member of his staff instead of his friend.

I'm not going to lie. His coldness stings my ego and bruises my heart.

"Isaac, I—"

Any further words preparing to seep from my lips are cut off from the stern glare he directs at me. His furious wrath causes the guilt I'm carrying to become more weighted.

"Not now," he demands while glaring at me. "This day is not about me or you. It is about Isabelle. I know you care for her." His jaw gains a twitch from his last sentence. "And she cares for you. So, for her, I'm willing to push aside the overwhelming urge to *destroy* you like your *betrayal* gutted me."

After witnessing him fight in a charity UFC match last week, I thought his fists were his greatest weapons. They aren't. His words and the desolate look in his eyes inflict more damage to my already guilt-ridden heart than his fists ever could.

"We leave in five minutes."

When I nod, he enters the living room at the side of the foyer. I move into the spare room and change into my work attire—a black suit and a crisp white dress shirt. My movements are sluggish, weighed down by the guilt strangling my heart.

After I'm dressed, I return to the foyer to await further instructions. My eyes float up from the floor when a tiny pair of feet padding down the stairwell sounds through my ears. Izzy stops halfway down the stairs. As her hand shoots up to clamp her mouth, her eyes well with tears.

After brushing away a stray tear clinging to her cheek, she gallops down the stairs and throws herself into my arms.

"Hey, Isabelle," I greet her while returning her embrace.

Deep down in my heart, I knew Isaac would take care of Izzy, but it still feels good to see her back to her carefree, happy self.

When I place her back onto her feet, her eyes roam my face. From the corner of my eye, I spot Isaac exiting the living room, carefully mulling over the exchange between Izzy and me. Even though his gaze remains static, I know he sees it. Izzy is like family to me. Nothing more. Nothing less. There are no fireworks or sparks. There's nothing but friendship and mutual respect.

When Izzy spots Isaac standing to the side, she gnaws on her bottom lip before she scurries across the room to greet him with the same enthusiasm she bestowed on me. Well, minus the kissing part.

Her gesture should settle any concerns Isaac has. The fireworks he was searching for while watching Isabelle and me are exploding before his very eyes—between him and Izzy.

"I'll bring the car around," I advise before slipping out the front entrance.

The heaviness of my stomps softens when my cell phone buzzes in my pocket. When I lug it out, my chuckle sounds over the gravel crunching under my feet. Ava snapped a picture of her and Joel playing Monopoly last night. Instead of using fake money, they used the multiple bags of Skittles I left in Joel's sock drawer as leverage.

As I move to the garage at the side of the main house, I punch out a reply.

Me: *Lucky his mom is a dentist?*

There's no doubt who the real estate mogul is in the photo Ava snapped. Joel's pile of candy is almost bigger than his head, whereas Ava only has a small scattering of Skittles that wouldn't even fill half her small hand.

Ava: *Lucky he agreed to save his candy gorging until his daddy returns.*

As I type a message, ellipses trickle over the screen. A grin stretches across my face when my message is sent at the same time Ava's is received.

Me: *I miss you guys.*

Ava: *We miss you.*

I've only been gone for a few hours, but I'm already missing them more than I could ever express. That proves, without a doubt, my life will not be complete until they're in it. Both of them.

When I hear Isaac and Isabelle walking toward the garage, I quickly type out a message and hit send before housing my phone back into my pocket. I rush to the driver's side door of one of Isaac's many town cars then crank the ignition.

Halfway to the private airstrip Isaac instructed me to drive to, my cell phone buzzes. Since I'm dying to know what Ava's reply is, I shift my eyes between the road and my trousers while retrieving my phone. My hearty chuckle traps in the front half of the car since Isaac has the privacy divider lifted between us.

Ava: *That was even more pathetic than that time in your office.*

It takes me several tedious minutes to type a reply since I'm gripping the steering wheel with one hand and typing with another.

Me: *Come on, cut a guy some slack. I've never done this before.*

I can't wipe the grin off my face when I pull into the private airstrip on the outskirts of Ravenshoe. It isn't because we've arrived so I can type with two hands. I'm loving Ava's reply.

Ava: *Well, for one, you missed a box.*

Me: No, I didn't.

Ava: Yeah, you did.

I scroll up the screen to check the original message I sent her: *Will you go out with me? Yes or Maybe... To dinner. I meant to say, will you go out to dinner with me?*

Me: I don't see what the problem is.

Ava: Imagine a rolled eyes emoji here if I could work out how to do them on my new phone.

Me: LOL. Ask Joel. He would know.

Ava: I can't believe you type LOL. How old are you? Anyway, you forgot the 'no' box.

Me: *And? What's wrong with that?*

Ava: You can't ask a girl out without a no box.

Me: Hell yes, I can. Saying I can't do something is pretty much daring me to do it. And we both know, I never back down from a dare.

I peer up from my phone when one of Cormack's private jets Isaac regularly uses taxis toward us. Realizing I need to wrap things up, I get desperate.

Me: There isn't a no box as I'm not going to take no for an answer. Come on, Ava. It's dinner. A guy's got to eat.

Ava: *What if the restaurant stops serving breakfast at 11 in the morning?*

I chuckle.

Me: We'll go to another restaurant.

Although I'm loving Ava's playful banter, on the inside, I'm dying. I haven't inhaled a full breath since her first reply was received.

I stare at my phone's screen, willing for it to hurry up and deliver Ava's reply. Thankfully, I'm not left waiting for long.

Ava: Alright. Let me know the day, and I'll ask Mrs. Mable to watch Joel.

Fuck, yes!

Me: *I'll take care of everything.*

When the door of the private jet swings open, my eyes lift from my phone. My brows hit my hairline when the guy who was dancing with Izzy steps out of the jet with a little girl wrapped around his legs. Wanting to gauge Isaac's reaction to being confronted by the guy who had every intention of adding Izzy's name to the notches on his bedpost, I snap my eyes to Isaac.

My brows furrow when he seems oblivious to the man's significance in Izzy's life. His reaction can't be true. He's always watching Izzy. *Always.*

I return my focus back to my phone and quickly type out a message.

Me: *I gotta go, babe. I'll call you later.*

Ava: *Okay. Talk to you later.*

I sit in the car for several minutes, quietly watching the exchange between Isaac, Izzy, and Izzy's half-sister, Callie. You'd think witnessing Isaac spend millions of dollars to secure Callie would be the most admirable thing I've witnessed him do the past five years.

It isn't.

Not even close.

But since they're making their way back to the car I'm helming, I'll have to save the stories for another day.

After settling Callie into her new room, Isaac strides into his office. His brisk pace slows when he notices me standing at the side of his desk, glancing at a photo of Izzy he has there. He seems to have an odd obsession with watching her sleep as this is only one of many photos he has of her dozing.

I place the photo on his desk then turn around to face him. "You knew what Izzy was going to do. You knew why she went to the Dungeon." Although you could construe my statement as a question, it isn't. I know Isaac. I know him *very well*. So I'm well aware my statement is factual, not fiction.

Isaac unbuttons his suit jacket, removes it, then slings it over the coat rack in the corner of the room. Remaining quiet, he saunters to a crystal bar set up at the edge of his desk and pours a generous serving of whiskey into a crystal glass.

"You intuited Izzy's next move before she even knew what she was going to do." *Just like I knew Ava would accept my invitation to dinner before I sent the message.*

The corners of Isaac's lip crimp in a wry smirk. "A game of chess is not a hard game to win if you study your opponent in great depth."

My eyes widen. "So you sent Ayden in knowing he'd kiss her?"

His smirk vanishes, and a set of hard-lined lips ruefully take its place. "No," he growls. "I sent Ayden in to *stop* Isabelle from kissing someone." He pivots on his heels to face me. "Isabelle knows me better than anyone. She knew I had kissed Ophelia without me needing to confess. In her heart, she knew I betrayed her, so she went to the Dungeon to exact her revenge. Ayden was the closest man I had on the ground. I sent him there to *stop* her kissing another man."

He slams his whiskey glass onto the desk so roughly, the crystal chips from his brutal force. His nostrils flare as he inhales deeply with the hope of filling his thrusting chest with air. "Ayden had one task... use any tactic he could to keep Isabelle safe until you arrived. What I didn't expect was to be blindsided by the man I trusted. I never suspected the man I would have bled for would be the one to cut me open and *tear* my heart straight from my chest."

The heaviness in my chest turns lethal. "Isaac, I did—"

"You did it because you knew I'd be watching," he interjects, his tone lowering to a vicious snarl. "Because you wanted me to see it." His face lines with anger when I nod, agreeing with his statement. "What I can't comprehend is why you did it. I've seen you with Isabelle. I know you care for her, but I never suspected it to be anything more than friendship. I've only seen the spark of admiration in your eyes once before. It wasn't directed at Isabelle."

"Izzy is my family, Isaac. Just like you," I declare while staring into his pained eyes.

His face reddens, and his jaw muscle spasms. He doesn't believe a word I'm speaking, so I bring out the truth instead. "I wanted you to fire me." I step closer to him, putting myself in the danger zone by moving within reaching distance. "After everything you did for me, I didn't feel like I could leave your empire of my own free will, so I took the coward's way out. I forced you to do it for me."

Isaac's stern eyes bounce between mine, but he remains quiet, allowing his eyes to demand an explanation.

"I have a son," I enlighten him. Even in the seriousness of our conversation, I can't stop the smile tugging on my lips. Isaac's strengthened posture weakens, and he eyes me as if he misheard what I said. "Ava was pregnant before I snatched Roberto from the compound," I explain, still smirking.

Isaac inhales a quick breath before shaking his head. "No, she couldn't have been. I had a family member keep an on Ava the weeks following your disappearance. I wanted to ensure Col wasn't aware of her significance to you."

"I know that." Isaac would have ensured she was safe. "Ava didn't discover she was pregnant until she was nearly six months along. Joel is my son, Isaac. Even without a DNA test, there's no doubt in my mind."

He swallows harshly before scrubbing his hand along his jaw.

After a small stretch of silence, he walks around his desk and takes a seat in his leather chair. This is the first time I've seen him look wholly stumped. He isn't used to being divulged information secondhand. He's normally the informant of vital information, not the receiver.

His leather chair creaks when he leans back and lifts his eyes to me. "If I'd known, I would have never—"

"I know," I interrupt before taking the chair across from him. "I didn't kiss Izzy because I thought you hid my son from me. I kissed her because I didn't take the time to properly judge the repercussions of my actions."

The deep V groove in between Isaac's eyes smooths. "I've warned you before. Haste decisions—"

"Cause unforgiving mistakes," I fill in, nodding. I rest my ankle on my trouser-covered thigh. "I don't expect you to ever forgive me. What I did to you was wrong, but I need you to understand why I did it. I was hurting as I thought Ava was going to take my son away from me. I let my anger get the better of me... as did Izzy."

Isaac shifts his eyes to the side of his office like he can see Izzy through the walls separating them.

"I made a foolish mistake and stupidly threw Izzy under the bus with me. You don't need me to tell you this because I can see in your eyes that you are already aware, but I'm going to say it anyway. Izzy is your Achilles heel just like Ava is mine."

He returns his eyes to me. The catastrophic storm brewing in them earlier has been downgraded to a tropical shower.

"I wasn't man enough to talk to you last week, but I'm man enough to admit I made a mistake. I'm sorry for what I did to you, Isaac. For breaking your trust and messing around with the best thing that has ever happened to you. I don't expect you to accept my apology, but I hope one day, you'll understand if I had the chance, I'd go back in an instant and fix all the wrongs I've done. Not just this week, years ago as well."

Isaac inhales a ragged breath as he stands from his chair. He paces around the desk and props his hip on the side. His arms are crossed in front of his body, and his jaw is ticking, exposing his agitation, but the pain in his eyes has eased from my confession. "I'm only going to say this once, so you better listen." His voice is rough like his throat is raw and bleeding. "I was once told family isn't the people related to you by blood. It is the people you chose to be a part of your life that makes them family."

I smile and nod. I've quoted that saying to him numerous times over the past five years.

"No matter what happens, Hugo, you'll always be my family." He coughs, clearing his throat of any encumbrance. "But in saying that, I'll *fucking* kill you if you *ever* touch Isabelle again," he warns, glaring into my eyes to ensure I'm aware his warning is not an idle threat. If I so much as touch a strand on Izzy's head, he will slit my throat.

I swallow the brick lodged in my throat before nodding. Smirking at my agreeing gesture, Isaac pushes off the desk and takes his original position behind it. After running his eyes over a barrage of paperwork in front of him, he lifts them to me. "Are you planning to sit there all day?" When I shake my head, he says, "Then get the fuck out of my office. Some of us actually have to work for a living."

Even exulted by him using part of a quote he said to me many years ago, my brows furrow. I'm happy I've repaired some of the damage I instigated between us, but I can't just step back into my old role. My family needs me, but even more important than that, I need them.

Sensing my hesitation to leave, a smirk etches on Isaac's mouth. It is only small but large enough to appease some of the guilt maiming my heart. "Go back to your family, Hugo," he responds to my silent thoughts. "Mark might have pulled in the female clientele back in the day, but he's shit at operations. My clubs in the New York region are taking a hit with him behind the wheel. Maybe with someone steering him in the right direction, I might not have to fire his ass."

A broad grin stretches across my face. I'm not bragging, but when I was at the helm of operations in New York five years ago, Isaac's clubs saw substantial growth. *Alright, maybe I am bragging.*

When I stand from my chair, Isaac gestures his head to the door. "Make sure you say goodbye to Isabelle before you leave."

He tried to suffocate it, but I didn't miss the slight smear in his tone, but I appreciate his effort in lessening the vehement jealousy he has when it comes to Izzy and me being friends.

Never being the talkative type, Isaac returns his eyes to the paperwork spread on his desk as I amble to his office door.

"Hugo," he calls out just before I exit.

I crank my neck back. "Yeah?"

His gray eyes stare into mine. "You should consider upgrading your suit. It looks tacky walking around in a thousand-dollar suit when you have over two million dollars in your bank account."

I stare at him, more confused than ever.

He does his best to alleviate my bewilderment. "Those checks belong to you. What I did for you and your family wasn't under the stipulation that you had to repay me. I did it because I wanted to."

A smile curls on my lips before I curtly nod. Isaac has always been generous, but I never felt right accepting his money. For the past five years, he has fed me, sheltered me, and kept me safe. What more did I need than that? So instead of cashing his checks he printed every month, I shredded every one of them, apart from the original one he gave me over five years ago. I kept it as a memento of how far I'd come and what I'd given up to get here.

My eyes float up from my shoes when Isaac bridges the gap between us until he stops directly in front of me. "Ravenshoe has grown substantially the past few years." I nod. Under his guidance, it's grown phenomenally in the five years I've lived here. "A rapidly developing city could use a world-class dentist," he suggests, his tone rapidly changing from my boss to my friend.

A vast grin stretches across my face. "I'll talk it over with Ava. See what she thinks." I don't have a chance in hell of hiding the excitement in my voice. Although Rochdale was where I was born and raised, Ravenshoe became my home in the last five years. It wasn't the location that earned it that title. It was the people who live here. People like Isaac.

Spotting my slack-jawed expression, Isaac smirks. "I'll have my team look into suitable locations. Just in case Ava is interested."

Not giving him the time to react, I throw my arms around his shoulders and give him a quick bro hug. Although he stiffens, he doesn't pull away from my embrace. That is good enough for me to accept.

My brows meet my hairline when he strengthens his grip around my shoulders. "If Ava is your Achilles, pull your head out of your ass before you lose the best thing that's ever happened to you."

I crank my neck back and peer into his eyes. "You were close, but I said, 'pull your *fucking* head out of your ass before you lose the best thing that's ever *fucking* happened to you,'" I say, quoting what I said to him the night he was arrested by Izzy.

Isaac shrugs. "Extending your vocabulary with offensive language doesn't make you any more of a man." His lips curve into a smirk. "Besides, my memories of the night are a little fuzzy, hazed by a liquor bottle or two."

I chuckle. "True," I drawl out. I'd never seen him so intoxicated.

When he drops his arms from my shoulders and locks his eyes with mine, his twinkling gaze spears me in place. It is the same spark his eyes had when I collected him from the airport the day he met Izzy. The glimmer that told me he had just met his match.

"Don't waste a day, Hugo. Because when you breathe your last breath, it won't matter how many breaths you took but how many moments took your breath away."

TWENTY-FOUR
AVA

My office chair squeaks when I slump into it and swivel around to face the window in the corner of the room. I've officially been operating my practice for the past week. Thankfully, for the most part, the experience has been positive. With keeping my prices reasonable for the average Rochdale community member, I've secured a handful of new patients. I even snagged a few loyal clients from Gardner and Sons who prefer the appeal of quality dental work over a lavish office space. Although it's been a good trading week, I have a long way to go before I'll be turning a profit.

"Even Bill Gates had to start somewhere," I mumble to myself.

A sigh spills from my lips when I peer down at my phone's screen and discover it's void of any missed calls or text messages. Ever since our exchange of text messages this morning, Hugo has maintained radio silence. The craziness of my day ensured I only sneaked peeks at my phone every thirty minutes instead of every minute of the day like I did the months following his disappearance.

I'll be the first to admit it will take me some time to adjust to

Hugo's conflicting work schedule, but it's a compromise I'm willing to make if it maintains his relationship with Joel and me.

Hugo has only been gone a little over twenty-four hours, and I'm missing him like crazy. Even though we are not an official couple, my moods have already become dependent on his presence, which sounds like a terrifying notion.

After being controlled by my father, I grew up striving for independence, often vowing no man would ever have that type of hold over me again. Although some may see my dependency on Hugo in such a short period of time as a negative, I see it as anything but. The fact we have years of friendship as the foundation of our unique bond undoubtedly proves our relationship isn't based on propaganda. It is founded on mutual respect and admiration.

The past week has been surreal. Hugo stepped into the role of devoted spouse and father without a single qualm seeping from his lips. He's mastered the school drop-off without getting any citations from the parking mothers who govern with an iron fist, and he even attended a PTA meeting with me Tuesday night. Although I'll admit, from the blank, desolated look he wore during the meeting, I'll have more chances of getting him in my dental chair than to another PTA meeting.

Although he's only been back in my life for two weeks, it feels like years have passed. Our relationship has always been like that. Small moments make a lifetime of memories.

Don't read my admission with foggy glasses. I know Hugo is anything but perfect, but for years, he has been my drug of choice. And just like every addictive drug, he's been the cause of life-altering highs and devastating lows in my life. But like all things in life, I greedily accept the good and wade my way through the bad. It is the sacrifice every woman makes for the man she loves.

I rub my throbbing temples before stretching my arms above

my head. After an exhausting day, I'm dying for a long, hot shower and a nice glass of wine. I dump my phone on my Ikea desk and crank my head to the side when a knock sounds on my office door.

"Come in," I say, my high tone exposing my interest. It is a little after six on Friday night, so my office doors are officially closed for the weekend.

My excitement dampens when Belinda glides through the door with an imploring look on her face. "I know we're closed, but we've just had an emergency case come in. Do you think you could squeeze them in?" Her nose screws up as she stares at me with pleading eyes.

Even though I'm beyond exhausted, and I've reached my quota of peering into smelly mouths for one day, it would be injudicious of me to turn down a prospective new client. Strength and growth only come through continued effort and struggle.

"Sure, just give me five minutes so I can advise Mrs. Mable I'll be late collecting Joel, then send them into the exam room," I instruct.

A big grin carves on Belinda's mouth before she nods and exits my office, closing the door behind her. I leave a quick message on Mrs. Mable's home phone when my call is sent to voicemail. I'm not shocked by her failure to answer. She can barely hear Joel's earth-shattering screams, let alone a telephone ringing.

I'm scrubbing my hands in the washroom's sink when the examination room door attached to my office creaks open. "Hi, I'm just washing up. Please take a seat in the dental chair, and I'll be right with you," I call out while snagging a paper towel from the dispenser mounted on my right.

After thoroughly drying my hands, I crumple the paper towel and throw it into the bin before walking out of the washroom. The ghastly dentist smell I've always hated hits my senses when I step into the sterilized treatment area at the side of my office. The space is deadly quiet—only gloves being removed from a cardboard box are heard.

After tying a facemask around my head and putting on my gloves, I delve further into the room. My breath hitches halfway between my lungs and my throat when I discover who is sprawled on the dental chair. I cough and wheeze, struggling to breathe through the saliva now sitting in my lungs instead of my throat.

Hugo's panty-wetting smile sags when he hears my breathless coughing fit. "Are you okay?"

Through watering eyes, I nod. I try to speak, but the shock of seeing him sitting in *my* dental chair is too great for me to harness. My mouth can barely move, let alone relinquish words. Hugo *hates* dentists. Not a small dislike, he openly admits that he hates, *hates* them.

Even putting aside the shock of his sudden arrival in my office, I only dropped him at the airport yesterday afternoon. And although I wished for him to return soon, I never fathomed it would be the very next day.

After rolling my shoulders, I level out my erratic breathing and try to portray that I am a responsible, career-oriented twenty-nine-year-old woman, not the teenage, braces-mouthed girl Hugo's presence always incites. Although my posture alludes to professionalism, my shaking steps and quickening pulse give away my deceit.

"What has brought you to my practice today?" I ask after finalizing the last three steps between us. I catch my eyeroll halfway over the dimness of my words. Anyone would swear I'm performing dental work on Beyoncé for how much my voice is juddering.

"I have a toothache on my lower left molar," Hugo mumbles, his words low and croaky.

And just like that, the professional obligation to my patient overtakes my nerves.

The butterflies impinging my stomach settle when I notice beading of sweat glistening on Hugo's forehead. He appears even more rattled than me. After switching on the dental operatory light above my head, I take a seat on my swivel chair and roll in close to Hugo's side. He remains as quiet as a church mouse as I adjust the height of the dental chair, but his lips tug into a seductive grin when I clamp a drool cloth around his neck and hand him a pair of protective glasses.

His cheeky smile is wiped off his face when I gather a dental mirror and probe from the sterilized stainless tray at my side. "Open up," I instruct when I spot his clamped-shut mouth.

Through quivering lips, he does as instructed. Leaning over, I glance into his wide-open mouth. My lips purse. For someone who *loves* sweets and *hates* dentists, his teeth are beautiful.

He must be a regular flosser.

After a deep exploration of his mouth, I fail to locate anything that would cause him concern. There are no cavities or shadows that allude to an internal problem. His mouth is clear of any signs of an abscess, and his gums appear healthy.

Perhaps it's a sinus issue?

More times than not, some dental pain is associated with severe sinus infections.

"I can't see anything pointing to a reason why you're experiencing pain. Can you explain what the pain feels like?" I ask, mumbling through my facemask. After placing my probing tools back onto the tray, I yank down my mask. "Sometimes sinus infections can cause—"

My words stop, halted by a delicious pair of cinnamon-flavored lips. After licking the seam of my O-formed lips, Hugo's tongue dips inside to explore every inch with more vigor than my cavity search of his mouth. His tongue dances with mine in a toe-curling kiss that renders me breathless. He kisses the living hell out of me, bestowing me with a kiss that makes every other kiss I've experienced pale in comparison.

He holds nothing back, and neither do I.

I've wanted this and so much more the past week, but no matter how many corny one-liners, seductive poses, or inappropriate teases I did, nothing could deter Hugo from his resolve to give me time to process my failed relationship with Marvin.

In all honesty, at the start, I was confused about my ease of leaving a relationship without feeling a morsel of remorse, but after my deep and meaningful in my car with Mrs. Marshall, any doubts festering in my mind vanished. The facts were as clear as the sun shining in the sky. I never loved Marvin. I've always loved Hugo—even after years of absence and more tears than I can count.

A minute, an hour, or a week of deliberation will never change that fact.

Hugo is my one and only true love.

When Hugo pulls his sinful lips away from mine, my head is dizzy, stuck in a crazy blur of lust and devotion. His eyes dart between mine before his kiss-swollen lips curve high in the corners. After running his index finger over my tingling mouth, he stands from the dental chair and moves to the middle of the room. I watch him, more stunned than ever. I am shocked he can function so normally after a mind-hazing kiss. I can barely breathe, let alone walk.

"You coming?" he asks after grasping the handle of the door separating my office from the treatment area.

Nodding, I slip off the stool and step toward him. The shake of my knees increases with every stride I take as does the grin on Hugo's face. Once I'm standing in front of him, he runs the back of his fingers down my cheeks before swinging open the door. My heart leaps out of my chest and tears prick my eyes when a splendid scene unfolds before me. Joel is standing in the doorway, swamped by a giant bunch of long-stemmed red roses he's holding. His usually unmanageable hair has been wrangled into glossy curls, and he's wearing a pair of dark blue trousers and a buttoned-up shirt. He looks adorably cute and grownup all at the same time.

The rest of my office has vase upon vase of long-stemmed roses in every color you could imagine—pink, blue, yellow, white. It is like a rainbow of color, and it smells divine, overpowering the ghastly dentist smell I hate.

The tears welling in my eyes escape when Hugo kneels on one knee in front of me before he gently grasps my left hand. The glistening of moisture in his eyes gathers my attention, but the admiration beaming out of them secures my utmost devotion.

"The biggest mistake I ever made was letting you walk away the first time, but the past cannot be changed, forgotten, edited, or erased... it can only be accepted. I've learned from my mistakes, and I refuse to let them happen again. I never want to be away from you again. Not a second, not a minute, not a single day. This ring is a symbol of my promise to you. A vow that I'll always be there, standing by your side, supporting you, loving you, and cherishing every single inch of you until the end of time. I can't change the past, but I can shape my future. I want to shape it with you, Ava. My very existence begins and ends with you. Will you do me the honor of becoming my wife?" He cracks open a red heart-shaped box to showcase the beautiful dusty pink diamond ring nestled inside.

I run my hands over my tear-drenched cheeks before nodding. I don't need time to formulate a response or an objection or to evaluate his proposal. All I need is him.

Smiling, Hugo places the ring on my finger then stands from

his crouched position as Belinda captures the entire precious moment with her phone. Joel squeals excitedly before dumping the roses onto the floor and encircling his arms around mine and Hugo's thighs. His elated cheers dull into a hum when Hugo seals his plump lips over mine, finalizing the most romantic proposal of all time with an even more heartfelt kiss.

"Thank you so much for watching Joel," I say while wrapping my arms around Belinda's shoulders.

After Hugo proposed, he took Belinda, Joel, and me to a fancy restaurant in the middle of New York City. I won't lie. When I saw how much they were charging for a regular glass of wine, I choked on my spit. Then panic set in. If a standard glass of wine cost hundreds of dollars, how much would a sparkling glass of water set me back? It was only when Hugo assured me we were paying wholesale prices as he knew the owner did my flipping stomach settle and excitement took over.

As we exited the elegant restaurant, I spotted two limousines at the curb. Hugo explained that one was to take Belinda and Joel home and the other was for us. "Our night of celebrating is only just beginning," he muttered in my ear after bidding farewell to Belinda and Joel.

Memories of our first night we went out dancing at the club flooded my mind when Hugo gathered me under the crook of his arm and dashed to the black stretch limousine. Those memories turned into real-life flashbacks when the limousine pulled onto the curb at the exact club he originally took me to.

Even though it was over five years ago, the vibe at the club was as exciting as it was the first time we visited it. It was a wild mix of sex and seduction, but even more intoxicating than the thumping club was the boyish grin on Hugo's face. It never once waned, not even with us being bumped and elbowed as we danced for hours.

Tonight was the most carefree I've been in the past five years.

My clipped wings grew back, and I was once again free to fly.

It was perfect.

"You're welcome, sweetie," Belinda replies while returning my embrace. "I'm just sorry I didn't get Joel settled for you so you could enjoy the rest of your night in peace." Her lips purse as a heavy set of lines indents her forehead. "I think I'll adhere to your advice about lowering his sugar intake after dinner. That boy goes a little bit crazy when the clock strikes eight."

I laugh while stepping to my front door to open it for her. Crazy is an understatement for Joel's antics when he stays up too late. Instead of his tiredness wearing him down, it seems to heighten his excitement.

"I'll see you Monday?"

Belinda nods before slipping out the door. "Have fun."

After ensuring she enters her car and exits my driveway safely, I amble down the hall. My brisk strides slow when I hear Hugo trying to whisper. When I reach Joel's room, I lean against the wall and prick my ears.

"So, if you hear Mommy calling out, don't worry, I've got her covered," Hugo whispers, his tone self-assured with a dash of cheekiness.

Interested in what their conversation is about, I sneakily peer into Joel's room. His brows are furrowed together tightly as he looks at his dad with confusion in his eyes.

After a beat, he cautiously nods.

"Do we have a deal?" Hugo asks while peering into Joel's anxious eyes.

"Yep," Joel replies, his words muffled by a big yawn.

"Alright, but let's go over it one more time just to make sure you have the details right."

Joel nods. "If I stay in bed *all* night, I get five dollars."

My brows arch high at the same time a dash of euphoria pumps into my veins.

"Uh-huh," Hugo mutters softly.

I lean deeper into the hallway when Hugo slants his head to the side and glances out Joel's door to check that the coast is clear. Once his focus returns to Joel, I peer back around the door.

"And?"

Joel rubs his droopy eyes. "And if I ask Mommy to make pancakes in the morning, I get ten dollars," he confirms after resting his head on his pillow.

"That's right," Hugo praises before standing from his bed to tuck him in. "That's called a bonus. An incentive for a job well done."

"I like a boganus," Joel replies, his lips quirking.

I laugh quietly over his mispronunciation of the word.

Once Joel is tucked in tight, Hugo places a kiss on his forehead, switches on his night light then heads for the door. I spin on my heels and sprint down the hallway, vainly pretending I wasn't eavesdropping on their private conversation.

When Hugo spots my contemptuous face, his long strides down the hall slow. His head angles to the side and his brow curves high. "You heard that, didn't you?"

"No." I overdramatize the short word before nodding. I've never been good at deceit.

Hugo cockily winks, not the slightest bit concerned I heard

him bribing our son to stay in his room. I'm not shocked he devised a tactic for us to have uninterrupted adult time. I'm just astonished I didn't think of it first. It would have been helpful when I was attempting to seduce Hugo last week. At times, my ploys seemed to be working until we were interrupted by the patter of little feet.

With a crass grin, Hugo recommences his original journey.

I quirk my lips. "Sounded like someone was planning on sleeping over?" I try to keep the excitement out of my voice. My attempts are fruitless.

"No," he replies, shaking his head.

My bottom lip drops into a pout at the same time a pathetic whimper ripples through my lips.

My fret is unwarranted. "Neither of us are going to get any sleep, so I can't really call it a sleepover."

My eyes drift between the beast of a man prowling toward me and my dowdy work attire-covered body. Hugo is dressed in a well-fitted black suit with a light gray pinstriped dress shirt. His jacket has been removed and slung over the rock-hard couch he slept on weeks ago, and the sleeves of his shirt have been rolled up to the elbows. Even with every inch of his alluring torso covered, I can't miss the mouth-watering ridges of his chiseled abs and pecs as he prowls toward me like a lion on the hunt.

My brows furrow when I take in my clothing selection. I'm wearing a black pleated pencil skirt with sheer black stockings and a white blouse with decorative cuffs. My waist-length jacket has been hung on the coat rack in the entryway along with my heavy wool coat.

I'll be the first to admit, I'm panicked. I didn't thoroughly evaluate all avenues when I attempted to seduce Hugo last week. My brain was too overwhelmed with unbridled horniness to think rationally. Now, while watching the muscles in his thighs flex as he struts toward me, I realize I should have given it a little more thought.

In both good and bad ways, I'm not the Ava Westcott Hugo remembers from five years ago. I've changed. Some things have improved, like the strength of my backbone and my sense of self-worth. Others, mainly my body... not so much.

"I've changed," I warn, slowing Hugo's fast pace. "My body is no longer that tight twenty-four-year-old body you're used to seeing."

I straighten my slumped posture when his eyes run the length of my figure from the tips of my toes to the top of my head. He studies every inch in great depth. When his eyes return to my face, my breath hitches. His gaze is uninhibited and brimming with lust. It quickens my pulse, but not enough for me to forget my objectives.

"My boobs hang a little lower, and my stomach isn't as flat as it used to be," I advise him, wanting to ensure he fully comprehends my warning. I've given birth—no woman's body bounces back to its original perkiness after that.

After arching his brow, Hugo glares at me. "Insult yourself one more time, Ava, and your ass will be as colorful as my tattoos by the time I'm done with you."

My breathing pattern quickens as my lady garden throbs. I stand frozen, openmouthed, and bristling with excitement.

When Hugo spots my eagerness, a beguiling grin etches on his sinful lips. "I need to devise a new punishment for you. You like spanking too much for it to be classed as a reprimand."

Blood surges to my pussy when he bands his arm around my waist and pulls me in close. My pussy grows wet when I feel what his avid inspection of my body has done to him. He's thick, hard, and rip-roaring ready to go.

"Your body incited that fully clothed." He rocks his hips

upward so the crown of his cock rubs my throbbing pussy. "Imagine what seeing you naked will instigate."

Leaning in, he presses a kiss to the side of my mouth before lowering his dedication to my neck. His teeth sink into the sensitive skin above my collarbone before his tongue soothes the sting. I slant my head to the side, giving him full access to my neck. Soft, provocative moans spill from my lips with every gentle nib and suck he does.

After gripping the back of my thighs, he encourages my legs to wrap around his waist. A breathless pant erupts from my lips when his thick cock brushes against my sensitive clit.

After sealing his lips over mine, he walks us to my room at the end of the hall. By the time we make it down the hall, fumbling with each other's clothes on the way, any doubts festering my mind have vanished. If the desire in his eyes isn't enough to assure me he's attracted to me, the thickness of his cock is a sure-fire indication.

When he places me down onto my feet, a grunt leaves his parted lips. On the short walk, he nimbly undid all the buttons on my blouse, which exposed my Carmina black and red push-up bra. Growling, he tugs down my bra's cup before he sucks my budded nipple into his mouth. Desire floods my nether regions when his teeth graze over the sensitive bud as my hands shoot up to weave through his hair. I secure his wicked mouth to my breast that's been aching for his attention for nearly five years.

While keeping my nipple in his mouth, Hugo wraps one arm around my waist then steps back until the duvet on my bed brushes my stocking-covered legs. His stealth moves cause my blouse to slip off my shoulders and plunge to the floor around our feet.

After releasing my nipple from his mouth with a pop, he stares at me with a heavy-lidded gaze. After a cheeky smirk, he pushes my shoulder, sending me toppling onto the bed. My hair fluffs out as a breathy huff escapes my lips, but any laughter preparing to spill from my mouth are hindered in my throat when Hugo removes his dress shirt before fisting his undershirt and yanking it over his head.

I don't know what it is, but there's nothing sexier than the way men remove their shirts.

I take that back.

There's nothing sexier than Hugo biting on the corner of his lip as his eyes rake my half-dressed body. His gaze is predatory, and it sets my pulse racing.

I assess him with as much vigor as he's instilled in me when he undoes his belt and lowers the zipper in his trousers. Even covered by an immense number of colorful tattoos, I can't miss his chiseled abs, rock-hard pecs, and drool-worthy V muscle. Every inch of him is hard. And by every inch, I mean every goddamn rock-hard inch.

While raising my eyes from his thick, glorious cock he's just freed from his trousers, I lick my lips. My knees curve inward in the hope of settling the throb between my legs from the panty-wetting visual in front of me.

Hugo's seductive grin enlarges when he places his knee between my thighs, denying me the ability to ease the tingle that may have me falling into ecstasy before he's even touched me. He stares at me with wild eyes while undoing my skirt's fastener. His eyes absorb my thrusting chest as he pulls down the zipper on my skirt. He drinks in every inch of my body as he glides my skirt down my waist and hips. His lusty gaze compels a peppering of goosebumps to form on my skin and for wetness to saturate the area between my legs.

"Beautiful Ava, every inch of you is perfect," he praises, his words deep and tempting.

A rush of heat forms on my cheeks nearly as quickly as an inane smile stretches across my face.

Hugo hisses when my skirt glides past the matching garter and lace-topped stockings I'm wearing.

"Fuckin' hell," he mutters under his breath.

When his eyes rocket to mine, I bite my lower lip. His gaze is full of desire, and it sends my libido to an all-time high.

"I wanted to be prepared for your return," I inform him, my tone a low purr that shamefully exposes my pleasure about the approving look beaming from his eyes. "Since I didn't know when that would be, I bought a week's worth of supplies. This is day one of my seven-day lingerie selection I prepared for you."

The desire pumping into my veins thickens my blood when a seductive growl emits from his lips. "If I'd known you were wearing these the entire time we were dancing, we wouldn't have made it past the club's storeroom."

I throw my head back and gasp when he flicks the suspender. It slaps my skin with a pleasurable jolt of pain. The pounding of my clit matches the hammering of my heart from his playful tease.

"Nothing's changed," Hugo murmurs in a low, deep tone. "Not a single fucking thing."

I call out when he slips my panties to the side and runs his tongue along the seam of my pussy in a slow, tantalizing motion. Although shocked he hasn't removed my panties, I'm also happy. He did the exact same thing the first time we slept together—the night we conceived Joel.

When his tongue delves inside my quivering labia, I fist the duvet and arch my back. He tongue-fucks me with as much eagerness as his cock usually instills when he fucks me. The battle to keep my erotic squeals to a bare minimum ramp up when he devours my pussy like a man who's never been fed. It's a mind-hazing blur of licks, sucks, and bites that have my orgasm building at a rapid pace.

When he slides his index finger into my throbbing pussy, adding another mind-blurring element to the already overstimulating mix, my teeth gnaw on the side of my palm. I battle to hold in my cries of pleasure because the last thing I want is another interruption.

Before I have the chance to warn Hugo of its arrival, a climax shreds through my body, hard and fast. An ear-piercing scream erupts from my lips as my body quakes. As my pussy trembles around his finger, my cries switch to a low, long moan. I ride the intense wave that feels like it will never end while moaning on repeat.

"Please. Oh god. Please. I."

Constructing complete sentences is above my caliber at the moment. I can barely breathe, let alone formulate a response for the excitement coursing through my veins. It overheats my body with feverish heat and makes me a sticky, sweaty mess.

Hugo continues to devour me in a torrent of greedy lashes and gentle nips, not the slightest bit impeded by the sudden arrival of my orgasm. He holds down my bucking hips when the intensity of my climax becomes too much for me to bear—too overwhelming.

"I want every drop, Ava," he mutters against my trembling lips, sparking even more ardor to surge through my body. "Every sweet drop of your cum belongs to me."

Like it could get any stronger, my climax gains momentum. I snag the pillow at my side and throw it over my head. I try to suffocate the erotic screams shredding from my mouth as a second climax claims my body. My efforts are woeful. I've never experienced an orgasm with this much intensity, let alone two so close together. Not once. Not ever.

I've only just returned from the clouds when Hugo places one last lash on my clit before he rises from his kneeled position at the end of the bed. When the room falls into silence, I flutter open my eyes before removing the pillow from my flushed face. My excited breathing lowers to a pant when I catch sight of Hugo's hard, thick cock fisted in his hand.

With his eyes arrested on my shimmering bare mound, he runs his hand down his engorged length to the tip before he glides it back to the base. His cock is thick, hard, and undoubtedly beautiful. I can't wait to be claimed by it—again.

A new type of anticipation courses through my veins when I see the precum beading on his knob. After scampering off the bed and falling to my knees, I wrap my hand around the base of his fat cock and lick off the drop of excitement from his crown.

A groan tears from Hugo's throat as his knees buckle. After weaving his fingers through my hair, he guides my pace. The sting of pain from his tugs spurs on my pursuit to unravel him as he just unraveled me. I lap him up, drinking in every inch of him—his seductive scent, the warm silkiness of his glorious cock, and his delicious taste. *God, I've missed his taste.*

I draw him in deep, working hard to untangle him, wanting him to lose all rational thoughts. The corners of my mouth burn as they stretch to accommodate his girth, but nothing can snuff my enthusiasm. I glide my moist lips over the smooth crest of his cock, then down his shaft with palpable eagerness. My tongue flicks and teases his knob while gathering up every drop of his enjoyment. My cheeks hollow, revealing my keenness to suck him dry.

"Slow down, babe, I don't want to come yet," Hugo demands, his words throaty. "We've got all night."

I increase my pace, loving that I can push him to the brink as quickly as he can me. While staring up at him, past the muscles of his impeccable six-pack, I take him to the very back of my throat. My hankering eyes advise him that I have no intention of slowing down until I've swallowed every drop of his cum, not to mention my gag when I try to swallow him whole.

A cocky grin carves on Hugo's mouth when he spots the determination in my eyes. "Be careful what you wish for, babe," he mutters before he rolls his hips forward, plunging more of his cock inside my mouth.

Before I have time to prepare my throat, hot, thick cum spurts out of his silky-smooth crown. He drenches my mouth with his magnificent goodness while grunting like a wild animal. I moan before vigorously swallowing. I make sure every bit of his cum is consumed. I don't want to waste a single drop.

The throb in my pussy intensifies when the hardness of his cock doesn't lessen any, even with every drop of his cum expelled. If anything, it gets thicker, more veined.

I guide his still rigid cock out of my mouth before staring up at him wide-eyed and highly aroused. Smiling, he bands his arms around my waist and places me back onto the bed. His eyes absorb my naked, feverish skin as he glides my panties down my legs. When my panties are dumped to the side, my thigh muscles sweep open to accommodate his large frame kneeling between them.

My body tenses when the crown of his cock hovers over my drenched pussy. He stares into my eyes as he sheaths me one glorious inch at a time. I'm so wet, he can slide in without too much hindrance. When he finalizes the last three inches, my breathing stills, and a nib of pain rockets through my body. I'm so full, taken, and very much overwhelmed that tears prick my eyes and dribble down my face before I can stop them.

Upon spotting my tears, Hugo intakes a quick, sharp breath. "Babe—"

"I'm fine." My voice is husky, strangled by an upwelling of emotions. "I'm more than fine. Please don't take my tears the wrong way. They're sentimental tears, not ones of pain. I'm just overwhelmed that you're here, with me, doing this."

He bounces his concerned eyes between mine, seeking any untruth in them. The strain hampering his gorgeous face relaxes when he sees the candor spoken by my eyes. Every word I spoke was the truth. I can't believe he's here, in my bed, in my home, and I'm not dreaming.

I may have pinched myself earlier just to make sure.

"I'm not going anywhere, Ava. Never again," he assures me when he intuits what caused my sobs.

Fresh tears well in my eyes when he kisses away the ones that fell down my heated cheeks. Once every teardrop has been lapped up, he seals his mouth over mine and kisses me senseless. He expresses his promise with actions instead of words, and I believe every single one he hands me.

By the time he pulls back, my heart has as much fluid surging through it as my lady garden. I'm drenched, but Hugo still patiently waits for my body to adjust to his sheer girth while also ensuring no more tears sneakily spill from my eyes.

Only once I nod, giving him permission to move, does he slowly withdraw his cock.

My pussy ripples around him, greedily trying to hold him inside. It doesn't care about the bite of pain shooting through it, all it cares about is being consumed by him.

"Fuck, you feel so good, Ava. Tight, wet," he mutters, his eyes burning into mine. "You feel even better than I remember."

His words have me on the brink of another mind-hazing orgasm. I just need a little more to push me over the edge. Reading my body's desires without a word needing to seep from my lips, he rocks into me harder. He pumps in and out of me on repeat until I'm on the verge of screaming his name, then he tilts my hips and wraps my legs around his sweat-slicked waist.

A husky moan rumbles through my lips when his V muscle grinds my pulsating clit with every stroke he inflicts. Our bodies mold together and move in sync like two pieces of a puzzle, perfectly matched for one another.

Over time, my skin dampens with sweat, and my body overheats, but nothing can weaken the excitement coursing through me. I've dreamed of days like this. Hell, I prayed for days like this, and now, it is coming true.

I run my nails down Hugo's sweat-slicked back before manhandling his perfect ass. Just like every other part of his body, it's gotten better with age. His body moves with such ease, showcasing how in tune he is with himself. He's a sexual creature who holds nothing back as he possesses and claims every inch of me, both inside and out.

The tightening of my coil strengthens with each precise stroke he inflicts. He's like a machine, designed to unravel me. The room is thick with humidity, and the smell of sweat and sex filters through my nose as his body guides me to a core-shattering climax. His name tears from my throat, and goosebumps prickle my skin as my orgasm hits fruition. I claw at his back as I fight through a blinding scattering of stars forming before my eyes.

A carnal groan sounds from Hugo's parted lips when my pussy squeezes his cock, greedily begging for his hot cum. My earth-shattering orgasm sets him off. He sheaths me to the very root of his cock before he stills. I moan when hot, violent cum spurts from his cock like lava exploding from an active volcano. Unlike me, he keeps his cries of ecstasy to a bare minimum. Although from the strained look on his face and the way his veins are bulging, it's a hard-fought battle.

When Hugo withdraws his still-throbbing cock several long shudders later, I snuggle into my pillow, beyond exhausted and eagerly anticipating a few hours of sleep. Hugo arches his brow and peers into my sleepy eyes. "No sleep, babe. I'm not even half done with you yet."

A squeal emits from my lips when he flips me over and yanks my ass into the air. Dynamite explodes in my womb when he rubs his cum into the cleft of my pussy with his hand. He coats me with his slickness to lessen any friction before he slides his *still* rock-hard cock inside me.

Shocked, I crank my neck and peer back at him, both shocked and incredibly aroused by his determination. Any thoughts on catching a few hours of sleep turn into a forgotten memory when the crack of his hand spreads a fiery heat across my butt cheek. His spank was the perfect final act to confirm our fire-sparking reunion.

TWENTY-SIX
HUGO

My heart pounds my ribs as my lungs fight for air. I feel like I'm dying, suffocated by the heaviness weighing down my chest. The face of a monster is before me, snickering as he seeks his revenge. He's evening the score between us. I took his son. Now, he's taking mine.

Joel's big blue eyes stare at me, pleading for me to save him from the devil holding a knife to his throat. Even with tears flooding his eyes and his body uncontrollably shaking, he maintains a brave front with the hope of appeasing the fear of his mother standing beside me.

"It's okay, sweetheart, Daddy will save you," Ava stutters through the tears streaming down her pale face.

When Joel is jerked backward, I pull through the heaviness asphyxiating me with fear to lunge for him. I outstretch my arms, frantically trying to reach him, but no matter how hard I fight, no matter how far I stretch, I can't reach him.

Col is too quick.

"No!" My back arches as a tormented scream shreds from my

throat. "Please, don't hurt my son." I plead as Col drags Joel through a sea of black, soulless shadows. "I'll do anything you want, just don't hurt my son."

I thrash against a heaviness entangled around my legs, fighting to be released from their stranglehold.

I *need* to save my son.

I *must* save my son.

I suck in a quick blast of air, filling my lungs with oxygen as I race toward Joel. The ice-cold fear clutching my chest impedes my usually lengthy strides. My thighs burn as I chase the white Range Rover that has an unconscious Joel in the back seat. My lungs are heaving, and my entire body is covered in a dense layer of sweat, but I don't give up.

I'll never give up.

Confusion envelops me when I race past distinguishable land-marks in Ravenshoe—Harlow's bakery, the office building where Izzy worked, and the Dungeon nightclub flash by as I sprint down the narrowing street.

The heaviness on my chest increases when the Range Rover vanishes before my eyes, not leaving a trace of its existence.

"Joel!" I shout, shocked.

As I spin around in a circle on Tivot street, I run my hand through my hair. My brows furrow when a volley of confusion steamrolls into me. Only now do I realize Joel was snatched from his bed in Rochdale, not Ravenshoe.

My bewilderment intensifies when an image of a blond-haired man resuscitating another surfaces before me. I dart my wild eyes up and down the street, seeking assistance. Surprisingly, the usually packed sidewalks of Ravenshoe are empty. Not a soul is in sight.

I return my focus to the two men in the middle of the street when the blond man furiously pumps on the chest of the unconscious man sprawled on the ground.

"Come on, Hugo," he commands before thumping the unconscious man's chest with his enclosed fist.

When I shift on my feet and slant my head to the side, unsure exactly how I can aid them, the air is forcefully removed from my lungs when I discover who the blond man is resuscitating.

It's me.

"Don't give up! Do you hear me? You're *not* allowed to die!" screams the resuscitator.

I step around the scene, wanting to see the face of the man saving me. I don't recall the events after I was shot. All I remember is landing on my backside with a sickening thud and waking up to the devastated face of Izzy. Everything in the preceding seven hours was a complete blur.

When I peer down at my rescuer, my pupils dilate to the size of dinner plates. "Blondie?"

I crouch down on the ground, unable to comprehend what I'm seeing.

The son of the man who ruined my life is saving my life.

What the fuck?

As sirens approach, the buildings surrounding me distort before I'm suddenly swamped by eerie blackness. It's so dark not even a star in the sky can be seen.

My head cranks to the side when a familiar voice screams through the darkness. "Hugo, wake up!"

I stand from my position and walk toward the voice. "Ava?"

I shelter my eyes when a blinding light streams through the darkness.

"Wake up!" Ava screams again.

I jerk awake, gasping for air. My massively dilated eyes shift around the unfamiliar room as I suck in big breaths. It takes several moments for me to realize where I am. I'm not in my apartment, my childhood home, or Regan's penthouse. I'm in the guest room of Jorgie's home. Ava's bedroom.

Gratitude envelops me when I discover the bed is empty. Catching sight of the alarm clock on the bedside table, I see it is a little after seven. Ava and Joel will most likely be in the kitchen getting ready to start their day.

I kick out my legs, breaking free of the sheets wrapped around me before I run a trembling hand over my head. My body is cool from the combination of sweat and the remnants of my nightmare still clinging to me.

A new type of fear clutches my heart when my surveillance of the room stumbles upon Ava crouched on the floor halfway across the room. Her hand is covering her mouth, and fresh tears are staining her cheeks.

"*Ava.*"

I scramble off the bed and kneel in front of her. Grief and despair smack into me when I see the terrified haze clouding her beautiful eyes.

"Did I hurt you?" I ask, panicked as my eyes rake every inch of her, seeking any injuries from the brutality I can display in my dreams.

Ava shakes her head. "No," she whispers, her voice hoarse. "I remembered what Dr. Avery told me about ensuring I'm at a safe distance before waking you."

I peer into her eyes, seeking any untruth in them.

I inwardly sigh when nothing but honesty reflects back at me. After wrapping my arms around her quivering shoulders, I slump onto my bottom and lean my back against the bed. The pain twinging my heart weakens when Ava presses her cheek onto the sweat-drenched skin on my chest. She nuzzles in close, not the slightest bit concerned about the dampness. Her sobs are quiet. So discreet, if her tears weren't adding to the wetness on my chest, I wouldn't be aware she's crying.

I gather her hair off her cheeks and lift her tear-stained face to me. Her lips twitch, itching to speak, but no words spill from her mouth. I already know what she's going to ask without her needing to speak. Ava's eyes have always been expressive, revealing way more than her mouth ever could. Today is no different. But even if I couldn't read her eyes, she knows me well, better than anyone. She would have determined what my nightmare was about the instant she heard my tormented screams begging for Col not to hurt Joel.

My voice shakes as I begin to speak. "I tried, Ava. I swear to you, I tried every legal avenue available. When that failed, I took matters into my own hands. I couldn't let him get away with it. He killed Jorgie and Malcolm but was free to live his life how he saw fit. He didn't suffer at all. I'd already seen Gemma endure the injustice of the courts. I wasn't going to let the same thing happen to Jorgie."

Ava's moisture-swamped eyes stare into mine, but she doesn't speak. She doesn't need to. The understanding in her eyes is all I need to see to ease my concern about revealing a secret only a handful of people know.

"I wanted him dead. I wanted him to suffer the way Jorgie suffered. The way *we* suffered." I peer into her forgiving eyes as my chest rises and falls with every inhalation I take. "I wanted to make him pay."

Ava takes a quick breath, but she remains as quiet as a church mouse as I share my story...

I load .38 caliber bullets into the magazine of my gun before clicking it into the chamber. After sliding across the safety mechanism, I house my gun into the back of my jeans, swing open my truck door, and walk toward the compound I've been surveying the past two weeks. I have one plan on my mind—exact revenge on the man responsible for killing my sister and unborn nephew.

I tried the legal channels. I spoke to the DA, the detectives assigned to Jorgie's case, and I even pleaded with the media.

No one listened.

Jorgie's killer was a free man, exonerated of all charges.

That's about to change.

Calm settles over me as I jog toward the warehouse surrounded by a six-foot steel wire fence. A Rottweiler charges out of a kennel at the back of the compound, barking and growling. His fang-baring snarl only lasts as long as it takes for me to throw a juicy bone over the fence. He gnaws on the half-frozen turkey leg as I cut a hole in the mesh with a pair of bolt cutters.

After returning the bolt cutters to my duffle bag, I conceal it in a bush at my side then climb through the hole. When I enter the unsecured grounds at the edge of the warehouse, I take a sharp left. I've witnessed the same routine every day the past two weeks at this compound. Three men enter the complex at nine, two guards and one asset—my target.

One armed man stands at the front entrance of the warehouse while the other follows the asset inside. Within ten minutes of entering, the second armed guard cranks open a door on the left-hand side of building, his nicotine habit too strong for him to overcome the desire for a quick hit.

Within twenty minutes of arriving, my target leaves the warehouse flanked by the two guards and carrying a black briefcase in each hand. Their routine hasn't altered the past two weeks I've been watching them.

Their complacency is about to cost them dearly.

When I reach the edge of the warehouse, I slow my steps, ensuring my heavy stomps don't cause the gravel under my feet to crunch. I lean my back against the sun-heated outer wall of the warehouse, vying for a prime opportunity to react.

When the door next to me cracks open not even five minutes later, I pounce. Grabbing the handle, I yank the metal door forward before slamming it back with brutal force. A grunted noise echoes in the quiet, closely followed by a hard thud.

Gliding my hand into the back of my jeans, I retrieve my revolver before peering around the door. A man easily six feet tall lays sprawled on the dirty concrete floor. A nasty bump is forming on his forehead, his eyes are closed, and his half-lit cigarette is dangling from his mouth.

As I crouch down to remove the two semi-automatic weapons strapped to his hip and a knife wrapped around his thigh, my eyes scan the inside of the warehouse. After housing his Glock and Bulpap into the back of my jeans, I brace my gun in front of my body and move slowly through the warehouse.

The smell of freshly printed Benjamin Franklins filters through my nose the closer I amble to an office on my right. Years of sniper training ensure my fast pace goes undetected. I push open a heavily weighted wooden door and sweep my eyes over the room. Roberto's suit-covered back faces me as he piles bundles of money from a black safe bolted to the floor into an open suitcase sitting on a polished wooden desk.

"Give me another five minutes, and I'll be ready to go," Roberto instructs when he senses my presence.

I aim the barrel of my gun at the back of his head before saying, "How about we leave now."

He freezes. "Do you have any idea who you're robbing? Leave now, and this matter will remain between us."

"I'm not here for your money. The only asset I want to secure is you."

As I stare at the flashing red light in the corner of the room,

Roberto spins on his heels, his movements steady and alert. A V grooves between his brow as his rich brown eyes scan my face. His expression remains static until he registers the similarities between Jorgie and me—same nose, same eyes, same smile. No one could deny we were siblings.

Roberto's throat works hard to swallow before his lips spasm, preparing to speak.

"Move." I nudge my head to the door, not giving him the chance to protest.

He had his chance to speak up when he was arrested at the scene of Jorgie's accident for driving under the influence. If he'd pled guilty, I wouldn't be standing before him.

I follow him out of the warehouse with the butt of my gun aimed at a patch of gray in his dark, clipped hair. When we exit the frosted glass door at the front of the compound, the armed guard spins around, clearly shocked by Roberto's early arrival.

When he notices me standing behind Roberto with a gun pointed at his head, his hand slips into his suit jacket, no doubt to reach the gun he has holstered on his waist.

"Roberto will be dead before you remove your gun," I warn, my words rough like they were dragged through a whole heap of gravel before spilling from my lips.

The guard's dark eyes shift between Roberto and me. His gaze is vehement, fueling my agitation.

"Unless you want splatters of Roberto's brain on your fancy suit, unclip the Seven Eagle strapped to your hip, remove the bullets, and throw it into the bush," I instruct before motioning my head to the thick bush at our side.

Other than his eyelids twitching, the guard remains motionless, refusing to follow my demand. He only does as solicited when I squeeze in the trigger. Sweat rolls down the nape of Roberto's neck as he shakes in fear. Through gritted teeth, his protective detail removes the gun holstered to his hip and empties the magazine chamber.

"Now the magnum strapped to your ankle," I demand while glaring into his thinly slitted eyes when he dumps his first gun into the prickly bush.

His lips set into a hard line before he bobs down to remove the magnum strapped to his left ankle. After dumping the bullets from the barrel of the .44, he throws it into the bush and pivots around to face me. "You're a dead man walking," he snarls, his tone vicious.

I snicker before pushing the barrel of my gun deeper into Roberto's skull. I use its pinch to direct him to my truck parked at the side of the compound. The guard's threat causes me no concern. I'm already dead. An empty, soulless man who has no chance of emerging from the hell I'm living in.

That is why I didn't bother covering my face. I want everyone to know I'm the man who made Roberto Petretti pay his repentance.

"Do it." Roberto glares at me over the gun's barrel pointed at his head. "Do it already! I killed your sister! I ran her down!"

I slam the butt of my gun into his left temple with vicious force. His head ricochets to the side, and a trickle of blood streams down his face, pooling at his bound feet.

"Shut the fuck up." My angry words reverberate around the desolate basement in Jorgie's house.

In the haste of my decision, I didn't properly evaluate what I was planning to do once I secured Roberto from the Petretti compound. I acted on impulse, knowing it may have been the only viable time I could secure him. Rumors were running rife in our hometown that Col was moving his underground fighting circuit to a new location. I couldn't run the risk of losing my tail on Roberto.

I also couldn't stand the thought of another day of injustice rolling by. Needing a place free of any encumbrance, I brought him to Jorgie's house. Roberto has been bound to the water boiler in her basement for the past two hours. I only left him twenty minutes ago to call Ava.

When Roberto's head returns front and center, he smiles a blood-tainted grin, seemingly pleased to have sparked a reaction out of me. He spent the majority of the last two hours goading me, not caring that his very existence is balancing precariously on the edge of a steep cliff. Just from his taunts, I can tell he has chosen death by suicide, but instead of using a gun as his weapon of choice, he's using me.

I push a gag into his mouth, not just to stop his callous words but to also ease the pain shredding my heart, crippling me with grief. Snubbing the shake of my hands, I squash the barrel of my gun against the skin between his eyes. Unable to speak through the gag, his eyes beg for me to issue the punishment the courts failed to decree. To free him from his miserable existence.

I push the barrel in closer, pinching the wrinkled skin on his forehead. When I lower my finger to the trigger, Roberto closes his eyes, accepting his fate with a sense of dignity.

After gritting my teeth, I squeeze the trigger.

Blood roars in my ears when a metal click bellows over the rampant beat of my heart.

Seconds felt like hours as I stare at Roberto, shocked I claimed another man's life.

My shock doesn't last long.

I take a step backward, exasperated when Roberto's eyes flutter open.

I pulled the trigger.

He should be dead.

It is only when I sense a presence at my side do I realize the clicking heard wasn't my gun firing. It was the old bolts clanking together in Jorgie's basement door.

My eyes swing to the side of the room, closely followed by my gun. Isaac stands at the entrance of the basement. He's wearing his standard suit, accentuated with a murderous glare. His stance is firm, not the slightest bit concerned about having a pistol pointed at his chest.

One slip of my finger, and he would be dead.

"You need to leave," I say before returning the barrel of my gun to Roberto. "This is between me and Roberto, not you."

"You're my family, Hugo. What happens to you affects me," Isaac responds, his deep timbre booming around the room.

My nostrils flare as I glare into the eyes of the man who killed my mom's spirit. He left a shell of a woman I no longer recognize. The man who tore her heart out of her chest, threw it onto the stained floor, and stomped on it.

The man who shattered her soul.

"He killed my family. He tore them apart."

"No," Isaac argues, his composure stern and unwavering. "He didn't kill your family, but you will if you don't leave now."

My neck cranks to the side faster than a missile being launched out of a jet. I stare into Isaac's eyes, unable to comprehend any of the words coming out of his mouth.

"The instant you took Roberto, you signed your family's death certificates. Trust me, Col will not stop hunting you until you have suffered the same loss as him," Isaac explains to my confused face.

My stomach lurches into my throat when I see the truth relayed by his frank eyes, but nothing can lessen the fury blackening my veins. "He deserves to die. He killed my sister. My nephew!" I roar, my veins bulging with every syllable I speak. "I want him to suffer!"

"He will suffer," Isaac declares, stepping closer to me. "I'll *make sure of it. I will take care of this." He stares into my eyes. "He won't get away with it. You have my word," he assures me. "There are two types of people in the world, Hugo. Healers and hurters." Before I can react, he snatches my wrist holding the gun, then says, "You're a healer. I am a hurter..."*

Ava remains cradled in my lap with her eyes flicking between mine, staring but not speaking. Although the stretch of silence passing between us is thick and somber, the unspoken words relayed by her beautiful eyes are the greatest ally in repairing the damage my foolhardy mistake made.

Even crammed with qualm, the glimmer her eyes get every time she looks at me hasn't dampened from my confession. They reveal she understands the reason I reacted the way I did. She empathizes with the pain I went through because it wasn't just parts of my soul that vanished the day Jorgie died. Ava's did as well.

TWENTY-SEVEN
AVA

I want to say I'm surprised by Hugo's confession, but I'm not. When news circulated about Roberto's disappearance, I suspected Hugo was involved in some way. Mr. Marshall had raised his sons to protect their mother and sisters. That notion didn't stop because Jorgie passed away. Even after her death, I knew Hugo would continue to defend her. I just hoped the justice system would issue Roberto's punishment so Hugo didn't have to. But once again, the legal system failed him.

Although I would have preferred that he seek justice in a legal manner, I can understand what he was going through all those years ago. He was riddled with so much grief, he was unable to form a rational decision. I still recall with crystal clear memory looking in Roberto's eyes when he was placed in the back of the police cruiser on the day of Jorgie's accident. Even with his eyes jammed with remorse and a gold cross hanging around my neck, I cursed him to death. I wanted him to suffer the way Jorgie did when she held my hand and cried because she couldn't feel Malcolm moving. I prayed for him to experience the pain that was shredding my heart, crippling me with devastation. So I understand what Hugo was going through because, at the time, I also wanted Roberto dead.

My opinion on the matter only changed when Joel was born. When I was looking down at his little face and big, worldly eyes, I realized it wouldn't matter what he did, no matter how heinous, he would always be my son, and I would always defend him.

It was in that instant I realized Roberto wasn't just the man who killed Jorgie, he was someone's son. His mother would have grieved his death as deeply as Mrs. Marshall grieved Jorgie's. No mother should go through the pain of losing a child, not even one who gave birth to a monster.

Hugo's eyes dance between mine as he removes my tears from my cheeks. Once they're cleared away, he locks his eyes with mine. "If I'd known my hasty decision would have the consequences it did, I would have evaluated it with more diligence. I would have taken the time to properly assess the repercussions of my decision." Guilt darkens his eyes. "But I was hurting too much. Losing Jorgie and Malcolm, then you... the pain was too great. It killed any chances of my grief-riddled brain forming a rational decision. Losing Jorgie gutted me, but losing you utterly destroyed me." His words come out gravelly and deep.

From the regret in his eyes, I have no doubt if he could take back every wrong he did, he would. *All of it.* Not just hurting me and missing out on the first four years of Joel's life. *Everything.* Even what happened to Roberto.

Hugo's sorrowful eyes peer into mine. "I wanted to punish Roberto, to issue the penalty the courts failed to administer." He exhales an uneven breath as his eyes flick between mine. "But when I peered into his eyes, all I could see were yours looking back at me."

I gulp in a jagged breath as my wide eyes dart between his, searching for the answer to the question my mouth is failing to ask.

"I got close. I held the gun to Roberto's head, and I pulled back the trigger, but no matter how strong the desire was to make him pay, I couldn't do it. I couldn't fully compress the trigger."

I release the breath I'm holding in as a mass of salty liquid swamps my eyes. "You didn't kill him?" My words come out in a tremor as a torrent of emotions flood into me.

Tears roll down my cheeks when Hugo shakes his head. "I couldn't. I didn't want you to *ever* look at me the way I was looking at him. I didn't want you to think of me as a monster."

"I would have *never* looked at you like that," I declare while cupping his jaw and staring into his eyes to ensure he can see the honesty in mine. "You not being able to pull the trigger proves how strong you are."

My gut twists when Hugo shakes his head again. "I'm not strong. I might have failed to pull the trigger, but I didn't stop the man I knew could." My breath snags halfway to my lungs when I see the dishonor clouding his eyes. "I was a coward who left the integrity of defending my baby sister to a man who was a stranger only months earlier," he mutters under his breath. "I didn't even ask Isaac what he was going to do to Roberto because, at the time, I didn't care. Isaac said he would take care of him, and I trusted he would. That not only makes me a coward, but it also makes me just as much of a monster as Roberto."

I viciously shake my head, sending tears flinging into the air. "No. That does not make you a coward or a monster. That makes you a man with morals. A man who was raised right. *Not* a coward. Even with your soul shattered, you still knew the difference between right and wrong. That makes you a man, Hugo. That makes you *brave*."

He stares at me in shocked silence, unable to relate to what I'm saying. I return his stare minus the calamity his eyes are sparked with. I stare at him with nothing but love and admiration, wanting to ensure he's aware his confession hasn't altered my opinion of him. I love him. I always have, and I always will. Nothing he could ever say or do would change that fact. Not one single thing.

As a stretch of silence crosses between us, the cloud dulling his usually impish eyes dissolves, but even with his mood shifting toward his regular persona, it isn't enough to ease the pain festering in my heart from his melancholy expression.

Deciding to test Hugo's theory of using actions instead of words, I press my mouth against his stern, snapped lips. The muscles in his thighs tense when my tongue brushes the ridges of his lips to wordlessly request access to his mouth.

His unease only lasts for a fleeting second before he parts his lips and accepts my kiss. I delve my tongue into his warm, inviting mouth in a slow, sweeping wave. His tongue follows the pattern of mine, tasting and devouring every inch of my mouth in lengthy, gentle strokes. Our kiss expresses all the emotions surging through our bodies—our sorrow and anguish and my understanding of why he initially reacted the way he did. It is a controlled and emotionally-packed kiss that relinquishes my heart from the stranglehold that's been asphyxiating it the past five years. Our kiss mends wounds I never thought could be healed. I should have known only Hugo's touch would have the chance of doing that. Only he can return the parts of my soul I lost when Jorgie passed away.

Inhaling deeply, I breathe in his scent. My senses savor being engulfed by his familiar woodsy smell. He smells heavenly. *He smells like home.*

When I pull back from his delicious lips, his eyes slowly flutter open. Our kiss has removed the fog obscuring the eyes I fell in love with well over fifteen years ago. They're the clearest they've been since he returned to Rochdale four weeks ago.

He runs the back of his index finger over my cheek in a slow, tantalizing maneuver, prickling my nape with goosebumps. I lean into his hand, wanting every inch of my skin to be touching him in some way. The muscles in his stomach contract when I run my hand along the bumps of his abs, over the Princess Peach and Luigi tattoo inked above his right hipbone, and by the replica of the tree I engraved our names into at Lake George over fifteen years ago covering most of his left ribcage.

Every tattoo that adorns his god-crafted body is a reference to our life together. Whether it is the pair of black, thick-rimmed glasses floating on top of a pool of water, the *Friends* sitcom logo on his right shoulder blade, or the three letters of my name integrated in multiple locations on his body, every tattoo has some significance to our time together.

Snubbing the tears forming in my eyes, I press a kiss on the outer edge of the bullet wound scar on his chest. My lips land just to the side of Joel's freshly-inked name above Hugo's heart. My breath hitches when I pull back and catch the cajoling look in his eyes. Gone is the cloud of remorse and despair replaced with a new voracious look only my kisses incite.

My pulse quickens when Hugo rocks his hips, ensuring I'm aware of what my simple peck did to his body. I'm not going to lie, I love that I can spark such a carnal desire from him caused by the meekest brush of my lips against his bare skin, but even with the desire to throw caution to the wind and undertake crazy wild sex on the floor of our bedroom, I won't. Not because I don't want to, but because I refuse to relinquish my eyes from Hugo's demanding gaze. He's staring at me with zero restrictions or complications. Nothing but love and awe is beaming from his devoted eyes. This affects me more intensely than any earth-shattering orgasm ever could.

The unbreakable connection between us only bends slightly

when little feet padding into the room sound over the furious beat of my heart. Warmth blooms across my chest when Joel sleepily rubs his eyes before he plops onto the floor next to us and leans his crazy curl-covered head onto Hugo's forearm.

A giggle bubbles up my chest when his tired eyes peer up to Hugo, and he asks, "Do I still get a pancake boganus since it's Monday?"

Hugo cranks his neck back and laughs. "Yeah, buddy, if you can convince Mommy to make pancakes, you'll still get a bonus."

Joel's little eyes widen before they dart to me. His lips pucker as he gives me his best puppy dog eyes. Like a dog rolling over and begging for my tummy to be scratched, I nod. A squeal emits from Joel's lips before he jumps up from the floor and charges to the door. "I'm going to wash my hands!"

He charges out of our room so quickly, nothing but a blur flashes before my eyes.

Laughing, I drift my eyes back to Hugo. "You know you'll go broke if you keep bribing him."

"It will be worth it. Besides, it's not bribery. It's an *incentive*," he retorts with a grin.

I screw up my nose. "An incentive to stay in his room so you can screw his mom senseless before you gorge on pancakes?"

Hugo doesn't attempt to answer my question.

Lying has never been his forte.

EPILOGUE

HUGO

Six months later...

"And just like that, Hugo Marshall is undead."

After a few more lightning keystrokes, Hunter snaps the screen of his laptop closed and puts it back into the hemp bag dumped at the side of the chair where he's sitting.

"Was it that quick to make me dead?" I ask, shocked it only took him five minutes to undo something that caused Ava years of pain.

Hunter arches his brow and stares into my eyes. "I didn't make you dead," he advises with a shake of his head. "If I did, you'd have no chance of being resurrected."

I peer at him in shock. For the past six months, I'd assumed he made me dead to keep me hidden from Col Petretti. If it wasn't him, who was it?

Hunter throws his hemp bag onto a chair before scrubbing his hand along his scruff-covered jaw. I eye him even more curiously when a sly smirk peeks out from behind his scraggly beard. Before

I can ask what his odd look is about, his spine straightens, and his dark eyes shift to me. "Did you want me to file the paperwork for you today? Or do you want to do it the legal way?"

I smirk and slap him on the back. "Now that I'm undead, the legal way will be great."

Snubbing the confusion muddling my brain, I move to the corner of the room and check my tuxedo in the full-length mirror. Today, Ava and I are getting married.

Putting it bluntly, I shit bricks the day I asked her to marry me. It wasn't a fear of commitment that had me quivering like the earth was shaking beneath my feet. It was the fact I had to lure Ava away from her office long enough to give Belinda and Joel the chance to decorate it with the two hundred long-stemmed roses I'd purchased that caused my greatest concern.

It's no hidden fact I'm not a fan of dentists. I love Ava, but my fear of sitting in her dentist chair is the cause of my greatest panic. Thankfully, Ava's constant reminders to make sure I floss regularly were implanted into my brain from a young age, ensuring her dentist drill remains holstered on the side of her dentist chair and not buzzing in my mouth.

While I'm being forthright, I'll admit my proposal to Ava was brazen, particularly since we weren't even an official couple, but I'd already lost so much time with her that I didn't want to miss one more moment. Since my last two attempts at asking her out were pathetic, worse than any fifth-grader could have conjured, I either had to go big or go home.

I went gung-ho.

Thank god she said yes.

After loosening the constricting bowtie around my neck, I run my hand through my hair to fix it into place. I grimace at the small scattering of gray hairs forming on my temples.

Getting old sucks.

Even with the room air-conditioned at seventy degrees Fahrenheit, a beading of sweat glistens my forehead. My eyes shift to the side when a white handkerchief is placed on my tuxedo-covered shoulder. With a grin, I accept the handkerchief and run it over my sweat-drenched head before spinning on my heels to face the smirking face of Isaac.

"Why are your shoulders so tense?" he queries, his voice its normal deep, demanding tone. "You and Ava are already a family. Nothing screams of lifetime commitment more than raising a child together."

I cock my brow and stare into his jeering face. "Who are you trying to convince? Me or yourself?" I ask, my tone doused with cheekiness.

Isaac's nostrils flare as his face lines with anger. Although he's tried numerous times the past six months to drag Izzy down the aisle, her feet have remained firmly planted on the ground and outside of the church. I don't see her strong stance budging an inch until Isaac takes the pre-nuptial agreement he had Regan draft off the table. Since I don't see Isaac's position weakening anytime soon, I don't expect to hear wedding bells for them in the near future.

When I catch sight of Isaac's furious scowl, I cockily wink. Most men would be shaking in their boots from the wry look he's directing at me, but I know his threat doesn't hold any heat. No amount of scowling can hide the massive heart he has in the middle of his chest.

"Don't make me fire your ass," he warns in a vicious snarl when he spots my grinning face.

"Again! What will that make it? The sixth time he's fired you the past year?" Hunter asks in a cheeky tone. "That's nearly a new record, even for someone as fire-able as you, Hugo."

His boisterous chuckle bounces off the wall and jingles in my ears when I punch him in the bicep.

"It's not my fault Izzy is always up to mischief," I mutter.

Neither Isaac nor Hunter attempt to refute my accurate claim.

Hunter is still rubbing his arm, feigning injury when my mom enters the room. Her hair has been pulled back in a fancy up-do, and she's wearing a pale light blue dress.

"We will meet you out there," Isaac advises while gesturing his head to the door my mom just entered.

Once Hunter and Isaac exit the room, my mom moves to stand in front of me. With tears in her eyes, she adjusts the collar of my light blue dress shirt before running her hands down the lapels of my jacket, smoothing everything into place. When her eyes lift to my face, a smile curls on my lips. Nothing but pride is projected from her eyes.

There's my mom I remember.

"Ava is five minutes out. Are you ready?" Her voice shakes with both nerves and excitement.

I nod. "I've been ready for at least five years."

The hammering of my heart kicks up when we exit the vestibule at the side of the church and amble down the aisle Jorgie and Hawke walked down six years ago. This is the same church Chase, Helen, Jorgie, and I were christened in. And the same church Jorgie and Malcolm were laid to rest.

My heavily weighted strides down the white carpet come to a standstill when the suit-clad man standing next to Isaac turns around to face me. I shake my head, certain my brain isn't registering the prompts my eyes are relaying.

Even after a brisk shake, the unbelievable image remains.

Hawke has returned to Rochdale.

I'm not going lie, my nose is tingling, and fresh tears are pricking my eyes.

After assisting my mom into the front pew next to Mrs. Mable, I span the distance between the congregation of wedding attendees and the altar, only stopping when I'm standing directly in front of Hawke.

"You came," I mutter, bouncing my eyes between his.

Ava sent Hawke an invitation with a note attached stating we understood his reluctance to return to Rochdale and he was under no obligation to attend, but neither of us felt right not inviting him. When he failed to RSVP, I assumed he decided not to attend.

Hawke's lips twist before he nods. "Couldn't miss seeing my best mate getting married."

Although his voice cracks, exposing the surge of emotions pummeling him, I can also see sparks of the old Hawke in his eyes. This is, no doubt, a tortuous step for him to take, but it is a step in the right direction. A giant, scary leap toward healing his heart and giving him the chance to move on from his grief.

My eyes drift from Hawke to the end of the aisle when "All of Me" by John Legend begins playing over the speakers. Hawke, Isaac, and Hunter take their spots next to me as the bridesmaids commence walking down the aisle.

The pounding of my heart increases when Belinda, Izzy, and Helen make their way down the aisle to take their positions on my right. As they glide past the pews of attendees, my eyes spot a flurry of blonde. A smile curls on my lips when I see the smiling face of Gemma. Our reunion occurred not long after my return to Rochdale.

When she walked into my office nearly six months ago, I automatically assumed Ava tracked her down. It was only when I saw the look of surprise on Ava's face when she arrived at my office not long after Gemma did I realize she didn't have the faintest clue who Gemma was. Ava's claws were sheathed when I promptly introduced her to Gemma. They've been close friends since that day.

My hearty chuckle rumbles over the beat of my heart when I spot the sight of Joel charging down the aisle. Nothing has changed these past seven months. He still doesn't know how to walk. He dumps his frilly satin ring-bearer pillow halfway down the aisle, making me glad I succumbed to Ava's pleas for Isaac to look after our platinum wedding rings and not put them on Joel's pillow.

When Joel reaches the end of the altar, he wraps his arms around my thigh and turns his eyes to the end of the aisle. My lungs take stock of my oxygen levels when the song switches to "How Would You Feel" by Ed Sheeran. This song reflects Ava and my relationship to a T. I just wish I got to tell her I loved her years earlier.

My breathing halts the instant Ava steps out of the alcove of the church. Just like the first time my eyes landed on her at Jorgie's wedding, she takes my breath away and renders me speechless. She's beyond beautiful, a unique mix of innocence and seduction with big, rich eyes, gorgeous, tanned skin, and a body created with the sole purpose of making me drop to my knees, but even with having off-the-Richter-scale sexiness, her heart is one of her most admirable assets. And thankfully, it belongs to me.

When Ava reaches the end of the altar, she kisses my dad on the cheek and hands her bouquet of flowers to Belinda before pivoting around to face me. The smile on her face eases the nervous cramps hammering my stomach, and the happiness in her eyes smothers the agitation over the previous times I visited this church.

Only Ava can calm any storm building on the horizon before the first cloud has even formed.

I gently run the back of my fingers over her pale cheeks before lowering them to brush by her beautiful, rounded belly. "Is she being a good girl for Mommy?" I query, only loud enough for Ava to hear.

Ava's face scrunches as the color in her cheeks drains even more. Unfortunately, she's been suffering dreadful morning sickness from the day she discovered she was pregnant with our little girl, exactly four weeks after we first slept together.

Although we caved and found out the sex of our baby, we haven't informed anyone that we're expecting a daughter. Joel is already struggling with the concept of sharing his parents' devotion in two months' time. We're moving to Ravenshoe at the end of the month, so we don't want to add more uncertainty into the mix by declaring the baby brother he so desperately wants is actually a baby sister.

I'm sure with some time and a good dose of candy, he will adjust to the idea of having a sister. If not, he has a fifty-fifty chance of getting a brother in the next round. With how easy Ava gets pregnant, I have no doubt the odds of her being pregnant within a year of giving birth swings the pendulum in Joel's favor of having a large family. He's happily declared on numerous occasions to anyone willing to listen that he wants five brothers.

Ava screws up her nose. "Don't even think about it," she reprimands me while glaring at me like she can hear my private thoughts.

I smile, loving that she can read me so easily. I shouldn't be surprised. She's always been the only woman who can see through my bullshit. Well, except for my mother, but she doesn't count.

The flutter of Ava's pulse spasms up my arm when I enclose my hand over hers and glance into her beautiful eyes. Every uncertainty, concern, or worry I've ever had vanishes the instant she peers up at me with her uniquely beautiful eyes. I have no doubt she is my beginning and end. *She is my everything.* And although we've lost years we can never get back, in a short period of time, we've created enough memories to last us two lifetimes.

People will often quote that there are no guarantees in life, but I'm *certain* Ava and I will never be parted again. Because although there are no guarantees, you can't fight fate.

The story of Hunter Kane. You can find it here: Spy Thy Neighbor

ALSO BY SHANDI BOYES

Perception Series

Saving Noah (Noah & Emily)

Fighting Jacob (Jacob & Lola)

Taming Nick (Nick & Jenni)

Redeeming Slater (Slater and Kylie)

Saving Emily (Noah & Emily - Novella)

Wrapped Up with Rise Up (Perception Novella - should be read after
the Bound Series)

Enigma

Enigma (Isaac & Isabelle #1)

Unraveling an Enigma (Isaac & Isabelle #2)

Enigma The Mystery Unmasked (Isaac & Isabelle #3)

Enigma: The Final Chapter (Isaac & Isabelle #4)

Beneath The Secrets (Hugo & Ava #1)

Beneath The Sheets (Hugo & Ava #2)

Spy Thy Neighbor (Hunter & Paige)

The Opposite Effect (Brax & Clara)

I Married a Mob Boss (Rico & Blaire)

Second Shot (Hawke & Gemma)

The Way We Are (Ryan & Savannah #1)

The Way We Were(Ryan & Savannah #2)

Sugar and Spice (Cormack & Harlow)

Lady In Waiting (Regan & Alex #1)

Man in Queue (Regan & Alex #2)

Couple on Hold(Regan & Alex #3)

Enigma: The Wedding (Isaac and Isabelle)

Silent Vigilante (Brandon and Melody #1)

Hushed Guardian (Brandon & Melody #2)

Quiet Protector (Brandon & Melody #3)

Enigma: An Isaac Retelling

Twisted Lies (Jae & CJ)

Bound Series

Chains (Marcus & Cleo #1)

Links(Marcus & Cleo #2)

Bound(Marcus & Cleo #3)

Restrain(Marcus & Cleo #4)

The Misfits

Russian Mob Chronicles

Nikolai: A Mafia Prince Romance (Nikolai & Justine #1)

Nikolai: Taking Back What's Mine (Nikolai & Justine #2)

Nikolai: What's Left of Me(Nikolai & Justine #3)

Nikolai: Mine to Protect(Nikolai & Justine #4)

Asher: My Russian Revenge (Asher & Zariah)

<u>Nikolai: Through the Devil's Eyes</u>(Nikolai & Justine #5)

<u>Trey</u> (Trey & K)

<u>The Italian Cartel</u>

Dimitri

Roxanne

Reign

Mafia Ties (Novella)

Maddox

Demi

Rocco

Clover

Smith

<u>RomCom Standalones</u>

Just Playin' (Elvis & Willow)

<u>Ain't Happenin'</u> (Lorenzo & Skylar)

<u>The Drop Zone </u>(Colby & Jamie)

Very Unlikely (Brand New Couple)

<u>Short Stories - Newsletter Downloads</u>

Christmas Trio (Wesley, Andrew & Mallory -- short story)

Falling For A Stranger (Short Story)

<u>One Night Only Series</u>

Hotshot Boss

Hotshot Neighbor

<u>The Bobrov Bratva Series</u>

Wicked Intentions (Katie & Ghost)

Sinful Intentions (April 25)

Devious Intentions (June 13)